PASSION'S PRISONER

By

Trudy Thompson

Futuristic Romance

New Concepts   Georgia

Be sure to check out our website for the very best in fiction at fantastic prices!

When you visit our webpage, you can:
* Read excerpts of currently available books
* View cover art of upcoming books and current releases
* Find out more about the talented artists who capture the magic of the writer's imagination on the covers
* Order books from our backlist
* Find out the latest NCP and author news--including any upcoming book signings by your favorite NCP author
* Read author bios and reviews of our books
* Get NCP submission guidelines
* And so much more!

We offer a 20% discount on all new Trade Paperback releases ordered from our website!

Be sure to visit our webpage to find the best deals in e-books and paperbacks! To find out about our new releases as soon as they are available, please be sure to sign up for our newsletter (http://www.newconceptspublishing.com/newsletter.htm) or join our reader group (http://groups.yahoo.com/group/new_concepts_pub/join)!

The newsletter is available by double opt in only and our customer information is *never* shared!

Visit our webpage at:
www.newconceptspublishing.com

Passion's Prisoner is a publication of NCP. This work is a novel. Any similarity to actual persons or events is purely coincidental.

New Concepts Publishing, Inc.
5202 Humphreys Rd.
Lake Park, GA 31636

ISBN 1-58608-790-8
© Trudy Thompson
Cover art (c) copyright 2006 Eliza Black

NCP books are available at special quantity discounts for bulk purchases for sales promotions, premiums, fund raising, or educational use. For details, write, email, or phone New Concepts Publishing, Inc., 5202 Humphreys Rd., Lake Park, GA 31636; Ph. 229-257-0367, Fax 229-219-1097; orders@newconceptspublishing.com.

First NCP Trade Paperback Printing: June 2006

OTHER PRINT TITLES FROM NCP BY TRUDY
THOMPSON:

HOSTAGE HEARTS

PROLOGUE

Gustoff climbed stone stairs up a passageway much used over time. The lumalantern he held caused flickers of ghostly light to creep up the ancient walls. Smoke and ash teased his nostrils as he gained the top of the stairs. He reached out from beneath long purple sleeves to tug off his cowl. Heavy, silver-gray locks fell to his shoulders.

He sat the lantern on a dust-covered table, bent to place several more small sticks on a fire in the pit at room's center, then walked across the tower to a barrel beside the far wall. He filled a battered bucket with water, returned to the cauldron, and added liquid to that already bubbling over the pit.

Gustoff took a seat in a huge wooden chair beneath the lone tower window to await the appointed hour. As he waited, his thoughts traveled back over time and gathered strength from his memories. He made a mistake in discharging his duties as Guardian. Had he destroyed the emerging evil force when he had the opportunity, he might have prevented the destruction foretold and altered the path of Fate over the next decade.

Instead, this night marked the beginning of events that would eventually complete the task he had forsaken. His Guardianship would end, and a younger, more agile being would finish the battle he had fought for fifty-eight of his seventy winters.

He thought about Thea, daughter of Lars Asvaldr, Ruler of Glacia. Guardianship of the Sphere of Light would now be passed to her because her father no longer abided by his legacy inherited from the Ancient Ones, and ruled the Glacian people by the Articles designed by the Elders.

The shuffle of footsteps disturbed his silent musing. He tilted his head. The chamber grew brighter as approaching footsteps brought another lantern and a tiny figure covered in gray from head to foot. The figure paused on the top step and, with her eyes cast in darkness by the hood of a cape, searched the chamber.

"Gustoff?" A soft whisper pierced the silence as the covered head turned from side to side. "Gus, are you here?"

"Enter, Thea." Gustoff smiled as the figure edged forward and paused before his chair. He squinted until his eyes grew accustomed to the light of the lantern held suspended from the sleeve of gray.

"Is it time?"

"It is time," he answered. He stood slowly. He extended his hand to rest upon the shoulder before him, then raised it higher to push back the cowl and expose the trusting face. He grasped an offered hand.

"Everything you have been taught has had its purpose. Tonight you will learn the reasons. Come with me."

Gustoff led Thea into the light. The glow of the fire caught shafts of russet and sent flares of gold around her still-bent head. Tendrils of long, dark hair escaped the gray cape and cascaded forward over the cape ties, falling to the evidence of budding breasts hidden beneath the folds of wool.

"Sit," he ordered, and pointed to a stool beside the warmth of the fire. Knowing she would do his bidding without question, Gustoff turned to a table against the wall and removed one candle. He dipped the wick in the pit and shielded the gathered flame with his hand as he placed the candle in a holder at the center of the table.

"Hold out your hands."

He waited until her slender hands were cupped, palms up, before him. He reached back to the table, drew the candleholder into his left hand, and with his right captured the flame in his fingers. The fire continued to flicker as it danced on the tips of his fingers, not charring his flesh, but becoming a part of his extended hand.

Gustoff closed his eyes and mumbled words in a tongue familiar only to the Ancient Ones. When he opened his eyes, the tiny flame had grown into a blazing white light that covered the palm of his hand. The sphere pulsed with life and energy, grew in intensity until its luminescence flooded the tower.

Reaching forward, he placed the Sphere of Light onto the girl's upturned hands, stepped back, and whispered yet another incantation as he placed his hand on the top of her head.

"Hundreds of years ago, long before the Articles by which we now live were written, the Ancient Ones ruled our world. In their time, there was no separation of peoples. All lived as one. But there were devious men among the populations. Men dissatisfied with the teachings of the Ancient Ones. Their words caused great unrest. Soon revolution spread. War followed. Blood ran like water into the sands of Solarus, through the jungles of Borderland, and froze in the Tundra of Glacia. Still the usurpers were not satisfied. They killed hundreds of thousands of people, destroyed everything in their path, and finally met the Ancient Ones on the field of battle.

"Because the Ancient Ones held the Sphere of Light that enhanced their powers far beyond the knowledge of the men who thought to destroy them, the battle was short lived. All of the leaders who sought to obliterate peace were executed.

"Decades passed. Then another, Queen Shakara of Borderland, sought disharmony. The Ancient Ones again destroyed forces working against world peace.

"Because their numbers were few and the distance they ruled far, the Ancient Ones elected a Council of Elders to help govern so they might be forewarned of any upheaval taking place in the world before such destruction took place again.

"The Elders became more accessible to the general populace and, after a few decades, grew in power. They disagreed with the Ancient Ones rule. In order to prevent another revolution, the Ancient Ones relinquished rule to the Elders and assumed the position as Guardians of the Sphere.

"The Elders then designed the Articles and split our world into three different regions. They chose hundreds of Messahs to go forth over the three regions and teach the knowledge of the Articles to all people.

"The people of Glacia and Solarus were eager to accept the Elders teachings and abide by the Articles, but the warriors of Borderland, staunch supporters of their deceased queen, Shakara, refused the Messahs admittance into their lands.

"Decades again passed, and the Ancient Ones, being mortal men, gradually decreased in number, unheeded and ignored by the populace. Yet, the Sphere of Light burned on. To protect the last magical talisman of their forefathers against the forces of evil, the remaining Ancient Ones selected the most worthy of their members and entrusted Guardianship of the Sphere into his keeping. Over the years that followed, protection of the Sphere has passed through the dwindling numbers until now only a few may control it.

"As the Elders passed and were replaced by new generations, interpretations of the original Articles were altered until laws of docile neutrality and male supremacy, to prevent another female leader from gaining enough power to create a revolution, were established in the lives of all who followed the Elders teachings.

"Now, as we enter into a new decade, warned by the Ancient Ones that it will be filled with death and destruction, the gentle society the Elders created will be powerless to prevent their own demise. Once again, through Guardianship of the Sphere of Light, the Ancient Ones will be called upon to save our world from disaster."

Gustoff had seen the future. He knew what trials she would face. His heart ached at the pain she would suffer, but he could not change what was now predestined. He touched her forehead with two fingers.

"Evil will once again spread over our world like a pestilence, Thea. Blood will flow like water over the snows of Glacia, the sands of Solarus, and the jungles in between. The Sphere of Light holds our salvation. I have kept it safe since it passed to me when I reached two and ten. Now, on the eve of your second and tenth winter, I pass its safekeeping to you."

Gustoff closed his eyes. "The passing of the Sphere of Light gives you the magic of the Ancient Ones to be hidden in the depths of your mind until the demand for such magic surrounds you. When needed, a voice will come, whispered through thousands of years by generations. You will seek wisdom and find allies in the most unlikely places. Comrades will guide you along your chosen path. The heritage passed to you from your forefathers will find victory in our cause.

"But know this. The task is for you as one of the last known survivors of the Ancient Ones. No one will be able to assist you over the threshold, or be able to assume your responsibilities, though there are those who will try. Trust only those who earn your trust. Confide only in those trusted, and remember, while not in physical form, I will always remain at our side.

"Take this Sphere into yourself. Use its power wisely and keep it safe until the time comes for its next passing. Cherish the truths and faiths you were taught, for if you allow doubts and uncertainties to fester and grow, the power of the Sphere will weaken. Bless you, Thea, daughter of the Ancient Ones."

Gustoff then spoke the words told to him many years before. He opened his eyes as Thea repeated the words, and watched as the Sphere of Light grew smaller until it finally disappeared.

Satisfied the Sphere had diffused itself into Thea's body, he lifted the two fingers still on her forehead and placed his hands on her slim shoulders.

"Open your eyes, Thea." She stared at his face, entranced. "You will go on with your life as it was meant to be until the special powers within you are needed. I will continue to help you control the gifts you possess until I join the Ancient Ones.

"Go with love, my child."

CHAPTER 1

Borderland
A Decade Later

Exhaustion threatened to collapse his aching lungs, but Galen Sar ran on. The harsh clang of metal against metal combined with cries of the injured, shouts of battle, and the woeful wail of mourning to play a dreadful symphony inside his head. His people were in danger. His skills, and those of the thirty warriors with him, were desperately needed.

Adrenaline surged, giving another burst of energy to his depleted muscles.

Galen glanced at the men standing near. He signaled for his warriors to spread out, and began to run again.

Sweat beaded on his brow, accumulated dirt from the smudges covering his face, and dripped into his eyes. Not breaking stride, Galen used his shoulder to wipe away the salty mixture blocking his vision.

A half league. Another quarter. The terrain beneath his feet became rockier, the vegetation more sparse, the air cooler. The city of Cree lay beyond the next bend.

"Galen! Behind you."

Galen turned to find a warrior cloaked in robes the color of sand poised to strike a lethal blow with his broadsword. The warrior's fierce cry echoed through the jungle. With no time to draw the sword belted to his waist, Galen sprang forward, blocked the downward thrust of the warrior's arm, and deflected his sword.

Shorter by several spans and lighter by at least two stones, the warrior stumbled, then fell beneath the force of Galen's blow to his midsection. Galen straddled his prone foe, forced the sword from the warrior's hand, and used the interloper's own weapon to end his life.

"Aheeee!"

Galen turned at the alien war cry. Three more warriors blocked his path. He lunged, locking sword hilts with the first warrior. Jakar, his second in command, stepped to his side, blade flashing in the slivers of waning sunlight that filtered down through the dense jungle foliage. A third Creean warrior joined the battle, but his opponent turned and ran back toward the city.

Quickly dispatching his charge, Galen kicked the body of his victim aside. "That warrior will warn of our approach."

Jakar wiped the blood from his sword on the side of his leg. "Perhaps, we should--"

A woman screamed.

Thoughts of strategy scattered. Running headlong, Galen and the warriors of Cree rounded the bend and entered the city.

Galen could barely contain the stampede of emotions that pounded through him. Hundreds of his people lay dead or dying in the clearing that formed the main thoroughfare of Cree. The smell of fresh blood and burning flesh hung in the air as thick as the smoke that billowed from the houses lining the avenue. Enemy warriors, perhaps fifty, looted and pillaged the buildings that remained, strewing clothing and household articles in their wake as they moved from one abode to another.

"Galen!"

Galen pivoted at Jakar's warning in time to ward off the blow of a pike aimed at his head by a warrior whom he'd not heard approach. He stepped back, stumbled over the body of another foe who'd been defeated by one of his warriors, and deflected the oncoming blow by raising his foot and kicking his attacker in the stomach.

Jakar finished the man and Galen pressed forward.

"Gaaaalen!"

His mother's voice reached him over the din of battle. Galen turned to discover his father lying on the steps of the Temple, his body covered with blood and dirt, his golden head cradled against his mother's breast. Galen stumbled toward them, but another warrior attacked viciously, swinging his bloody sword like a club. Galen dropped to one knee and thrust his own blade upward, burying it beneath the warrior's breastbone, plunging it in to the hilt.

A movement from the corner of his eye caught Galen's attention. Turning, sword raised, he found Jakar had stepped to his flank. Jakar engaged a charging foe, clearing the way for Galen to make his way to his parents.

"Gaaalen!"

His mother's garbled scream tore at his innards.

A warrior was at his mother's side, gripping her hair, holding her head back to expose the tender white flesh of her throat, sword poised, prepared to strike.

Less than fifty spans separated them, but it might as well have been five hundred. Galen ran, fighting the agony that crushed his heart, knowing he'd never reach her in time. He sidestepped the blood-covered bodies of children, slipping and sliding in the sticky wetness that soaked into Borderland's fertile soil.

"Ahheee!"

The warrior's battle cry echoed in Galen's ears. A bloodied sword raised high in one hand, his mother's head in the other, the warrior of the desert had but one second of triumph before Galen's sword ripped into his midsection and punctured his heart.

Galen fell to his knees before the mutilated bodies of his parents. Tears slipped unchecked down his cheeks. He reached out, disentangled the dead warrior's fingers from his mother's platinum hair, and then closed her eyelids with trembling fingers. He clasped his father's lifeless hand and brought it to his cheek.

"I swear I will avenge you both. I pledge this with every beat of my heart, each breath I draw into my body."

A hand touched his shoulder.

"Galen, by the Gods, I'm sorry. The invaders have been defeated, Galen, but several escaped into the jungle. We were able to capture one. He told us all this was Berezan's doing. Berezan sent his army to Borderland in search of some mysterious Sphere of Light."

Galen closed his eyes. He trembled with grief and rage. For many sunrises he'd warned his father not to ignore the rumors of unrest and violence from Solarus. He insisted the warriors of Cree remain home instead of leaving the populace vulnerable while they went on their semiannual hunting trip. But Omar Sar had cast aside Galen's worries, maintaining the rumors from Solarus were only rumors, that Berezan would never be foolish enough to attack Borderland.

The senseless murder of his parents, his people, could have been prevented if he'd been stronger, more insistent.

"Don't blame yourself, Galen. You couldn't have foreseen this." Jakar bent and slipped a golden chain from Omar Sar's neck. He held it out to Galen. The bronzed sun-shaped medallion suspended from the chain glistened in the last afternoon light. "The warriors who escaped may bring back reinforcements."

Galen pushed Borderland's symbol of leadership away. "We need to bury our dead, help the wounded, and see that the survivors are taken to our hiding place." Galen rose, wiped the blood from his sword on the beige robe of the fallen warrior at his feet, then sheathed his weapon.

"Galen? Take this." Jakar held out the bronzed medallion. "It's your place to lead."

Galen shook his head. He lifted his father's body from the Temple steps. "I have no right to accept the emblem of leadership or the position of Regis until I've avenged our people's deaths. Come. There's much to do before I depart."

"Don't be foolish, Galen. After our people are seen to safety, your warriors will go with you."

"No. I won't wait. Berezan is mine."

* * * *

The pounding of hooves and the angry shouts of Galen's pursuers somehow penetrated his brain over the loud drumming of his heart. He couldn't let Berezan's henchmen capture him again. Couldn't stand any more torture. Galen shook his head to ward off the wooziness. With an effort, he pushed away from the tree that lent support, almost sagged to his knees, recovered his balance, then stumbled forward.

The center of his world became the effort it took to place one foot in front of the other. Galen was oblivious to the snow beneath his boots, the rising wind that whipped over his bare arms and chest.

He had no idea how long it had been since he'd last eaten. Thirst dried his mouth, making it impossible to draw a deep breath. He panted, gasping for what little oxygen he could force into his lungs, and continued.

Another league. Two. His teeth chattered. Fever burned his brow. Chills shook his body.

Galen cursed his own stupidity. He should have heeded Jakar's council, stayed, taken his place as Regis and seen to the welfare of his people.

Instead, he'd followed the fleeing members of Berezan's army. Alone. And he'd fallen into their trap.

Pain obliterated his sense of time. How long had it been since he'd heard his mother's pitiful cry of anguish as she held his dying father in her arms?

Galen shook his head to clear the memories. He looked around. He was in the middle of nowhere. Blinding whiteness glared at him from every direction. Cold penetrated so deep his blood felt sluggish. He could no longer feel his legs, couldn't force his feet to move.

His last coherent thought before he fell to the snow-covered ground was that he was going to die and there was nothing he could do to prevent it.

* * * *

Glacia
A mooncycle later

Thea Asvaldr glanced into the black night sky as she considered the dangerous plan she and her mentor, Gustoff, had undertaken to save Glacia from the peril now facing her homeland.

Two full mooncycles ago, her father had died. Erik, her adopted stepbrother, had been summoned by the Elders from his home high in the mountains surrounding Glacia to rule in her father's place. A full mooncycle past, Thea and Gustoff received word from a private messenger that Erik had met with an unfortunate death on his journey to Glacia. By telling the people of Glacia Erik had been delayed in his travels, Thea and Gustoff had been able to rule in Erik's place by relaying messages to the Messahs in his name.

But they couldn't keep up the ruse indefinitely.

Word had come from Solarus that Berezan planned to visit Glacia within two full mooncycles. Berezan had already overthrown the House of Japier, leaders of Solarus, to claim the deserts of the south as his evil domain. With Erik dead, Thea, the surviving heir, a woman, could not succeed to power under the stipulations of the Articles drawn because of Shakara's war.

The Articles had been drawn forbidding the citizens they governed to participate in violence, and this precluded the Elders from any act of revolution. Therefore, Berezan could seize control of Glacia by placing his appointee in officer to rule as Berezan himself commanded.

In desperation, she and Gustoff had undertaken a frantic search over the past mooncycle to find someone who could impersonate her stepbrother long enough for Gustoff to go to the Borderland and try to form a secret alliance with the rulers of the jungle against Berezan.

"After ignoring Glacia for years, why has Berezan sent word he'll come now? Unless, of course, he's learned of Father's death." Thea groaned, raised her eyes to the heavens, and whispered, "Help me."

* * * *

Gustoff stood beside the thick tapestries that shielded the chamber from the cold beyond the archway. He studied Thea as she paced the balcony.

With a heavy heart, he whispered incantations and called upon the Ancient Ones to guide him through the next few mooncycles. "I have lied, Ancient Ones. Misused the gifts bestowed upon me to deceive the one person I should have been honest with from the beginning. Now, because of my duplicity, I must send my beloved prodigy into battle unequipped to meet the foe she must defeat."

A tear streaked down Gustoff's cheek to wet the hair of his beard. "Thea, lovely Thea. Chosen to defend those who will never honor you. Too much rides on your ability to protect Glacia, the whole of our world, to confess my mistakes at this late date."

Gustoff closed his eyes. The power of the Sphere of Light relied on Thea's strength of conviction, her sense of wrong and right, and her distinction between good and evil. Were she somehow to discover her own true brother was behind the malevolence she must meet and destroy, her faith in him, and all he had taught her, would be obliterated.

Gustoff shook his head and backed away from the tapestries.

* * * *

The faint rustle of her long silken robes whisked through the moonless night to blend with the soft tattoo of impatient feet. A blustery wind shifted the light snow that capped the chest-high stone wall of the balcony and sent white powder skittering over the frozen floor. Whiffs of smoke and ash rose from chimneys a hundred spans below. Tinkling sounds split the near quiet when an icicle broke free from the edge of the roof and crashed onto the stone walkway surrounding the Governing House of Glacia.

Thea turned, drew a deep breath, and released it slowly. The thick tapestries shielding the arched entrance to the balcony parted. A sliver of light crossed the floor. Between the parted tapestries stood her mentor, Gustoff, the glow from the chamber outlining his deep purple robe, but hiding the features of his aging face.

She placed her hand upon his arm. "Were you successful?"

"Be patient, Thea. Come," he whispered, then backed into the chamber.

After Thea entered the chamber and made sure the tapestries closed, Gustoff nodded. "Be comfortable and listen carefully. There is not much time."

With a motion of his withered hand, he pointed to the chaise and waited while she took a seat. "Your lessons serve you well, Thea. Only a few short winters ago, you would have bombarded me with impatient questions."

"It's not easy," she confessed. "Please." She patted the side of the chaise next to her and took Gustoff's hand as he seated himself. "Don't make me wait."

Gustoff closed his eyes and sighed. "His appearance is similar, but I cannot attest to his mental abilities."

Thea tapped her foot. Gustoff had a way of prolonging explanations. "Does he or does he not look enough like Erik?"

Gustoff raised his hand to stroke the long white whiskers on his chin. "He has the same light eyes and hair. His height is sufficient, so my sources tell me. Yet...."

"Yet what?"

"His physical condition, as well as his mental stability, are somewhat in question."

"Why?" she prodded. Gustoff would get to it eventually, but she couldn't wait.

"He is a Creean Warrior."

"And?" The fact he was Creean gave her a mental picture of the man under discussion. Born of the Borderland

jungles, the Creeans were the fiercest race of people to
inhabit their world. Men and women grew to towering
heights and were known for their physical prowess and
stamina. However, this man's capacity seemed to be in
serious doubt. "He was found wandering alone in the
Tundra a mooncycle ago, nearly frozen and with no
memory of how he arrived. He has been held at Dekar
Facility in the lower ward."

Thea inhaled sharply. "With no memory?"

"Precisely."

"I wish to see him."

CHAPTER 2

Snow-covered mountains jutted high into a black sky, now lit by a full moon that was just beginning to climb. Not a wisp of cloud marred the star-studded beauty of the sky. The ground glistened with a new coat of snow as the moon rose higher, sending long furrows of light across the pearly surface. Dark shadows hid most of Glacia, but tiny dots of light blinked in clusters from the cliffs above her head.

Thea adjusted the fur cape around her body to ward off the chilled Nordic air. She cast a hurried glance at Gustoff, expecting to find him faring far worse. Yet, Gustoff, even with all of his years, seemed impervious to the cold.

"Are we riding in that?" Thea pointed to the rickety coach drawn by a pair of equally old mules.

"Trust me. It is important we arrive thusly to support the ruse I have perpetrated to gain the man's freedom--should he meet our specifications."

Thea nodded. Gustoff always had valid reasons for the things he did.

"We will reach Dekar Settlement in a short while. Pull that hood over your head and keep it there. Should anyone recognize us sneaking about like thieves in the night or entering the Facility, and report out activities to the Elders, our mission will be exposed before we have the opportunity to place your plan into action." Gustoff waited while she covered her head, then took her hand and assisted her into the coach.

* * * *

Thea drew back the fur on the window and gazed out at the frozen valley. Located at the foot of the mountains four leagues north, Dekar and its surroundings were a part of her country she knew little about. Most of the villagers who lived beyond the fortress walls worked for the Facility, either by cultivating foodstuffs consumed by those within the walls or by furnishing ironworks for implements the likes of which she'd never seen used.

A shiver ran the length of her spine. The Settlement around Dekar was dark and forbidding as the Facility itself. Gustoff told her families of persons working inside the enormous fortress inhabited ramshackle dwellings in the shadows.

Could the man she needed possibly be found in such a place?

Did she have a choice other than accept him if he was? She was desperate to the point of recklessness. Time grew shorter and shorter with each turn of the wheels that buoyed the old coach.

Forcing down the lump that rose to her throat, she reached to turn up the fur flaps of her heavy boots. The wooly clothing Gustoff borrowed from one of her servants chafed against her legs. With a sigh, she reached for the thickly lined gloves in her lap and drew them snuggly onto her fingers.

Gustoff tapped on the roof as a signal for the driver to halt.

"How are we going to get inside?"

"It was not easy to find a guard I could bribe. Only the late eve watch was approachable. A greedy guard named Moog was obliging enough to offer us entry for ten crystals." He clasped her hand.

Thea gasped at the enormous amount her mentor paid to gain entry into an establishment that she should have been able to inspect freely. Should have--if she were male and permitted to legally assume the position she'd secretly held for over two full moon cycles. She pushed away the anger that always followed such thoughts and looked around.

Inside the Settlement, bright fires burned in huge metal vats. Sparks rose like geysers into the darkness. Around each blaze, clusters of people hovered for warmth. Others milled idly on slippery roadways.

"It is not a long walk." Gustoff assisted her down from the coach and aided her balance as she steadied her footing on the slippery surface.

Out of nowhere, two children almost collided with them, nearly causing Thea to lose her balance. She drew a determined breath to ward off the chill of fear that stung more deeply than the prickling cold. She wrapped the thick fur closer to her face and held tightly to Gustoff's hand.

They moved to the far side of the roadway, out of the flow of bustling dwellers.

They paused to rest and stood in awe as they leaned their heads held back and studied the hundreds of icicles dangling from heights almost thirty spans overhead. They hung down at different lengths and, at the edge of the building, tiny pools of ice formed beneath their feet.

Thea turned away from the beautiful spectacle that seemed foreign to a place so decadent. She stomped her feet and raised her gloved hands to rub her cheeks. Exhaling a frosty breath, she said, "I'm near frozen. How much longer must we wait?"

Gustoff bowed his hooded head. "I think sufficient time has passed. We will proceed, but I must warn you again. Do nothing to give away who you are. Do not look directly into the guard's eyes and do not utter a sound. I will speak for us."

His warning was perfectly clear. The Elders believed a female incapable of controlling power and had decreed that a woman's place in society should be subservient. Because of this ridiculous notion, she was ignored whenever she attempted to offer her opinion or answer a question, except by her staff and Gustoff. Everyone else treated her with the reverence due her family because she was the daughter of the Ruler of the Governing House of Glacia, but entirely discounted her as an individual. Anger again threatened to surface, but Thea held it back. It would accomplish little.

With a reluctant nod, she agreed.

Moments later they huddled inside a tiny guardroom. The lone lumalantern on the debris-strewn table cast little light to brighten the stone structure. For this one occasion, Thea was glad. It didn't take much imagination to know what made the skittering sounds she heard streak across the floor, or guess at the condition of the surface beneath her feet. She resisted the urge to reach down and lift her skirts higher, and forced her attention to Gustoff and the man behind the table.

After a few grumbled exchanges and the obvious sound of crystals placed upon the dirty table, the guard stood and preceded Gustoff through a heavy metal door. Gustoff cast another glance at her over his shoulder. The weak light of the luma defined with shadows each line on his face, every year of his advanced age, and his deep concern for her.

Thea made sure her hood shaded her face and walked slowly toward Gustoff. He turned. She followed.

They traveled cautiously down a long, dark corridor. Thea gazed from side to side and up tall walls of hot, rough stone. The guard explained to Gustoff that, centuries past, the stone had been cut high in the mountains surrounding Glacia and hauled down rutted roadways by the very inmates who inhabited the structure as each section was completed. They made numerous detours around debris accumulated over years of neglect, and around odd objects Thea could not identify.

Before her lay an enormous stairway leading down even farther into the hellish pit. She could hear the sound of running water. Steam rose from the bottom of the stairway. Moog stepped back to avoid two other huge guards as they approached and passed.

Thea's heart pounded in her ears. She feared the questions they would have to answer should their identity be discovered, but a calm presence filled her as Gustoff touched her mind. She was not alone.

She blinked when Moog shoved aside a heavy wooden door, opening to a dank chamber. A lone luma gave little light to the stone floor and the solitary figure huddled on a tiny cot at the far side of the chamber.

Closer! Touched by her thoughts, the guard stepped across the floor until he paused about four spans away. More light, please! Time appeared to stretch as the guard moved the lumalantern until she could see the man clearly.

"This him, Messah?"

Thea's gaze shifted quickly to Gustoff's face. You told the guard you were a member of the Elders staff? Oh, Gus, what would the Messahs possibly want with a prisoner? His gaze met hers. Gustoff shook his head.

"This is he," Gustoff whispered. The guard stepped back against the door to allow a better look.

Thea followed Gustoff's concerned gaze. She suddenly stared into beautiful eyes fringed with gold-tipped lashes that met her gaze without blinking. A glaze covered the surface, distorting the color of his iris so she couldn't determine if his eyes were blue or gray. Thousands of questions pushed into her mind. Again, the gentle presence touched her. Gustoff understood and would answer everything later.

Breaking the hypnotic trance, she studied the prisoner's face. A thick beard covered the contours of his jaw and cheekbones. His nose was straight, classic, mustache hid his mouth completely. Heavy, matted hair swept his shoulders. She knew his hair to be of a light color because the wisps that clung to his forehead were almost golden in the light, yet the rest was so dirty....

Her gaze slipped to his broad, hunched shoulders, then the strange fur vest that hung open on his chest. She contemplated his slumped body and counted each band of muscle stretched across his broad chest. She swallowed and searched lower, noted the corded mass of his long legs and the condition of the dark leggings that covered his frame.

A gentle hand took her elbow and tugged. "I will send word within two moonrisings," Gustoff advised the guard.

The guard nodded and replaced the lantern. Thea and Gustoff hurried back ahead of the guard, not bothering to wait for his assistance.

As soon as they were safely in the coach, Thea blinked, shook her head, and stared into the light reflected from the two tiny lumas attached to each side of their dilapidated transportation.

"I had no idea such horrible conditions were possible. Was my father aware such things go on inside Dekar?"

"Dekar was erected by your forefathers at the direction of the Ancient Ones after the bloody wars that resulted in the split of our world into three alien regions. Its original purpose was to house the hostiles who fought against the lasting peace the Ancient Ones sought. Over the years, I fear, it became a place our rulers, your father included, used to confine those deemed unfit to reside in Glacia's docile society."

"Are there others like that warrior?" Thea tore her gaze from the light to meet his.

"Many," Gustoff confessed, sadly. "But only the lower levels of Dekar are occupied. The majority of the fortress is empty."

"We must do something about Dekar, Gus. We can't condone people being treated worse than animals."

"In due time."

"This can't wait. We must act now while we're still able to use Erik's name."

Gustoff stroked his beard. "What do you suggest?"

Thea lifted the fur at the window and gazed outside. "You saw the living conditions in the Settlement. We must order the empty chambers of Dekar refurbished to house these people. We must also see that the remaining prisoners are given proper nourishment, ample exercise, and cleaner living quarters.

"We must take care of this matter immediately, before our ruse is discovered or Berezan arrives to thwart our plans. I'll ask Elijah for help as soon as we return to Glacia. He can assist me in organizing the stone mason's and the other tradesmen necessary to carry out this task. This is not something we can postpone. We must begin as soon as possible for the safety of all our people and the inmates who inhabit Dekar."

Gustoff nodded. "I will prepare a directive for the Guard Captain of Dekar immediately. It will be delivered as soon as we return to Glacia."

Gustoff touched Thea's hand. "Our most pressing problem at the moment is Berezan. The Creean does not seem to be the answer. He is barely alive. For moon after moon, he has been forced to swallow food and kept drugged to stop him from doing harm to himself. He has not spoken a word since they placed him in the chamber. Before that, he ranted and raved like a wild beast, threatening anyone that came near. He had no idea what he was doing. No idea who or what he was."

Thea shook her head. "The trip to Glacia might kill him."

"This is your decision, Thea. I do not wholeheartedly agree with your plan, but at this point, I feel desperate enough to try anything. But, if Berezan discovers our deception...."

Chills raced along her spine. She turned from Gustoff's kind face to stare out into the darkness of the passing countryside as the coach rumbled onward, nearer and nearer to her mountain home, high above the atrocities she'd witnessed.

"I must rethink this plan, Gus. Too many things could go wrong."

"Time is also our enemy. Berezan comes soon, and we have much to do. Do not allow sentiments to distract you."

* * * *

Thea rose from the chaise and crossed to the tapestries that shielded the balcony. Parting them slowly, she stepped outside into the darkness. She brushed aside a light dust of fresh snow, placed her hands on the edge of the balcony wall, and lowered her head to offer a silent prayer for guidance.

By the next full moon, she'd reach her twenty-second winter. Gustoff, her father's advisor, had been her constant companion since her mother died giving her birth. He'd been her nursemaid, her teacher, and avid cultivator of the fledgling powers she possessed.

Over the years of her life, Gustoff had guided her, employing his vast knowledge to hone her skills. She was special, he'd say. Chosen. One of the few remaining who possessed the abilities of the Ancient Ones. She had the capability to touch another's thoughts by weaving her own consciousness gently through theirs, the power to enter an out of body seeking trance and touch another's mind over a distance.

She could also use several of her gifts for self-defense. But, most importantly by her measure, she had the ability to heal another's hurts by absorbing their ailments into her body, then diffusing harmless energy into the air.

Because of these gifts, she'd been sheltered, her talents carefully hidden until needed. By Gustoff's own words, that time fast approached.

Her deep breath billowed into a frosty exhale. Thea shivered. Tonight she felt not the blistering cold, but the chill of fear at what she must do.

Centuries past, after the great war of Shakara divided their world into three parts, delegates were elected from each sector, and the Council of Elders formed to create laws to maintain world harmony. Governing Houses were established in each region to administer the Elders laws. The Elders chose Messahs to go forth over the world and convey their words to the masses. To work closely with the Governing Houses to preserve the peace proclaimed in the Articles all agreed to live by.

Thea looked down at the village. Governing House of Glacia sat on the mountainside, overlooking the majority of the city on the plateau below. The houses scattered over the frozen wonderland were dark at this late hour. The huge urns that burned on each cobbled street corner gave the only illumination to the ice-covered roadways.

She thought about the people of Glacia sleeping cozily in their beds, unaware of the danger fast approaching. Glacians were gentle people. Hydro-farmers, ironsmiths, stone crafters, and weavers. The Glacians had never been warriors, but had relied first on the Ancient Ones, and now the Elders to keep their land safe so they could raise their families in peace. They had no defense against Berezan's evil, none of the special powers she and Gustoff possessed, and no abilities beyond those passed on from their parents to make a good life for their children.

However, evil again threatened their world.

She turned and entered the chamber to find Gustoff on the chaise awaiting the decision she'd postponed for two eves.

"Is there any way we can keep Berezan from coming to Glacia?" she asked, pacing impatiently while Gustoff stroked his white beard. She felt her heart sink when he finally shook his head.

"We knew from the beginning our secret would never continue. We only bought time for Glacia by withholding word of Erik's death. As soon as Berezan arrives and discovers--"

"Bring the warrior here immediately."

CHAPTER 3

"You cannot bring that creature into this chamber!" said Nola, Thea's waiting woman.

The three servants struggling with their heavy burden paused at Nola's declaration.

Thea directed a glare at her waiting woman. The servants believed the man they transported was Erik and that he'd met with an accident on the way to Glacia. Nola knew the truth, but unless she kept her silence, their secret would be out.

"Ignore her. Place him on the bed and stoke the fire. He's near frozen."

Thea hurried across the room, threw back the thick fur on the huge poster, and fluffed the pillows to extra fullness. She eased around the bed, tying the heavy tapestries open with gilded cords so the fire could warm the room.

"Thea, you cannot do this," Nola challenged again.

"Hush," Thea hissed. "I know what I'm doing," she said, adding silently, "I hope."

A loud thump drew her attention as one of the servants dropped the man's leg and his booted foot hit the floor. "Be careful. He's not a sack of grain."

"Oh, please. Listen to me," Nola begged, tugging on Thea's robe. "He's...."

"Enough." Thea's sharp command stifled the woman's words. "We'll discuss this later," she whispered. More loudly for the benefit of the other servants, she said, "Prepare Erik's bed and make him comfortable."

"This is wrong, Thea. Very, very wrong. That creature should be in one of the lower rooms. Not Master Erik's bed," Nola argued softly.

"Thea?"

Thea watched Nola's lips press into a satisfied smile as she turned to the man leaning against the doorjamb.

"Hurry, I need help." Thea looked first to Nola, then to the three men bustling to do her bidding. She gestured for them to finish quickly, and watched Nola cast a reproachful glance over her shoulder as she brushed by Gustoff and left the chamber.

As soon as the servants deposited their heavy burden in the middle of the bed and stoked the fire, they hurried after her.

Gustoff pulled from his position against the jamb. His deep purple robe flowed around his legs as he walked. He paused beside the bed to gaze at the man sprawled there, unconscious. "Why did you bring him here? We should have kept him hidden until we were sure he would recover."

"I can't trust his well-being to healers, Gus. I must tend him myself. This way, I'll be sure he receives every possible care."

"Thea." Gustoff's raspy voice carried a warning tone.

"We've searched so long to find him. I can't take a chance something will go wrong."

"He is Creean, Thea. He could awake at any moment, discover you hovering over him, and become violent."

She gazed slowly over the large blond man, huddled in a bed so large it dwarfed the room. And, his body filled it almost to capacity. Thea thought about her deceased stepbrother. While he was certainly equal in height to the warrior, Erik did not share the warrior's body mass.

She then studied the grayish pallor of his skin, the dark circles under his eyes. Reaching forward, she pulled the thick fur from the bottom of the bed and spread it over his body, across his shoulders, until it reached his chin.

"The fact he's Creean will aid our cause, Gus. If I can convince him our goals are the same, perhaps he'll help us persuade the Creean rulers to join in our fight against Berezan."

Gustoff's hand settled on her shoulder and gave a light squeeze. "He is your enemy, too, Thea. The success of an alliance is doubtful. The Creeans do not trust the people of Glacia any more than they trust Berezan's followers. This warrior will try to kill you at his first opportunity."

Thea ignored Gustoff's words. "He's also Berezan's enemy. If he'll only give me time to explain--"

"This man is a son of the jungle. A savage. He will not allow you time to explain your dilemma or request his assistance. He will strike as soon as he realizes where he is being held."

"He's not to be treated as a prisoner. He's been through too much already," she whispered, remembering the conditions she'd witnessed at Dekar.

She reached across the bed to place her hand upon his brow. "I've tried to touch his mind, Gus. Using all of the knowledge I possess, I couldn't reach him. I couldn't get past the barrier that encloses his thoughts." With a gentle swipe of her warm fingers, she pushed a blond lock from his forehead. "He's our only hope, but until all of the narcotics they gave him at Dekar are out of his system, I can't help him."

Gustoff grasped her hand and pulled her fingers from the man's hair. "The drugs in his system weaken. Since he is no longer under sedation, only his physical condition holds him bound." With a gentle tug, he led her across the chamber and pulled her down next to him on the chaise.

"This warrior could mean more trouble than good. He might resemble Erik, but it will be nearly impossible to turn a half-wild beast into a genteel man who can impersonate your stepbrother," he whispered. "I am sorry I brought him here. I may have doomed us all."

Thea brushed aside Gustoff's comments. Her thoughts clung to an entirely different pattern. "What would a man of the tropic region be doing in Glacia? The difference in climate should've killed him long ago, especially dressed as he is." She recalled the taut leggings that hugged his legs, the strange fur vest that clung to his chest and shoulders and left his massive arms bare.

Gustoff rubbed his bearded chin. "We may never know. If he dies, the reason for his journey may be forever secret."

Thea gasped. "He won't die. He can't." She stood and turned to look into Gustoff's eyes. "He's the only hope we have to overcome Berezan's wrath."

* * * *

Thea climbed upon the stool that made access to the high bed easier and took a seat on the side of the thick mattress.

She touched the warrior's brow. "Your fever's down. The herbs I forced into you have replenished the fluids lost during your stay at Dekar. Your color is even a little better. I wonder how much longer you'll sleep."

Servants had bathed his huge body, shaved the growth from his cheeks, and washed his blond hair. The image the man now presented was nothing like the dirty miscreant she'd seen in the dark chamber of Dekar. His skin still held a strange pallor, but Thea knew from the darkness of his flesh that his normal complexion was bronzed by the sun. She suspected the fierce jungle sun also lightened the streaks of near white in his hair. The gold-tipped lashes that fanned his high cheekbones darkened until they were almost black near his lids.

Thea remembered his eyes when he'd stared blankly at her in the chamber of Dekar. She had been unable to determine if his eyes were blue or gray. Thea gazed upon his handsome face. The straightness of his nose, the strength of his jaw, the firm chin that bore a slight cleft all beckoned her fingers. She curled her hands into fists at her sides.

"You're too perfect," she whispered. "Erik was a handsome man and similar to you in coloring, but his face bordered on frailty. He was tall, but his shoulders weren't this wide." A glance from shoulder to shoulder confirmed her statement. "The people of Glacia haven't seen Erik in fifteen years. Will they accept Erik could have grown into someone who looks like you?"

The warrior's eyes suddenly opened and he appeared to stare right at her.

He tilted his head.

Thea eased away from the concealment of the tapestry until she stood in full view.

The warrior's eyes never moved.

Chills raced along her spine. An inner voiced warned caution. Ignoring the voice, she stepped forward. Her fingers shook as she raised her hand. He didn't blink until she touched his shoulder. Thea realized she had startled him. She understood he would be alarmed waking to find himself in a soft bed instead of the dank cell he'd occupied during his stay at Dekar. She took a step back.

He reached out to grasp her arm.

Thea concentrated on the pain in her wrist, and used her mind to strengthen her bones so the pressure of his fingers didn't crush her arm. "Don't hurt me."

His hold on her arm loosened.

She moistened her lips with the tip of her tongue. "I can help you. I mean you no harm. Do you understand me?"

"Who are you? Where am I? And, why do you hold me in darkness?" He tightened his grip.

Thea gritted her teeth to withstand the pain and replayed his words in her mind. His voice was deep, somewhat gruff, but she judged his vocal cords suffered from lack of use and probably thirst. "I mean you no harm. Please, release me."

His grip eased but he didn't release her. Instead, his light eyes sought her voice. The expression on his face showed he understood.

"Who are you?"

Thea smiled. He was still under the control of the drugs administered at Dekar. Possibly, those drugs altered his thought process. She remembered Gustoff saying he hadn't spoken a word since entering Dekar. The fact he'd spoken to her gave her hope.

She raised her free hand to stroke his cheek. "I'm Thea. I'd like to know your name."

A growl passed his lips as he pulled her so close she was almost in his lap.

"What have you done to me?" He relinquished his brutal grip on her arm to grab her around the back and hold her so tightly Thea couldn't breathe.

"I haven't harmed you. You--"

"Silence." He grasped her against his chest. "Why do you hold me in darkness and steal my memory?"

Her ribs felt as if they were about to puncture her lungs. She feared she'd black out from the lack of oxygen. "Please, I must have air."

Lightheadedness engulfed her. She remembered Gustoff's warning about the Creean warrior. He'd kill her without giving her time to beg his assistance.

She did the only thing she could think of that would disorient him enough to release her so she could breathe.

She touched his bare chest.

He pulled back. The pressure on her ribs eased.

In self-defense, Thea raised her hand to the fluttering indentation at his throat. She reached higher, toward the massive cords in his thick neck.

She inched her fingers across the top of his shoulder, buried her fingers into his long hair, and then slid her hand higher to rest in the hollow behind his ear. She heard him moan as she closed her eyes and heart to the flutter that stirred to life within her own body.

She pressed her index finger firmly against his flesh and instantly immobilized him.

Thea pressed her hands against his breastbone and shoved. He fell unconscious against the mattress.

"I'm sorry, warrior," she whispered to his sleeping form. "I had no other way to defend against your strength."

She scrambled down from the bed and walked to the hearth. She stared into the flames for the hundredth time in three risings.

"My only hope and he's blind. Gustoff warned me about his memory loss and physical condition, but neither of us could have expected this."

Thea glanced toward the warrior. She tried to visualize what he'd looked like before Dekar. She could imagine the bulging muscles in his massive body springing to life, flexing with each move, the proud swagger he'd have when he walked. With those long, muscular legs, it could be no other way. The vision of him standing tall, his head at a proud tilt, that glorious hair falling about his wide shoulders....

She walked back to the bed and stared at the handsome man sprawled across the softness. Memories rekindled the strange sensation she'd felt when she touched him.

With an unsteady hand, Thea drew the fur coverlet up until it draped over his chest.

Unable to resist another stolen touch, she raised her hand and traced her finger over his brow, then brushed the fan of his lashes.

"Even perfection is flawed. Obviously, you weren't always blind, but I have no idea what's causing your condition." She pressed her fingers against his temples. Closing her eyes, she concentrated on thoughts buried deep in his subconscious to awaken them from the effect of the drugs. After several seconds, she opened her eyes.

"How you must have suffered," she said. "I have no idea what caused so much anguish. I can't make sense of the jumbled thoughts in your mind, but I detect something very painful." She climbed up on the stool and sat on the edge of the bed. She watched him sleep. "I suspect whatever happened caused you to wander alone in the Tundra. Are you blocking out thoughts too painful to experience?"

Memories of her plight resurfaced to tug at her heart. "I need you, warrior. Glacia needs you. I can help you if you'll allow it, but in order to do so you must trust me. I don't know how I'll gain that trust. You already think I've done something to take away your memory. You'll be doubly hostile when you realize you're blind."

She touched his cheek. "I can use the gifts I possess to help you regain your memory, but I can't restore your sight." She brushed his brow. "Glacia and Borderland must prevail over Berezan, warrior. We must place our people before anyone and everything even if I must force your cooperation. I don't want to, but if it's my only option, I will."

* * * *

Galen opened his eyes to study every little nook, each shadow or fire-brightened corner of the chamber, before he focused on a chaise before the hearth. He tried to bring his hand up to his eyes to wipe away the vision on that chaise, but found his wrist restrained by a thick coil of rope. He arched his shoulders, only to find his other wrist also secured. He shifted his buttocks on the soft mattress and attempted to pull into a seated position.

He found his ankles also tied.

He dropped his head to the pillows and closed his eyes. Why would someone go to the trouble to bind him when he could snap the coils with one flex? The situation demanded study. He opened his eyes, and drew a deep, quick breath when he discovered the vision that rested peacefully on the chaise now stood at his side, looking at him with an expression that bordered on concern.

Shadows covered his face. He took advantage of his placement upon the bed and watched as she reached forward to rest her slender fingers upon his chest. He didn't count on his heart nearly jumping through his ribs when she touched his breastbone.

"Erik," she whispered.

He resisted the urge to pull away from her touch. Who is Erik?

"You must get well."

Her voice was like the gentle wind that rippled through the trees surrounding his home. At the thought of home, he wondered again where he was, how he'd gotten here.

Her fingers slipped higher to rest against the pulse that thundered in his neck.

His thoughts scattered.

The mattress sagged as she sat upon the bed. She placed her hand against his jaw, touched the area beneath his lashes, and then glided her fingertip along the cleft in his chin.

Fire coursed through is body, along with the urge to snap the futile binds and pull this enticing creature beneath him to appease his needs. He did nothing more than close his eyes when her fingers rose higher to stroke the plane of his cheek.

"I want you well, Erik. I want you to regain your memory, to find your sight. Sightless, you won't be able to help me."

He wondered at her strange words. He might feel weak, but he was in no way helpless. He could remember every little detail of the past three cycles. Berezan's murderers had invaded his homeland, killed his parents, his people, and....

He shoved those thoughts aside. For now, he was in no position to act on the anger that flushed through him. It took all of his strength to remain still while the beautiful creature beside him worked strange magic on his flesh with her warm fingers.

"Erik," she whispered again.

He stopped breathing. Did she believe him to be this Erik? That he was blind? Hadn't he gazed at her most thoroughly while she lay upon the chaise? He hadn't dreamed the abundance of burning hair that flowed over the side of the chaise until it pooled in thick auburn waves against the floor.

He couldn't have imagined the look of concern on her face as she neared the bed and cast her thick-lashed brown gaze upon him.

What strange game was this she played? His name was not Erik. He was Galen Sar, descendent of Shakara, and now that his father had been murdered by Berezan's warriors, Regis of Borderland.

He sensed danger, but couldn't fathom what harm might befall him at the hands of this enticing female.

He considered whatever reason she might have to believe he was blind. The only explanation he could come up with was his eyesight had temporarily been affected by the multitudes of drugs he had been forced to take while he was imprisoned.

Galen made a silent vow to learn all he could about his situation before he acted, to continue to be exactly what she thought him to be until he knew all of the facts.

CHAPTER 4

Solarus

Berezan discarded his heavy gloves on a table at the end of the long dark hallway, unclasped the golden closure at his throat, and threw the dusty emerald cloak into the arms of a waiting servant. He did not pause to pay heed to the dozen or so soldiers who had returned before him from Borderland and now sat around a table in front of the cold hearth. He shoved aside the servant struggling with his cloak, turned to the stone stairway at his right, and began a hurried ascent.

Hardly winded after climbing the hundred stone stairs, he pushed open the wooden door at the zenith with a force that caused it to bang loudly against the inner tower wall. Several brisk strides brought him to the room's center and an elderly man huddled over a table, working diligently on a scroll spread across the table's width.

"One more false prediction and you will draw your last breath, Elsbar." Berezan slammed his fist down upon the scroll, spilling a small bottle of ink. "I have wasted six mooncycles on another of your foolish assumptions and have nothing to show for my efforts."

The old man lifted his head slowly, ignoring the black discoloration that slid over the calculations he had spent years completing. "Borderland was the logical hiding place for the Sphere. Naro, the burning mountain of Cree, is the only force I know of powerful enough to shield the Sphere's energy."

Fury darkened Berezan's face and made his brown eyes flash. "Borderland has felt my power. I've all but annihilated the Creean race, searched every conceivable hiding place, and came away empty. We have waited long enough to confront Gustoff. Your foolish assumptions and predictions have caused us to lose valuable time."

Elsbar paid little heed to Berezan's ravings as he watched the younger man turn from him and stride toward the tower window. Elsbar studied Berezan's tall form, noted the tenseness in his muscular body, and felt the aura of fury that flowed around him like static energy. He shook his head at his pupil's impatience. The one lesson of discipline Berezan had never been able to master.

Elsbar had raised the young man from a lad of six summers. In fact, he owned him if all accounts were settled, for he had given six crystals to purchase the boy from the servant woman who had all but abandoned the child in the fierce desert sun.

Elsbar had been alone then, living out his life in exile in a cave at the border, banished because the previous rulers of Solarus had abided by the dictates of the Council of Elders and outlawed his practice of the arts of the Ancient Ones.

Berezan's arrival had given his life purpose. The servant woman had boasted that Gustoff himself had paid her to dispose of the lad, and when touched by Elsbar's mind probe, had inadvertently revealed the secret she'd sworn to go to her grave protecting.

The child was the true heir to Glacia, Lars Asvaldr's only son, betrayed by Gustoff's magic and, unknown to Glacia's ruler, cast off when Gustoff glimpsed the evil waiting to be awakened within the young boy.

Elsbar had seen traces of what the lad could become with the proper tutoring. He had spent the last twenty-five summers teaching the young Master all he needed to know to overthrow the rulers of Solarus, to become proficient in the skills necessary to meet and defeat Gustoff, and eventually to rule all denied him by Gustoff's act.

Through careful manipulation, Elsbar's own deep-seated lusts had driven Berezan's ambitions. Revenge had become a deadly game, the quest for power as necessary as breathing. Restoration of his honor, the reclamation of his heritage, his own brand of justice against those who ousted him--those were the driving forces within the younger man, as they were Elsbar's.

Berezan believed he needed only the Sphere of Light and the knowledge to wield it to attain his goal. Elsbar knew differently. He had not taught Berezan all there was to know. Berezan sensed that, thereby making futile the threats hurled at Elsbar in anger.

Elsbar blinked and clasped his crippled hands together in front of him on the table. He watched Berezan march back and forth for several moments.

"Gustoff is a very crafty opponent, Berezan. He would not be foolish enough to hide it within his person or in his domicile," Elsbar said. "No other host would be successful in cloaking the Sphere unless they were highly trained in the arts of the Ancient Ones. To my knowledge, there are only a few of us left."

Elsbar closed his eyes and brought his fingers up to press against his wrinkled temples. "Since Gustoff was the last chosen Guardian, Glacia is the only place left to search, my son, but great danger awaits you there. I see death and destruction, yet the visions are not clear."

"I'm not afraid of Gustoff, old man. I'm younger, far stronger, and with your help, wiser. Defeating the aged one will be simple. I'm already one step ahead of you. I've sent a message to Glacia to announce my intended arrival. As suspected, my intentions were not welcomed." A deep chuckle filled the tower. "Father is dead. Dear stepbrother Erik thinks to rule Glacia in my place. My place!

"Gustoff and the Elders will be shocked when Erik welcomes me into Glacia with open arms." Another devious laugh echoed off the stone tower walls. "Gustoff will rue the day he changed the path of my destiny, Elsbar. He'll rue the day."

"Even if you locate the Sphere, you may not be able to control it," Elsbar warned.

"Glacia and the right to possess the Sphere are mine!"

CHAPTER 5

Galen shifted to ease the ache in his shoulders. The pain persisted. He tried to raise his arms above his head so he could stretch his muscles, but he was still secured to the bed. He raised his buttocks off the mattress, and used the muscles in his thighs to push himself higher and relieve the tension in his lower back. He drew his hands into tight knots and willed all of his strength to break the ropes that held him prisoner.

Something tickled his stomach. Galen forced his body to relax and opened his eyes to find sunlight flooding through the parted tapestries. Bright light cut a wide path across the chamber, up and over the side of the bed to his prone form. He followed the path of light until his perusal ended at a length of rich auburn flowing over his abdomen. He studied the highlights that glistened in that thick mass. Red, yellow, gold, and white combined with brown to sparkle like gems against his flesh. He followed the length of one long strand to the top of a head cradled against his side.

Galen fought the instinct to groan when the silk-covered bundle stretched her leg against his and sent his blood into a frenzied flow.

What was she doing in bed with him? The last thing he remembered was her beautiful hair as she leaned over him and touched her warm fingers to his skin.

The need to touch her was uncontrollable. Galen tightened the muscles in his arms, bunched his fists, and pulled with all of his strength. The posts groaned in protest, but held firm as the ropes that bound his wrists strained, frayed, then snapped.

He wanted to roll his aching shoulders, to raise his arms above his head to flex out the stiffness. To rub his raw wrists. He resisted the urge to do any of those things. Unexpected movement on his part might wake the sleeping goddess sprawled half over his body.

She moaned again and stretched her leg, bringing it in direct contact with his throbbing erection. Heat bolted through his body. Galen gritted his teeth and resisted. He drew several breaths and grasped her about the waist. He tugged her pliant body forward and eased her up and over his chest until she lay on top of him. Her head now nestled into the side of his neck, her firm, full breasts pressed against his chest with nothing separating his flesh from hers but a thin layer of silk.

And, to his utmost discomfort, her woman's sheath was positioned against his erection.

Powerful need grew within him. It had been many sunrises since he'd taken a female to his furs, but Galen waited. He remembered she believed him to be weak and blind. Instead, he buried his nose in her hair. The scent that filled his mind was sweet, alluring and unfamiliar.

He could no longer deny temptation. He cupped her face. Flawless skin, white as the snow that covered the ground just past the border of his jungle home held his gaze. Her small nose turned up just a bit at the end. Her cheekbones were high, marred only by the dark smudges beneath the fan of her thick lashes, lashes that matched the color of her hair.

Galen eased the thumb of his left hand across her cheek to touch the darkness beneath her eye. She'd been awake last eve, watching over him. How many other nights had she been by his side? Why? Did she truly believe him to be the Erik she'd spoken of at his last waking?

His chest tightened. He wondered just who this mysterious Erik might be. A lover? Mate? The idea of this beautiful female sharing her body with another annoyed him, but he shook away the feeling with memories that he was someone's captive, as evidenced by the ropes that bound him to the bed.

Whose? Hers? The idea seemed ludicrous, but he couldn't discount the facts he'd already gathered.

She wiggled again. Her curves meshed against him and brought the blood in his veins to a heat that matched the burning rock of Naro, the flaming mountain that sheltered his home.

Galen drew a deep breath and held it until his lungs burned. He exhaled slowly. His breath raised the tiny curls that framed her forehead. He looked at her mouth. Her lips were full, pink, and so inviting that his mouth watered. He pulled her closer, felt each time she inhaled, drawing air over his face. He closed his eyes as his lips touched hers.

He used the tip of his tongue to moisten her mouth from corner to corner, the fullness of her bottom lip, the softness of the top. He tasted her. Nipped at her sweetness. Licked and sucked her mouth, foregoing the instinct to sink his tongue deep into the tantalizing depths and brand her with his need.

She wiggled again. Galen almost broke the binds that held his ankles when he strained against the effect she had on his body. She moaned, accepting his kiss, applying light pressure of her own until Galen thought he'd explode.

Her soft hands crept upward, buried into his hair, and entwined his tangled hair about her fingers. Her lips parted.

Galen took advantage of the offer.

* * * *

Thea resisted the urge to open her eyes and escape the dream that had taken her to unexplored heights.

Heat catapulted through every nerve in her body, soothing and relaxing each muscle until she felt liquid. Firmness settled against her lips, warm and searching. Something enticed her to meet this firmness, to test the warmth, to bask in its glow. Fire engulfed her body, yet magically called her nearer and nearer until she became a part of the flame.

She stretched, sighed, melted. She couldn't get close enough to the warmth.

Something invaded her mouth. Something slick, hot, and wonderful, glided over her teeth, around her tongue to capture even the small moans of pleasure that escaped her throat. Her senses were alive. Taste, touch and smell warred with her unwillingness to open her eyes and allow sight to explore the wonders taking her to a pinnacle she'd never reached.

A deep groan echoed through the fog that clouded her mind and brought her sense of hearing and self-preservation to full alert. She forced her eyes open to find she was held tightly in the warrior's embrace, his arms covering her back, his lips doing unbelievable things to her equilibrium. She sucked in a deep breath and pulled away.

Thea wiggled out of the warrior's embrace until she sat upon his stomach. Her cheeks burned fiercely, but she pushed past the feeling in an attempt to understand why she was in his bed, atop his body, and making such a fool of herself by taking advantage of the warrior's weakness.

She held her breath for several seconds, recited every lesson of self-control Gustoff ever taught her.

Nothing helped.

Thea finally stared down into the warrior's eyes. The gold-tipped lashes were open. His beautiful blue eyes were clear and bright. She studied his forehead. Tiny drops of perspiration dotted the smooth surface. She lowered her gaze to his nose, followed its length, and then slipped to his lips. She closed her eyes when she remembered the feel of his mouth against hers.

She didn't expect his touch upon her cheek.

* * * *

Galen knew he'd given away the fact he was unbound when he raised his hand, but he couldn't help himself. The need to touch her was too great. He skimmed the tips of his fingers across her lips, swollen and flushed from his kisses. At that moment, he wanted and needed her more than he'd ever wanted or needed anything in his life.

"Erik?"

The softness of her voice, that man's name, caused his fingers to freeze. Galen forced his gaze to remain upon her face and wished for a second he was Erik. The Erik who had the right to bury his body deep within the folds of her flesh and keep her one with him forever.

He blinked when he noticed her tears.

Galen fought for all of his faculties. He needed every wit he possessed if he was to carry off his intended ruse. She thought he couldn't see her staring down at him. Believed the flush of her cheeks and the hurt in her eyes went unheeded. It was everything he could do not to follow the path of her hand as she reached out for something.

Her soft fingers clasped his wrist.

Galen offered no resistance when she raised his arm. Pain shot through his forearm when she ran her fingers along the raw spots on his flesh where the rope had burned him.

"I told Gustoff not to bind you. Now, look what's happened."

Galen's mind worked at a frantic pace. How would a blind man react to her touch? Should he try to pull away?

He made a weak effort, but she reached forward to touch his cheek with her other hand.

"I won't hurt you. You must believe me."

He watched as she leaned down to press her cheek against the injuries on his wrist, careful not to let his gaze follow the motion. Her dark lashes closed. The fingers that rested gently against his cheek disappeared beyond his limited line of vision. He felt her wrap her small hands around his wrists.

Her body suddenly became rigid. Her chest rose and fell rapidly with each breath until she panted.

Galen studied the expression on her face, saw her teeth grip the flesh of her bottom lip, her brows furrow in pain. It was everything he could do not to shake loose of her hold and bring her into his arms to soothe away the agony she felt.

She sighed and relaxed. Her expression changed instantly from one of pain into one of bliss. Galen held his breath to keep from acknowledging her actions. He did flinch when her soft mouth touched his wrist.

"There," she said with a smile as she brought his wrist within view.

Miraculously, the raw spots had disappeared, leaving no trace of an injury. He subdued his urge to ask how she'd healed him when she grasped his other wrist. Within seconds, his flesh was injury free.

Galen studied her and realized she'd pushed away the incident of their kiss. He wished he could erase the effect she had on his body as quickly.

She scrambled to the side of the bed.

Galen didn't count on the sight of her lean thigh being exposed when her silken gown parted as she moved.

He watched her pace the chamber. Her gown flapped over in front secured by a golden cord that accentuated her tiny waist and the swell of her hips. The silky fabric clung to her body and glided seductively over her skin as she walked. Heavy locks of burnished hair cascaded over her shoulders to tease the fullness of her buttocks. Her bare feet left tiny prints in the gold carpeting as she walked across the floor.

He studied her face as she fidgeted with the tie on her robe. Not once did she gaze in his direction. Perhaps she was embarrassed by her actions. Maybe she'd never been intimate with Erik. The thought made him uncomfortable and dashed any hope of easing the fullness in his groin.

He groaned to see if she'd return to the bed.

She cast a timid glance in his direction before she hurried toward the chamber door.

Galen fought the effect she had on his body. He prayed for strength to resist the temptation she offered.

Voices filtered in from the direction of the closed doorway. He cursed the strange weakness that overcame him when he tried to reach his feet and remove the bindings from his ankles.

He couldn't remember the last time he'd eaten, and his empty belly told him he wouldn't regain all of his strength until filled. He considered asking the female for something to eat. Maybe if he allowed her to believe he thought he was Erik....

"Hurry."

Her soft voice floated over him. Galen closed his eyes and waited, knowing he couldn't stop his gaze from following her about the chamber.

The act he undertook might be the hardest thing he'd ever done. Could even prove fatal.

He didn't hear her approach the bed. He tensed as her warm fingers traced his forehead.

"His wrists are free, Thea."

Survival instinct came upon him full force when a raspy, male voice issued those obvious words.

"Yes. Remove the bindings on his ankles. I've already healed the burns on his wrists. I told you I wouldn't have him treated like this, Gustoff."

So, she was in command of his fate. How far would the unknown man go to appease her?

"Remove the binds," the male voice said.

The fur lifted from his feet. Cold air crept up his legs. Galen discovered he was naked under the fur. Memories rushed back with a shattering force. The entire time the beautiful woman lay upon his body, he'd been bare as the day he was born.

It took every drop of his willpower to hold still upon the bed.

Several pairs of hands worked at the ropes around his ankles as Galen fought the desire to stretch out his feet and ease the cramps in his toes.

"Erik, wake up." Her fingers dug through his hair. Galen couldn't hold back the groan that slipped from his throat.

He opened his eyes slowly to discover her face only inches above his own. He focused on her brown eyes.

"Get back, Thea. He may harm you."

Thea. Galen silently repeated her name. Erik should know her.

"He won't harm me, Gustoff."

Her hands were warm against his flesh when she grasped his shoulders and tried to lift him. Galen thought how futile her efforts would be should he decide not to cooperate, but he gazed into her eyes to allow his ruse to play out.

"Gustoff, Nola, stack his pillows."

Two figures stood on the other side of the bed. Galen was thankful he had good peripheral vision. He scooted back until a mountain of pillows cushioned him. She climbed up on the step and sat on the side of the bed. Erik's bed.

"Thea, Erik needs nourishment to recover his strength."

Galen fought the urge to strangle the man who'd spoken those words.

She shook her head, almost as if she remembered something, then slid away. "Gustoff will heal the rope burns on your ankles, Erik."

Galen almost jumped off the mattress when he felt cold hands grasp his feet. One ankle, then the other came under Gustoff's care. The old man moved away.

"Nola is bringing something hot for you to eat," Thea said.

Galen turned to find himself staring into the gaping neckline of her robe, the fullness of her breasts less than inches from his nose. The sound that left his lips was half-groan, half-growl.

"I think you should try to get out of bed. Mardus and Elijah will assist you."

Two men stood beside Thea. Only a few inches taller than she, neither male seemed dangerous enough to offer resistance if he decided to overpower them. Galen tucked that thought away when Thea leaned near the foot of the bed to gather something into her arms he hadn't noticed.

"I hope this robe still fits you. It's been a long time since you've worn it." She shook out the creases in a luxurious jade satin robe. "I'll help you slip it over your shoulders."

His control precarious at best, the last thing he needed was this mysterious woman touching him. "I'm not an invalid. I can dress myself." He hadn't meant the words to be so gruff, nor had it been his intention to hurt her feelings, but judging from the stricken expression on her face, he had.

His conscience argued to take back his harsh words, to ease her distress.

But a blind man couldn't see any pain he might inflict.

Until he had answers, he'd do whatever necessary to keep her away. If it took cruelty to make her keep her distance, so be it.

"Give it to me."

He held out his hand.

CHAPTER 6

Thea draped the silken cloth across his outstretched hand and backed away.

"Where are the two servants who are to help me?" Galen dropped his legs over the side of the high mattress. The fur slipped away, exposing his flesh to the cool chamber air. He looked down at his bare body, then up to see Thea's gaze drop to his groin and jerk away. She turned to set up his tray, but not before Galen noticed the blush that stained her cheeks.

The two male servants stepped forward. Though it galled him to pretend helplessness, Galen endured as the men paused at his side and assisted him as he stood. One of the servants grabbed the silken robe from his hand and shook it out before he slid one sleeve over Galen's hand.

Every muscle tensed as the garment was draped over his shoulders, flapped partially over his exposed chest, then tied at his waist with a cord.

"Help him to the chaise. Carefully," Thea ordered.

Galen closed his eyes and damned the charade she perpetrated. He wanted to shout at Thea he wasn't some weakling she needed to coddle, but he tensed his muscles instead. His circumstances were partially his own fault. If he'd never begun this ruse, he wouldn't be in this predicament.

Galen took several slow steps toward the chaise, guided by a pair of hands on each of his forearms. He made a concentrated effort not to look at Thea as he walked across the floor, studying instead the far chamber wall. He paused when pressure on his arms redirected his thoughts and sat as instructed on the chaise he'd seen Thea use as a bed.

"I've had something filling prepared for you, Erik."

He tried to assess the expression on her face as she tucked a smaller fur around his waist then draped it over his legs, but found Thea had turned her head to avoid having to look at the part of him she touched.

She placed a small tray on the chaise beside him and handed him a cup of some steaming brew. "Do you need my help?"

The tensing of his muscles, as well as the groan that left his lips, was involuntary. Galen accepted the mug from her hand and brought the hot liquid to his lips, not asking what the mug contained. The bitter brew scorched his mouth. He almost gagged as he controlled the impulse to spew the disgusting drink across the chamber.

"What is this?"

To his astonishment, she made a nasty face, then took a moment to compose herself before answering, "It's herb tea. Drink. It will make you feel better."

Galen almost laughed. Instead, he tipped the mug to his lips again, braced for the bitter concoction, and drained the contents before he held it out in front of him.

"Good. I'd like some more."

She stared at him, mouth agape.

"I'm hungry, Thea. Did I not hear you say you had something for me to fill this emptiness?"

Her expression changed immediately. "I don't have to put up with your surliness, Erik. I'll send Nola to help you with your meal." She turned away in a swirl of softness.

He couldn't let her leave. "I'm sorry. I'm not use to being so helpless." No truer words had he ever uttered.

Thea turned back to stare at him. A smile crossed her face. She returned to his side, lifting a bowl of something that caused a wild grumble from his empty stomach.

"I'll help you."

"You can help by answering a few of my questions. Things are very confused in my mind." Galen knew he'd touched a soft spot when she sat on the floor in front of him and stared up into his eyes.

"How much do you remember?"

Galen intentionally fumbled with the spoon she'd left in the bowl, then carefully brought it to his lips. He took his time, savoring the grain mixture. "Nothing beyond waking to discover you hovering over me."

Thea reached forward and placed her hand upon his knee. Her light touch scorched his flesh beneath the fur. "Do you remember that my father is dead, and you, his stepson and

heir, were traveling to become leader of Glacia when you
had your accident?"

Galen digested the wealth of information her brief words
offered. Glacia. Lars Asvaldr was dead. Erik, his heir, en
route to assume leadership, had met with an accident.

Erik was her stepbrother. Not a lover or mate. And as
such had no right to--

"Are you all right, Erik? You seem awfully pale." Her
fingers grazed his knee again. Galen almost jumped off the
chaise.

She folded her hands in her lap and stared down at her
entwined fingers. "There was an avalanche. In the frantic
flight for safety that followed, you were thrown from your
mount. Your men and animals were killed, your supplies
lot. Only a miracle saved you. A messenger sent to greet
your convoy found you unconscious and near frozen. He
brought you here. Gustoff and I have treated your illness."

She never looked into his eyes as the lies fell effortlessly
from her lips. But why?

"Berezan sent word that he will come to Glacia," she
whispered. "We have no idea why he intends to visit,
unless he's heard news of Father's death. It's imperative
you get well and regain your sight before he arrives.
Gustoff will help you. If you'll let me, I'll do everything I
can to see to your recovery. In your present condition, no
matter how much you disagree, Berezan can present an
ultimatum to Council that you're unfit to rule and...."

And what? Galen had no doubt Erik had somehow met a
tragic death en route to Glacia. Thea and the old man
Gustoff had then kidnapped him. Because they believed he
had no memory of his past, they'd tried to make him
believe he was Erik Asvaldr. He taxed his mind for
anything that might explain this desperate act.

He stared at Thea. Was she Berezan's pawn? Some
instrument of torture Berezan had devised to wrench the
soul from unsuspecting males?

Galen decided to use whatever Thea plotted to his
advantage. He could spend many cycles attempting to track
down Berezan and extract his revenge. If he stayed,
pretended to go along with whatever Thea planned, his prey
would come to him.

Bone-chilling cries of terror echoed through his mind.

Pain seized Galen's chest. As Regis of Borderland, it was his duty as well as his destiny to see those lives avenged.

"Where are my clothes?"

She glanced up at him with a startled expression on her lovely face. When she reached out to him, Galen jerked away before she could press her hand against his flesh.

"But, you're not--"

"I wish to clothe myself. Now."

She whispered to one of the servants. The servant hurried from the chamber and returned moments later with Galen's leather leggings. "I've had the leggings you were found in cleaned," she said. "I'm afraid there wasn't much hope for the other garments."

The servant tried to assist with his leggings, but Galen pushed him away and eased his legs into the soft leather.

He stood and stumbled across the chamber toward the bed. He bumped into the wooden side, turned, and collapsed across the width.

Caught in the throes of memory, he didn't hear Thea cross the floor. He suppressed a growl when the side of the mattress dipped and her warmth burned his side. He clenched his fists to still the desire to grab her and force her to tell him the truth, to explain why she persisted with such lies.

"Erik, don't be upset."

Galen attempted to ignore the tenderness in her voice-- each soft word weaving in and around his tormented visions, threatening to shred what little control he had left. He held his breath and allowed bitter memories to enthrall him, to shield him from the delicate pursuit of a conniving female.

Guilt bore through him like a lance. Had he been in the settlement when Berezan's men arrived, perhaps he could have done something to prevent the horrible massacre of his people.

Then, in his grief, he'd foolishly gone after Berezan alone. This, in the end, had brought him into Thea's hands.

"Gustoff will be here soon to assist you with your needs, Erik. I've other matters that require my attention." She hurried out of the chamber and down the hallway, not pausing until she stepped out onto the balcony of her own chamber and leaned against the stone rail.

* * * *

"Thea?" A sharp knock followed Nola's urgent summons. "Thea. Please, open the door."

Thea stepped through the tapestries framing the archway to her balcony and walked across the carpeting to the door. She slid back the bolt and turned the latch. Nola almost knocked her down when she pushed the wooden planks aside and hustled into the chamber.

"I knew bringing that beast here would cause trouble, but you wouldn't listen to me. You've never listened to me, no matter how smart my opinions might have been."

Thea studied Nola's hands as she twisted and knotted the woolen fabric of her white apron, the chalky pallor of her face, the terrified glossiness of her blue eyes.

Alarm streaked through every nerve in her body. "What's wrong? Is the Erik all right?"

Nola grabbed the hemline of her woolen apron and rolled it over in her hands until it hung near her waist like a muff. "They're here. I knew they'd come. I knew this scheme of yours wouldn't work. Now, we'll all be doomed."

"What are you talking about?"

"The Elders. They've sent two Messahs to meet with Erik. They're in the meeting chamber with Gustoff now. When the Messahs see that beast in Master Erik's chamber, in Master Erik's bed, they're going to know everything. Everything!"

Too soon. There hadn't been time to prepare the warrior to assume Erik's identity. No time to guide him through what he must say, how he must act. Why now?

Inhaling deeply to calm her racing pulse, Thea counted slowly to ten, then exhaled. She concentrated on Gustoff, desperate to seek his guidance.

She closed her eyes and focused on Gustoff's presence, the space he occupied, the visual aspects of the room. She remembered the three tall arches that led to the enormous balcony, the vermilion draperies drawn back to welcome the warmth of the sun, the long table where her father conducted many conferences.

When she opened her eyes her essence filled the meeting chamber, neither seen nor felt by the two men cloaked in gray who stood before Gustoff as he sat in her father's chair.

Gustoff's thoughts touched hers. *Thaddius and Jermaine are here to assure themselves of Erik's well being. They are demanding an audience with him. I have explained his condition and the circumstances that have endangered his health, but they will not be dissuaded.*

Jermaine continued with his argument, unmindful of Gustoff's communication with another being in the chamber. "We will do nothing to endanger Master Erik further, Gustoff, I assure you. But you must understand the Elder's concerns. With Lars's death, the population of Glacia is in turmoil. Word of Berezan's intended arrival reached Council and is rumored throughout the whole of Glacia. Master Erik's condition must be assessed so Thaddius and I may return with news that will appease the Elders so they might reassure the masses."

"We have been instructed to insist you abide by the Elder's wishes, Gustoff," the second Messah added. "We do not hesitate to remind you that, though Asvaldr inhabited the ruling house of Glacia, his heir must defer to the dictates of the Elders in all matters that affect world harmony. Should Master Erik be unfit to lead...." Thaddius shook his head.

Gustoff's thoughts again toughed hers. *Thaddius is delicately attempting to remind me that, under the Articles, without a male heir to rule the House of Asvaldr, Council must relinquish leadership of Glacia. Any individual powerful enough could seize control. In other words, Berezan's arrival could cause catastrophic repercussions.*

Thea felt the energy that sustained her weakening. She could not remain out of body for much longer without endangering reentry. The chamber around her began to waver and dim. Gustoff and the two Messahs appeared no more than shadows. Holding on with the last ounce of her strength, she probed Gustoff's mind one more time. *What can we do? How will we keep them from discovering the warrior is blind?*

Gustoff replied, *Go to him. Do everything possible to prepare him for their visit. I will give you all the time I can, but I am afraid I cannot postpone the inevita--*

"Thea! This is no time for you to slip away. Answer me."

Thea jolted. The firm pressure of Nola's fingers clinging to her shoulders captured her attention. She cast a hurried glance around to find herself in her own chamber, Nola doing everything in her power to make her answer some questions.

"I must go, Nola." Thea shrugged off Nola's grasp and hurried toward the door. Casting a glance over her shoulder, Thea said, "Have refreshments prepared and bring them to Erik's chamber."

"But--"

"There's no time to explain. Go now, and be quick about it." Thea closed the door behind her.

In the hallway, Thea paused, drew another deep breath, then offered a silent prayer for assistance before she walked down the luma-lit length toward Erik's chamber. Without knocking, she opened the chamber door and slipped inside.

Elijah, who'd been left to tidy up, turned.

Thea greeted him with a smile, then sought the warrior. She found the chamber empty.

Elijah motioned to the tapestries shielding the balcony.

Thea nodded and walked toward the open panel.

CHAPTER 7

Galen stared out over the frozen countryside, studying a region foreign to his jungle home. Vegetation was sparse. Only a few picea trees clung to the mountainsides and lined the avenues below. He knew from his studies of Glacia that the climate remained as it was now year round, the heavy snows never leaving the ground.

He knew nothing of the culture of the Glacians, how they earned their livelihoods, grew their food. Curiosity overcame him. He glanced again over the countryside. No gardens or hothouses were present, yet he'd eaten grain, drunk herbal tea.

Galen shook his head, adding yet another question to the many that needed answering.

Several equox-drawn carts rolled by, appearing as toys from his vantage point more than a hundred spans above the surface. People, tiny as insects, went about their daily routines, obviously unaware of the treachery inside the walls of their own ruling house.

Galen gazed up past the portal he'd exited to examine the construction of the dwelling. Built from blocks of the light gray, silver-flecked granite that formed the numerous mountain ranges crossing Glacia and Borderland, the structure sparkled in the sunlight. Suspended perhaps thirty spans above his head was another balcony, yet another floor. Beyond that, stone walls reached higher still until they were capped by deep eaves laced with immense icicles that sporadically broke loose to crash into the walkway below.

Glancing down, he noted the entire dwelling seemed to be located on a shelf carved out of the mountainside. He looked around. There didn't appear to be an outside entrance. Another question to add to his ever-growing list. A list that needed to be answered before Berezan arrived.

* * * *

Thea wondered how long he'd been standing in the cold. "Erik?"

He turned slowly, leaned against the stone wall, and crossed his powerful arms over his chest. He said not a word, merely stared at her, his light gaze penetrating deep into her being, though Thea believed he could not see her.

Thea took a step forward and placed her hand upon his forearm. "We have work to do, Erik. Come inside and warm yourself before the fire while I explain." She felt his muscles tense beneath her fingers.

Thea glanced up. The intensity of his gaze unnerved her. Held hypnotized, she studied his warm blue eyes and felt the stirrings of an emotion stronger than anything she'd ever experienced in her life.

His grip loosened, but he did not release her.

Using the powers of her mind to carefully school her thoughts and concentrate on what lay ahead, Thea jerked her hand away.

"The Elders have sent Messahs to meet with you. They are in the meeting chamber with Gustoff and have insisted upon seeing you immediately. Gustoff has tried to stall their interview, but they will not be dissuaded. Come with me. It's necessary to prepare you to receive them." Thea turned and walked inside, nodding to Elijah as he left the chamber.

The warrior followed her. "Will you remain in the chamber while they are present?"

"Thea?"

Nola's shrill voice caused the warrior to take a step back.

Thea turned and walked across the floor to her waiting woman. "Place the refreshments you've prepared on the table, Nola." She turned again, not waiting for Nola's response, and walked to the warrior's side.

"We have to get you into bed and make you comfortable before the Messahs arrive, Erik," Thea said as she raised her hand and placed it gently on his forearm. Glancing over her shoulder, she asked Nola, "Have they left the meeting chamber?"

Nola shook her head.

"Good. Erik, its best you not be found up and around the chamber." Thea tugged on his arm, wondering what she'd do if he resisted. She smiled when he allowed her to lead him to the bed.

While he slipped the robe from his shoulders, Thea piled the fluffy pillows higher against the headboard instead of gawking at his muscular body. She made a mental note to have more clothing prepared for him immediately.

A faint buzzing entered her mind. Thea paused, raised her fingers to her temples, and waited.

We are leaving the meeting chamber now, Thea. Be prepared.

She glanced toward the warrior and found he'd slipped into the bed and tugged the fur coverlet over his exposed flesh.

"Thank you," she said before walking across the room to pause before the table Nola had prepared. She placed her hands upon the tabletop to brace for the events to follow and offered a silent prayer.

All secret planning would be for naught if the Messahs exposed the warrior as an imposter.

She poured a goblet of sweet wine and carried it across the chamber to Erik's bed. "This is wine. Your favorite," she said as she placed the goblet into his hand.

"The Messahs don't know you've lost your sight, Erik. It's best that they don't. If they did, they might...." She couldn't face what might happen if their ruse failed. "I'll try to remain by your side as long as possible. If I'm forced to move away, I'll place myself between the Messahs. Direct your comments to the sound of my voice."

* * * *

Galen stared into Thea's eyes as he listened to her instructions. He allowed the many lies she'd already told to surge to the fore, reminding him of his own plans for revenge.

The Messahs offered a chance to evade whatever devious plot Thea and Gustoff created for him. They presented the opportunity to end the deception he'd begun by confessing who he was and how he'd come to be here in Glacia, posing as Thea's brother Erik.

A voice of caution echoed in his mind. The Messahs might be just another of Thea's devices to bind him more firmly into her schemes. Could he afford to give up the footholds he'd created by pretending to be blind and weak in order to have the freedom needed to explore Glacia?

He glanced around the chamber. Comfort and warmth surrounded him. If he disclosed the truth, would Thea move him to a dungeon to await Berezan's arrival?

Galen shifted until he could see Thea's face clearly.

Nagging doubts assailed him. Galen forced those doubts away. He decided to make his decision after he'd fully assessed the Messahs and their questions.

"Thea, Messahs Thaddius and Jermaine wish a moment of Erik's time," Gustoff announced as the two men followed him into the chamber.

Galen noted the lack of expression on the old man's face. The white hair that covered his head draped past his shoulders and blended with the snowy beard that touched his breastbone. He watched Gustoff's withered hands as he ushered the other gentlemen toward the chaise and motioned for them to have a seat. Gustoff then ordered Nola, waiting patiently by the door, to prepare refreshments for the Messahs.

"Thea, you are looking well, child," one of the men in gray on the chaise offered.

"Thank you most kindly, Messah Thaddius."

Galen watched as Nola handed a goblet to each man before returning to her station.

"Though your lovely presence always delights us, Thea, we are here to see Master Erik. Please remove yourself to another part of the chamber," the other man, obviously Jermaine, ordered.

Thea stiffened at the man's terse words, then cast a glance toward him before she stood and walked across the chamber. As soon as she positioned herself behind the chaise, she said, "Erik tires easily, Messah Jermaine. I hope your visit will not tax him too much."

Galen knew Thea's words were for his benefit. He fought the anger that flared inside when the Messah spoke such demeaning words to Thea. Still, this could be a part of her plans. To judge her reaction, he stared into her eyes. "Thea has been of great assistance to me, Messah Jermaine. Without her constant vigilance, I daresay my recovery might not have been so swift."

Fear widened Thea's eyes. Had he overstepped his privilege as Ruler of Glacia by chastising the Messah? Galen cast a quick glance at Gustoff. An expression of delight twinkled in the old man's eyes. Galen swore he saw the twitch of a smile raise the old man's beard.

"We did not mean to discount your sister's services, Master Erik. It is just that our visit is of grave importance, and we have been advised we cannot take up too much of your time." This from Thaddius as he glanced toward Gustoff.

"You wish to see for yourselves that the avalanche didn't do me any permanent harm, isn't that what you mean, Thaddius?"

The other man in gray stood abruptly and began to pace. "The Elders are very concerned over your health, Master Erik. When news of your accident arrived so soon upon the heels of Berezan's intentions to visit Glacia...." The man shook his head, obviously taking time to choose his words more carefully. "Needless to say, several members of Council panicked."

Galen took advantage of the opportunity. "Did Berezan give any indication why he plans to visit Glacia?" He studied Thea's face. She seemed as anxious as he to hear the Messah's answer.

"Berezan never gives reasons for the things he does, Master Erik. He believes himself above the Articles and forbids the Council of Elders any voice in Solarus. No one can second-guess his evil, but you should know that well enough."

A maelstrom of confusing thoughts bounced around inside Galen's head. Had Erik Asvaldr at one time encountered Berezan? Thea's stricken expression implied she had no idea. Were the Messahs suspicious of Erik for some reason? Could this be the impetus behind their interrogation? How well did Thea actually know her brother?

He didn't need any more questions without answers.

The silent pause stretched until tension crackled in the chamber air. The Messahs awaited his response, but Galen agonized over how he should answer. He took a moment to examine how he'd react if he were collaborating with an evil power to overthrow another region. The first item on his agenda would be to gain the trust of a powerful individual in that region. Second, he would learn all he

could about the inner workings of the hierarchy, then use
that information to his advantage.

"You have been away from Glacia for fifteen years,
Master Erik." The Messah Jermaine had stepped near the
bed until he could get a good look at what the shadows
created by the tapestries hid. "Those years have been kind
to you. One would never think the lanky, timid lad you
were at fifteen would mature into such a magnificent
specimen since you left Glacia."

More questions surfaced. Why had Erik left Glacia to live
elsewhere? Thea told him an avalanche destroyed Erik's
party as he traveled from his mountain home to assume
leadership, but she'd given no hint something had
happened between Erik and Lars Asvaldr to cause unrest.
Fifteen years of Erik's life were unaccounted for. Years in
which Erik Asvaldr might have sought revenge against his
father by plotting with Berezan.

"It is a pity your mother could not journey to Glacia with
you, Master Erik. However, I suppose a blessing kept the
dear woman at home and out of danger. Poor Thea could
not have stood the death of her stepmother so close upon
the tragic loss of her father."

Jermaine turned and propped his cloaked buttocks on the
side of the bed. His view no longer blocked by the man's
bulk, Galen glanced toward Thea to find she'd moved from
the spot she'd occupied behind the chaise.

A strange sense of caution streaked through his mind. Out
of the corner of his eyes, Galen noticed the Messah
Jermaine waved his hand slowly back and forth, almost as
if he tested Erik's vision.

"Erik is tiring, Messah Jermaine. I fear he must rest now."

Thea's words came from the foot of the bed. Galen turned
to stare into her eyes. Knowing there was no way she could
convey the Messah's gesture to a blind man without
describing his actions, Galen decided to alleviate her fears.

"Why is it I get the impression you are testing me?"
Galen almost laughed at the man's stricken expression.

The Messah stood abruptly. Guilt drew all color from his
face as he struggled to explain his act. "A hundred pardons,
Master Erik. It is just that--"

"Rumors reached the Elders that your sight was lost
because of your accident. You must understand how such

falsehoods fly around from one gossiping servant to another," Thaddius said, taking up the explanation when Jermaine appeared at a loss for words. "The Elders sent us to determine the truth of these rumors and to judge your ability to rule Glacia."

Nola cleared her throat loudly, reminding Galen she was in the room.

"The servants in the House of Asvaldr are trustworthy, Messah Thaddius. Not one would utter such lies," Thea exclaimed.

Galen tightened his fist to keep from reaching out and strangling the disgusting man. "Have I satisfied your curiosity? Do you believe I'm capable of ruling Glacia and, if necessary, defending our homes against Berezan? Or is there some task you wish me to complete before you are convinced?"

Thaddius rose from the chaise and hurried to Jermaine's side. "We are convinced you are in good health, Master Erik. We shall report our findings to the Elders at once."

Galen realized the ambiguity of the Messahs' statement. He would be pronounced physically able to assume the position of leader of Glacia, but not trusted until he proved himself worthy.

CHAPTER 8

The wooden chair grumbled under Gustoff's weight as he shifted for a more comfortable position. To stretch the stiff muscles in his neck, he gazed up through the lone tower window into the heavy-laden gray sky. Less than two hours ago, warm sunshine glistened over the hills and valleys. Now, unstable weather, normal in the mountains of Glacia, blew down from the higher peaks.

Studying the rapidly darkening sky, Gustoff sighed. How dismal the clouds appeared, much like the turmoil that rose and ebbed within his chest. The heaviness of the secret he had carried for so many years pressed hard upon him, threatening suffocation. Gustoff dropped his head into his hands.

"My weakness has doomed us all," he whispered.

Visions came unbidden into his mind. Through a haze he saw Thea, eager to please, hungry to understand the strange powers within her. The Creean warrior stood tall and powerful by Thea's side, not as a deterrent to her quest, but the strength she needed to see her mission through. Then, in a flash of yellow light, Gustoff witnessed his own passing. His body quaked as the breath of life slowly escaped from an open wound in his chest. His fingers grew cold. His blood, sluggish in his veins, appeared to harden.

The images vanished.

Gustoff opened his eyes and searched the chamber.

Another chill streaked through his body. To warm his aged bones, Gustoff stood and walked slowly around the tower. He paused only to gaze through the window at the threatening sky, now charcoal and indigo. He would not be physically present to offer Thea support and advice when she faced Berezan, or to explain he had exiled her brother because the Articles would have made him the next heir of Glacia. Thea would never know he had done what he believed at the time was right, or that the capacity for evil with the young Berezan was another part of the prophecy he passed to her.

Unless....

Since the beginning of the plot Thea created to deceive Berezan with an imposter, and especially since finding the Creean in the dungeons of Dekar, Gustoff had believed the warrior would ruin all they had planned.

His vision proclaimed otherwise.

For decades, he had discounted the Creean race as uncivilized, warriors bred of Shakara, unable to understand the intricacies of peace between nations or the powers greater than those in their jungle world working to defeat all of mankind.

Perhaps he had been wrong.

The warrior displayed keen intuition and cunning when handling the Messahs. Whether by intent, or ignorance of the power wielded by the Messahs, he outwitted them at their own game. He understood their methods of interrogation. The riddles cloaked by carefully chosen words, and held his own admirably.

Gustoff remembered Thaddius and Jermaine's stricken expressions when the warrior had all but ordered them out of the chamber so he could rest.

More importantly, why had the Messahs alluded to the fact that Erik might have contact with Berezan during his sojourn from Glacia. Though Gustoff never fully understood their ways, he knew the Messahs and Elders could discover anything they wished to know about events taking place throughout the world. He speculated their spy network reached everywhere, and must even be active within the walls of the Governing House of Glacia, for how else would they have suspected the warrior's blindness?

Gustoff thought about the past, and specifically, why Erik left Glacia shortly after Thea's second and tenth winter. Any reason at all that might shed light on the Messah's suspicions.

Lars Asvaldr never fully recovered from what he believed to be his only son's demise. In order to relieve some of his grief, Dimetria, Berezan's mother, tried for almost a decade to become pregnant and offer Lars another child to love. By the time Lars's seed finally grew within her womb, Dimetria had grown weak from the numerous miscarriages. The strain of Thea's difficult birth taxed her beyond her endurance, and she died shortly after.

Years later, after much suffering, Lars wed the widowed Nadia of the Peaks and accepted her only son as his heir.

Marital bliss lasted but a few years. Nadia, furious at her inability to take the place of Lars's beloved, grew shrewish and finally took her fifteen-year-old son back to his high mountain birthplace. Erik had visited Glacia secretly numerous times over the years, but no hint of any animosity had ever been present in the coltish young boy. Lars treated Erik with the greatest respect, took him under his wing, and prepared Erik to one day take his awarded place as ruler of the House of Asvaldr.

During those visits, Gustoff had been too busy instructing his own pupil to pay much attention to the comings and goings of young Erik. A mistake, he now realized. By his neglect, he may have overlooked something hidden within the boy that could have forewarned him of any mischief the heir to Glacia might have been involved in while under his hostile mother's care.

Gustoff shook his head. Erik Asvaldr's death might have been a blessing. Unknowingly, Thea might have welcomed Berezan's own puppet with open arms.

Turning his thoughts from the past toward the mooncycles ahead, Gustoff reconsidered Thea's idea to offer rule of Glacia to the Creeans of Borderland in exchange for an alliance against Berezan's threat.

Thea believed the Creeans would join Glacia, not Solarus, in a quest for world domination. His own vision still fresh in his mind, Gustoff wondered if her surety had come by prophecy from the Ancient Ones. Maybe she experienced a glimpse of the future and thought the premonition her own.

She had always been adamant in her desire for one world. The Elders ways did not set well with her perception of how things should be. The dictate location alone would be the determining factor to separate the races was as absurd as the laws regarding females. All beings should be treated equally and permitted to experience the snows of Glacia, the warmth of Solarus, the lushness of Borderland. Cultures could be exchanged. Enemies turned to allies.

However, as a female, Thea was of little consequence in the Glacian structure, and her words were never heard by anyone other than him. Though he knew he would never live to see it, Gustoff prayed one day Thea's world would exist.

Berezan would arrive in Glacia in twenty mooncycles. The time for his journey to Borderland to meet with the Creean rulers could no longer be delayed. Thus decided, Gustoff began to prepare for his departure, planning to advise Thea before first light.

* * * *

Galen shook with the intensity of anger tearing him apart. He cursed Thea, Berezan, everything that had taken him from his jungle home.

The game was over. He had no more time to waste playing invalid while he awaited answers to his questions. Berezan could arrive at any time, and he knew no more about Glacia than he had when he woke to find himself a prisoner. He needed to explore the House of Asvaldr, to make plans to gain his revenge, then escape to Borderland, as far away from Thea Asvaldr as possible before he did something he'd truly regret.

A light tap on the door drew his attention. Galen stiffened and watched in silence as the wooden panel opened and a sliver of light from the lumalanterns in the hallway crept across the chamber floor.

"Master Erik?"

Galen recognized the voice of the servant Elijah who'd sung merrily while he cleaned the chamber at yesterday's rising. Galen remained still. Elijah and another servant walked to his bedside, the swish of their copper woolen robes the only noise in the chamber.

"Who is it?"

"Elijah, Master Erik. Mardus is with me. Gustoff asked that we accompany you to the lower chamber and assist with your bath. He wishes to speak with you and believes you will feel more relaxed if you meet him in the steam chamber."

Not wishing to pass up an opportunity to explore the interior of the Keep, Galen threw back the thick fur coverlet and dropped his legs over the edge of the mattress.

Blindness did have advantages. No one would attempt to alter normal routines when he was about or hide whatever secrets the Keep might hold. He had escape plans to formulate. Vantage points to map. The charade that caused so much discomfort finally became a valuable strategic asset.

"It is a pity your possessions were lost in the avalanche. We will arrange something more suitable for you to wear after your bath.

"Come. I will walk slowly and advise you of every turn and stair long before the need arises."

Galen gazed about in awe.

The Keep was round. Numerous doors, all polished to reflect the lumalight and framed by intricate scrollwork carved into the rock, circumscribed the balcony.

Galen traced the waist-high granite wall that formed a railing.

"We are about to reach the first step down, Master Erik. Thirty more before the next landing. Please step now."

Galen paid little heed to Elijah's step counting, contemplating instead the stone stairs. There were no windows in the granite spiral. No source of heat he could see, yet the stone beneath his bare feet and the air around him was very warm.

An enormous chandelier, constructed of thousands of lumastones in black iron sconces, hung from the ceiling two stories above, and dangled almost thirty spans down the center of the circular stairway. Galen studied the core of the building. He counted at least three more floors and twenty more doors.

"We have reach the glide to the lower level," Elijah said.

"Hold on here." Elijah then reached around him to release a metal grate.

The floor began to sink, silently, effortlessly, into what Galen judged to be a cylinder cut into the granite.

Movement ceased. Elijah reached released the grate.

Galen stepped into a chamber that was three hundred spans in diameter. A series of granite walkways crisscrossed the interior, suspended over an enormous pool that appeared to be no more than two or three spans deep. The water frothed and bubbled, spewing clouds of steam upward. Beneath the surface, lumastones lit the liquid.

A conveyor system zigzagged the entire chamber ceiling. Thousands of different plants were suspended from the conveyers by cords that lowered each until the root balls were only several spans above the frothing pits so the steam could give needed moisture.

Vegetables, grains, fruits, nuts, and every imaginable source of nutrition danced above the glowing water. Several dozen servants worked the switches and levers that caused the conveyers to move the plants to a center station. Each plant was carefully handled. Leaves pruned, roots checked, then sent to another station where the bounty was removed and placed into baskets upon the stone floor.

Galen forced away his smile when Elijah tugged gently on his sleeve. The question of food now answered.

He followed the servant in the flowing copper robe down another series of hallways, deeper and deeper into the bowels of the mountain, anxious to speak with the old man alone.

He had something important of his own to discuss.

* * * *

Gustoff walked slowly around the pool in the bathing chamber. He ignored the steam that drenched his flesh and caused his purple robe to cling to his legs as he paused to close his eyes. In order to gain knowledge of Borderland and Omar Sar, leader of the Creeans, Gustoff had to break another of the Ancient Ones sacred laws. He must touch another's mind against his will, steal information locked away in the recesses of his subconscious and use that knowledge gained for his own purpose.

Footsteps echoed in the outside hallway. Gustoff opened his eyes and watched Elijah lead the warrior into the chamber. A suspicion he had nurtured proved to be true as the warrior's gaze devoured every inch of the chamber. Gustoff wondered if his sight had recently returned or if it was a ruse the Creean used from the beginning. He decided to gain answers to his question while the warrior was under his mind probe.

* * * *

Galen clenched his jaw to stifle the instinct to gape as he stepped inside the bathing chamber. Like everything else he'd encountered since leaving the bedchamber, this room was round. A short stone wall rimmed a deep pit hollowed out of the granite floor. Lush cushions of purple and red were piled upon the wall, forming benches wide enough to lie upon and soak up the warmth of the chamber.

The pool was similar to the one he'd encountered in the hydro-chamber, though much smaller. The water, illuminated by lumastones, spumed and bubbled like the hot springs he was accustomed to in the Borderlands. Steam clouded the air. The light of the lumas reflected off the beads of moisture, glistened on the flecks of silver in the granite walls, and set the entire chamber aglow.

"Erik?"

Galen turned toward the voice. "Gustoff?"

"Lead him to this side of the pool, Elijah."

Galen allowed Elijah to guide him by the arm around the stone walkway that edged the pool. When they reached their destination, Elijah bowed and backed away.

"Why have you summoned me at this late hour?"

"In due time, Erik," Gustoff said. "Elijah will remove your clothing. The steam baths are delightful and will ease the cramps and aches in your muscles that must have accumulated over so many days of dormancy."

Galen untied the sash as his waist. He shrugged his shoulders. The jade robe fell to the stone floor. "I'm not an invalid." He peeled the taut leggings from his body and stepped free.

"Nicely done, Erik. I appreciate the fact you feel angered by Thea's insistence that you are unable to handle even the most mundane task on your own. I know I would, were I in your place. Come, the stairway is here." Gustoff placed his hand on Galen's arm and led him to the steps.

Galen eased into the hot water, expecting the frothing liquid to burn his flesh but found the temperature perfect. Jets buried within the lumastones sent tiny bursts of air up through the water to massage his aching muscles, shoulders to toes. Galen couldn't help but relax as the tension ebbed slowly away.

He closed his eyes.

A gentle presence touched his mind.

* * * *

Sleep, warrior. While the pool works its miracles upon your body, I will take what I need from your mind.

Gustoff knelt behind the warrior by the side of the pool. He leaned forward, pressed his fingertips to the warrior's temples, and then closed his eyes. He felt muscles work to expand and deflate powerful lungs. Heard blood pump sluggishly through the warrior's body. Experienced every emotional or physical change that occurred within the warrior's body as he delved deeply into the man's mind, weaving slowly through every thought, pausing to examine more deeply when something of interest caught his attention, then pushing on.

Moments ticked by. Perspiration dripped from Gustoff's forehead. His arms shook, protesting the position he held them in for so long, but neither his fingers nor his concentration wavered.

Until he reached a mass of knotted emotions even his power could not breach.

Gustoff probed harder to shift through thoughts the warrior, even in deep sleep, fought hard to hide. Bits and pieces surfaced. The warrior's homeland in devastation. People dead and dying all around. Blood. So much blood. Torture. Pain.

Gustoff saw the warrior escaping the clutches of some unknown force.

Blood pumped furiously through the warrior's veins when the sensation of running hard came upon him.

Exhaustion. More running. Cold. So very cold ...

Gustoff began to tremble. Chills crawled over his flesh. The turmoil in the warrior's mind caused his stomach to quiver. He drew a deep breath and continued. Drugs entered his system, slowing his heart rate, making it impossible to move his arms or close his fists. Raising his eyelids became a monumental task.

Exhaustion.

More running. This time internally as his mind attempted to flee whatever had happened to him.

Gustoff's breathing constricted.

Thea's face appeared. Her expression full of concern and longing. Something within the warrior warmed, then blazed red hot.

Lust. Blood pumping frantically to the warrior's loins.

Gustoff's old heart raced to accommodate the flow.

Perspiration dripped down Gustoff's cheeks, pooled against the flesh of the warrior's temples, wet his fingers.

Something black and forbidding caused Gustoff to jerk spasmodically. Hatred. Deep. Consuming.

Berezan's face.

Blood. More blood. Then deep agony.

Gustoff opened his eyes. He released his fingers from the warrior's temples and sat back to steady his own frantic breathing. With the assistance of Elijah, Gustoff slowly gained his feet. He stared down at the warrior's prone form. "You will sleep for several more moments, warrior."

He turned to Elijah and whispered, "Leave the warrior alone. Allow him to depart the chamber unattended and explore to his heart's content. He cannot leave the Keep."

Elijah nodded.

Gustoff walked around the pool, cast a last glance over his shoulder toward the warrior, and then shook his head. If all he discovered was true, he must begin his journey to Borderland immediately.

He then turned to Elijah again. "I will need an equox prepared for a trip across the Tundra. I will also need supplies sufficient to sustain a journey of six days. Please, see that all is prepared before sunrise."

Elijah nodded again and back away from the bathing chamber.

Gustoff glanced over his shoulder to the warrior still sleeping beside the pool. He decided he would keep his true purpose from Thea, for he feared if he disclosed his plan too soon, Thea would insist upon joining him. At this point, he did not want her to know the full scope of Borderland's plight, or the impact it would have upon Glacia should he not succeed in his mission to unite Glacia and Borderland and see Berezan's reign ended.

He closed his eyes and prayed it was not already too late.

CHAPTER 9

"Thea."

A cold hand touched her bare shoulder. Thea adjusted her gown then grasped the coverlet and pulled it around her body. The sound of Gustoff's voice hadn't awakened her. Too many troubled thoughts occupied her mind. Sleep, and the wondrous escape it offered, had eluded her for over an hour.

"Thea. Wake up." Gustoff's voice echoed through the darkness. "Now, child. There is much you should know, and time is of the essence."

Thea sat up in bed. "I'm awake."

"Good."

The mattress sagged under Gustoff's weight. His cold fingers entwined with hers, offering comfort. "I must leave for Borderland this night, Thea. I may already be too late."

Thea rose from the bed. She felt her way across the chamber until she located the lumalantern on the table near the hearth and slid the cap upward. Weak light spread over part of the chamber. "What's happened?"

"I have had a vision from the Ancient Ones that demands I go to Borderland and discover firsthand the destruction Berezan has created so that we might make a more solid defense here in Glacia," he said. "I cannot go into all of the details now. It will take too long and we need to make plans for the moonrises ahead."

"Should I go with you?"

"Not this time. You must remain here in Glacia. The journey I take will be made in great haste for I go now to seek an alliance with the leaders of Borderland."

Thea nodded and returned to the bed. She grasped Gustoff's hand. "I've been giving Glacia's destiny a lot of thought, Gus."

Gustoff squeezed her hand. "Have you drawn any conclusions?"

Thea met her mentor's kind gaze. "Should anything happen to you or me, the people of Glacia must be protected. Without the powers of the Sphere of Light to guide them, we can't expect our gentle subjects to take up arms against Berezan. Unless we have some alternative, I fear they will become victims of Berezan's evil."

"Go on."

"Elijah has informed me that the reconstruction at Dekar will be completed within a few moonrises. After the people of the Settlement move to occupy the upper levels, Dekar will still be partially empty."

Gustoff rose and walked to the hearth. He placed several dried boughs into the grate, poked at the smoldering embers until a bright blaze filled the pit, then returned to her side.

"I have a plan to evacuate the people of Glacia."

"To Dekar?"

"Yes. I remembered the old tunnels the Ancient Ones created in the forests. With enough time, the people of Glacia could use those tunnels to flee to safety."

"What of the Elders?"

"What of the Elders? They have done nothing to alter the fate of our people. It's our duty, my destiny to protect all, whether or not the Elders consent."

Gustoff smiled. "I agree."

"I also have an alternate plan in the event our people don't have enough advance warning to flee." Thea sat beside Gustoff on the bed and grasped his hand. "I plan to solicit Nola's and Elijah's help again. They're well known among the people of the village, and if evacuation fails, they will be able to speak with the masses and caution them not to resist Berezan's takeover of Glacia, to acquiesce to his wishes, and do nothing to cause themselves harm."

"You will be committing the people of Glacia to slavery, Thea."

"Slavery's better than death. As long as the people live, there's hope."

Gustoff stood. "While you initiate your plans, I will be en route to Borderland. I think you should take special care of the warrior. See that the Messahs do not meet with him again." Gustoff considered telling Thea all he knew of the warrior's past then decided against it. To do so he would have to explain how he actually received such information. And, he was not proud of the method he had used as he broke one of the Ancient Ones sacred laws.

He weighed his discovery of the warrior's reaction to Thea against the response he felt holding Thea's hand, and decided to let destiny take its course. To do that he needed Thea to discover for herself that the warrior was not now and never had been blind.

"The warrior grows stronger by the day. He needs exercise. He should get out and about."

Thea nodded.

Gustoff released her hand. "I should return within six days."

"I pray your mission will be successful, Gus. Please, go with care. I love you," Thea whispered, but she knew her words went unheard.

Gustoff had left her chamber.

* * * *

Thea walked to her dressing table, picked up the brush, and tried to work the tangles out of her hair. Frustrated by the futile attempt, she dropped the brush, turned and opened the door of her wardrobe to snatch a clean gown from a hanger. Without a backward glance, she left her chamber.

She paused briefly before the warrior's door. Fighting the palpitations of her heart and the strange ache in her belly, she hurried down the flight of stairs to the glide. A warm bath would soothe her distraught nerves, wash the warrior's scent from her body. Thea shook her head. Water might flush away the warrior's touch, but nothing would erase the want, the need, from her heart.

She closed her eyes as the glide slipped silently downward. She wished she had someone to talk to, someone to explain what was happening to her body. Nola's sweet face materialized in her mind, but Thea brushed it away. Some secrets she couldn't reveal, even to her most trusted friend. The word lust slipped into her mind, and she realized exactly what she was doing. Lusting for the warrior, craving him with a hunger far deeper than anything she'd ever experienced.

Yet, her feelings were deeper, less easily defined. His welfare was foremost in her thoughts. Most of the time. She cared that he recovered from his ordeal at Dekar, wanted him to regain his sight, his memory. More than anything, she desired to erase the haunted look from his beautiful eyes.

The glide stopped. Thea opened her eyes. She drew three deep breaths, exhaled, then hurried from the glide, across the granite walkway into the hydro-gardens, down the corridor toward the bathing chamber.

She skidded to a halt at the arched entrance of the chamber. She had to grab the wall beside her to steady her balance.

The warrior stood naked in the bubbling water.

Thea exhaled slowly. He hadn't heard her approach. He was too intent upon scrubbing his chest and arms with a large bar of soap.

She bit her tongue to keep from gasping when he raised arms to work a rich lather through his hair. The muscles in his broad back bunched and relaxed. A trail of bubbles snaked slowly over his shoulder blades, down the curve of his spine, paused on his firm buttocks, his upper thighs, then disappeared into the pool.

Thea leaned against the granite wall, desperately needing the support her wobbly legs failed to give. Breathing was no longer a normal bodily function. Her heart felt as it if had stalled and now raced to catch up with the frenzied blood flow through her veins.

She tried to close her eyes, to block out the vision of the warrior before her, but her brain ceased to function and refused to respond.

The warrior dipped below the water to rinse the soap from his hair. He surfaced, standing tall and proud once again in the center. He shook his mane of blond hair and water flew from it.

Thea stood transfixed, unable to pull away from the supporting wall, incapable of retreating.

No. She had no idea she'd uttered the word aloud.

He turned.

Under different circumstances, Thea might have been amused by the expression that crossed the warrior's face when he realized he wasn't alone in the bathing chamber. But these were in no way normal circumstances. She wasn't in the chamber staring at him as he lay upon the bed, the fur coverlet hiding his muscular physique from view. Her sudden traitorous thoughts didn't help her situation.

"Thea?"

She gasped. All muscle control dissolved. She slid slowly down the wall until she sat upon the stone floor. She watched as he took a step forward.

"Come into the pool, Thea," he whispered. "You came for a bath and I have no desire to deny you that pleasure."

Thea could only stare at him in awe.

She swallowed hard. "No. I want…. I came looking for you." The steamy air filled with his masculine scent. She tried to look away from all of his golden, muscular flesh, but her body resisted the command of her brain.

He stepped out of the pool and walked closer.

"Thea," he whispered as his long, tanned fingers worked through the thickness of her hair to cup her chin. "Don't be embarrassed. Take my hand."

The heat that turned her muscles limp moments before was all but paralyzing her. She could only stare up at his proffered hand, wanting to accept it, accept him.

Her hand shook when she released her death grip on the fabric of her gown and lifted her fingers to meet the thicker, stronger ones awaiting her touch. She watched his fingers close around hers. She couldn't hold back the small sigh that escaped her lips.

"Your bath awaits." He bent and picked her up as if she weighed no more than a bundle of fleece.

Thea squeezed her eyes shut, willing away the waves of pleasure his touch evoked. This wasn't right. Not possible. She couldn't be falling in love with him. It would be unthinkable. He was her prisoner, held to portray her stepbrother in a charade to save her home, and his.

His steps were slow, careful, as he walked toward the pool. He descended the stairs before releasing her from the cradle of his arms and allowed her body to glide down the front of his. The warmth of his flesh, the steam and bubbles from the pool, the sensuous slide of wet silk against hot flesh caused Thea to tremble.

He released her and took a step back.

Thea groped for the edge of the pool. She looked around for a means of escape. She found only a wall of muscle, still as a statue, beautiful and godlike in his nudity between her and the chamber exit.

The mist and shadows and eerie pale light of the lumas surrounded them in an ethereal glow.

Despite the moisture in the air, her throat felt dry, her mouth felt like it was filled with cloth. Every breath she drew stretched the wet silk of her gown, sliding the fabric over her taut nipples, and sent spirals of pleasure to tingle between her legs.

Memories of what she was, who he was, dissolved. The broad expanse of his chest filled her gaze, lured her fingers like metal to a magnet. She reached forward to lay her palms against his chest, trace her fingers slowly upward, across the wide span of his shoulders to the broad base of his neck--higher to the lush fullness of his long golden hair.

Her lips trembled. She had no idea how to proceed. What to say to make him kiss her again as he had days ago when she lay upon his body in the bedchamber.

He reached forward to close his hands around her waist and drew her to his chest. His lips smothered her whimper of longing when he tightened his embrace. His mouth moved forcefully, possessively over hers then slipped over her chin, down her neck, and blazed a path of fire to the tautness of her silk-clad breasts.

Thea gasped as moist, suckling heat enclosed her extended nipple. She felt him lift her, recognized the hardness of the stone pool beneath her buttocks, and realized his large hands were tearing at the sash of her gown.

She couldn't find the words to deny him as he pushed the silk from her shoulders and bent to lave her bare nipple with his tongue.

He lowered his other hand to caress the contour of her leg from knee to the top of her thigh. He spread his large hand over her mound and pushed one strong finger inside her. Tremors raced through her body as his finger wove a special magic. He added a second finger, delving deep, retreating, deeper still.

She matched the rhythm of his intimate caress, unashamed at the wanton way she met each trust. Each withdrawal.

Something inside her coiled tighter and tighter. The friction from his fingers increased. Faster. Faster still until spasm after spasm of ecstasy rocked her body and threatened to destroy all traces of sanity.

She gasped for breath, yet she didn't give up her hold on his hair. Everything about her blurred. She felt as if she were floating, experiencing an out-of-body trance. When her world righted itself, she was lying on the pillows of purple and red that topped the wall around the pool. The weight of the warrior's body was upon her. His heavy erection hot and hard against her thigh. She instinctively tried to resist the force that coaxed her legs apart.

"Don't, Thea," he whispered.

Thea released his hair and clutched at his shoulders. She did not intend to resist him. Ever. She sighed when his weight bore down more fully upon her, welcoming, accepting him.

He breached her hard and fast, stretching her, filling her. The tiny pain she felt fled instantly as she met each wild thrust, moving with each surge--deeper and deeper--until he touched the very depths of her soul.

Galen heard Thea's cries of awe, felt the tearing of the thin membrane that sheltered her innocence, recognized his own astonishment when her untutored body arched to meet his. He was cognizant of her tightness, of how miraculously her body stretched to accommodate his. He slid his hands beneath her, raised her hips higher, filled her deeper as the quivers that mounted within the folds of her sweet flesh closed tight around him.

He flipped over to his back, bringing Thea to straddle him. He clamped his rough, callused hands over her buttocks and guided her movements until her climax ebbed and he found his own release.

As she lay exhausted in his embrace, Galen closed his eyes and cursed himself. He'd thought one taste of her would ease his lust and permit him to concentrate on his plans for revenge. Instead, as he clung to her as fiercely as she clung to him, he realized he'd never have his full of his enchanting keeper. She'd permeate his every thought, the very essence of his being, until he drew his last breath.

* * * *

Solarus

Berezan slapped a leather-riding crop against his satin-covered leg. He paced around the small table in the center of the tower, pausing at the window to shake his head, then continue. One final circle and he stopped before his commander. "Prepare my army to march immediately."

The tall man bowed his head in acknowledgement.

Berezan looked at Elsbar. "Elsbar will tell you all he knows of Glacia."

Again, R'han nodded. "All will be ready, Master."

Berezan grasped the other end of the crop and bent it until the brittle leather almost snapped. "Good. See to your men."

R'han rapped his fist against his chest three times, turned and left the tower.

Berezan threw the crop on the table. He walked across the tower to the window, clasped his fingers atop the sill and lowered his forehead to rest against his hands.

"I remember Governing House as if I last saw it yesterday, Elsbar. I see each corridor, the meeting rooms, and the hydro-gardens beneath the main floor. In my dreams, my nightmares, I have counted each granite stone, doorway, and step. I've even seen myself sleeping in my father's chamber, snuggled before the warmth of the carved fireplace."

"Two and a half decades are a long time to hold a memory, Berezan. You cannot rely on the visions of your youth to guide an invasion. Much will have changed in your absence. You must have facts. Gustoff may be old, but he is in no way stupid. His powers may have weakened slightly, but he is still a very dangerous adversary. He will know you are coming to Glacia to search for the Sphere of Light. He will use every available weapon to protect it."

Berezan raised his head. He turned to face Elsbar. "The Glacians are not the Creeans, old man. They have no armies to fight my warriors. Will Gustoff oppose me if all he knows and protects is threatened? I think not."

Elsbar folded his hands in front of him on the table and shook his head. "You take Gustoff too lightly, Berezan. The power of the Sphere guides him. No warriors, no weapons, no might of any type can defeat the ultimate

Light. Warriors in armor, men cloaked by magic, even you, will be destroyed if the power is unleashed against you.

"The Ancient Ones were educators. In our quest for retribution, we have twisted their scriptures, nurtured the darkness until it has grown into a living, dangerous thing. We have destroyed all who were able to stand in our way to this point, but we have not been truly tested."

"I have no intention of failing when the results will produce what I've desired my entire life," Berezan growled.

"You have grown insolent, Berezan. We cannot waste twenty-five years of hard work by allowing the hunger for victory to overshadow common sense. Caution is the key to success, not might. Do not forget my latest vision. I foresaw blood, death, and destruction so great it shook the world from axis to axis. I cannot say whose death the vision foretold. It could be yours or mine."

Berezan raised his hands and ran his fingers through his hair. He stared at Elsbar. Finally, after exercising what little control he had over his fierce temper, he walked across the tower floor, placed his hands upon the table where Elsbar worked, and leaned down until he was almost nose to nose with the old man.

"I will not fail, Elsbar. You have given me much, but I'm strong on my own account. I have no doubts I'll meet and destroy Gustoff. The Sphere of Light and the unlimited power it expends will be mine."

Elsbar stared up into Berezan's brown eyes. He studied the flush that turned the younger man's ruddy complexion a deeper hue of red, the disruption of his russet hair where his fingers passed repeatedly in frustration.

"You do not understand all you will encounter in Glacia. You refuse to comprehend the power of the Sphere and think you can bend it to your command. It takes many long hours of training to wield the powers of the Sphere. Some of the Ancient Ones were never fully capable of controlling the power it releases. You are trained in the Ancient One's arts, but you have not had the opportunity to actually feel the full scope of the Sphere's force.

"With the proper training, the magic of the Sphere can lay the whole of our world at your feet. Without the proper preparation, you could destroy our world completely. Yet you glory only in the limited knowledge you possess, and do not fathom how anything could be greater.

"You are young, Berezan. Power, and the ability to use it, comes with age. Do not allow the few petty victories you have gained thus far to inflate your ego further. These triumphs are but small skirmishes in our overall scheme. The rulers of Solarus were weak. They believed themselves safe simply because of their numbers.

"Annihilation of the Creeans came about because your warriors murdered old men, women, and innocent children. The warriors of Borderland did not arrive until your massacre was completed and all but a few members of your army had begun the journey home to Solarus.

"Your capture and torture of Sar's son after your attack against Borderland confirmed the Creeans have no knowledge of the Sphere of Light. The search you conducted also proved this."

Elsbar reached across the table and touched Berezan's hand. "The warriors of Borderland have not been defeated. They are still out there and, I fear, waiting. When Galen Sar escaped your henchmen, I am sure he returned to his home to unite with his warriors and plan your defeat.

"You did not heed my warning when I tried to prohibit your invasion of Borderland. Instead of gaining aid in your quest, you created more enemies, foes far more dangerous than those you will face from the gentle people of Glacia. The heir of Shakara will seek to end your life path before you reach your destiny."

"You cannot see my final destiny, Elsbar. You've told me this a hundred times. Should Galen of Borderland try to lead an army against mine, he will be exterminated as he should have been while I had him in my possession."

Elsbar ignored Berezan's threats against the Creeans. "Your life path is clouded. No definite course exists for you to follow to the Ancient Ones. I believe Gustoff knew this. I also think he had not the knowledge to turn your path according to his wishes. The old servant woman knew of your exile because of the evil Gustoff sensed. His fear of castigation by the Ancient Ones must have kept him from ending your life."

"His weakness, you mean."

Elsbar drummed his gnarled fingers against the wood of the table. Berezan's stubbornness tested his patience almost beyond control. "One more time. Gustoff is not weak, he is strong, and he can be quite devious. The Sphere of Light adds significantly to his power and will destroy you if you do not proceed according to the plans we have made."

"If I destroy Gustoff before he is able to reclaim the Sphere from wherever he's hidden it, Glacia will be under my power. I'll be able to search Governing House at my leisure. Without Gustoff to lead a resistance, no Glacian would dare take a stand against me."

"I will not be there when you attempt absorption."

"I know the words, old man. I understand the ceremony. I can control the Sphere. Glacia and the Sphere and all of its powers will be mine if I have to destroy every being upon this world. All will be mine."

CHAPTER 10

Thea tried to wiggle her legs free, only to feel the warm pressure of the warrior's hand spread across her upper abdomen, his fingers touch the underside of her breast. Warmth permeated her belly. Memories, vivid and wild, streaked along each nerve.

Awareness of where she was--lying naked in the warrior's embrace--caused her body to quiver. Three deep breaths didn't calm the escalating pace of her heart, or chase away the sense of panic that suddenly sent chills racing over every inch of her flesh.

What had she done?

She should've heeded Gustoff's warning and never given in to the emotions the warrior created. It might have been possible to use the powers of her mind to overshadow his magical allure, but she'd never truly tried to resist him. Even now, she longed only to lie in his arms, to forget the future and all the evil it held.

She closed her eyes and allowed the steamy air to caress her flesh, to experience again the pleasure of his hard body fused with hers.

In one moment of weakness, she'd seduced the man she'd kidnapped to portray her stepbrother. And, she had enjoyed.

She opened her eyes to glance around the chamber. The robe she'd worn lay at poolside, soaked. Her other gown, hastily chosen from the wardrobe before she left her chamber, lay on the floor in the center of the archway where she'd dropped it earlier.

She reached forward to lift his hand from her abdomen and position it on the pillow beside her. The urge to kiss his cheek was almost stronger than her will to resist.

She eased from his embrace, picked up the robe she'd discarded, and left the chamber.

* * * *

Thea stood in the middle of Gustoff's dark tower. She shivered when the cold air touched her. Wrapping her arms around her waist for what little heat they offered, she hurried to the other side of the tower and pulled a gray robe from the peg where Gustoff left it. The woolen cloak swallowed her up and brought renewed warmth to her body. She folded the cuffs over several times at her wrists, reached up, and covered her damp hair with the cowl, then turned toward the fire pit.

She added several, brittle pieces of wood beneath the cauldron Gustoff kept suspended over the center hearth, struck the tinder she found in the pocket of the robe, and watched as the dried boughs flared to life. After adding several more pieces of wood, she walked to the chair beneath the tower window and watched the fire grow, felt the flames take the chill from the air.

She leaned against the back of the chair and closed her eyes. Many times, she'd come to the tower with Gustoff. Each visit for another lesson in the strange powers she possessed. She thought about the words of caution that always preceded Gustoff's instruction, reminders of the danger she'd face if her abilities were discovered.

Repeatedly, she'd promised never to tell anyone what they did in the tower, never to reveal the secrets passed to her, and most of all, never to expose her talents to anyone.

Over the years, she'd kept all but one of those promises. She shook away thoughts of her most recent transgression with the warrior, and considered the summer of her fifteenth winter when Nola's younger brother had fallen and broken his leg. The Elders healers were summoned, but in the panic that ensued, she'd forgotten all of her sacred promises and touched the youngster's fractured leg.

Five servants witnessed her action.

In order to keep tales of her deed from spreading over Glacia, she and Gustoff had taken the servants into their confidence, explained the talents she possessed. The servants swore never to reveal her secrets to anyone, and to this day, no one else within the Keep knew of her special powers or her vulnerabilities.

Except the warrior.

Thea opened her eyes and stared into the graying night sky. Memories of the warrior filled her. She'd made another dreadful mistake this moonrise. She'd weakened to the strange cravings of her emotions and body, and accepted a moment's pleasure from the warrior's touch. The after effect of the warrior's lovemaking now left her confused.

She needed to work through what she felt for the warrior, be it love or lust. To understand the wonderful things that happened within her, the magical pinnacles she'd achieved.

Thea rose and walked to the table. She picked up the lone candle, touched it to the fire beneath the cauldron, and then returned it to its position on the table. Closing her eyes, she spoke words taught to her many years ago.

The candle flickered and flared. White light filled the tower.

"Help me, Ancient Ones," she whispered. "I've taken a man into my body and offered him my love, though I have not spoken the words. I have dreams. Fantasies. I suddenly want things I've never imagined. I know my life is predestined. I realize I'm for a greater purpose.

"Is it selfish of me to want love and happiness?

"Things aren't so easily defined as they once were. Help me see the future, know what fate awaits me. Gustoff has taught me all he can, but I feel I'm not fully prepared to undertake the quest you've set before me."

The light grew brighter.

"I try to understand what is expected of me, but I don't know how I, one person, shall accomplish such a task without help."

The light dimmed until its luminescence filled no more than a hand's span of space. Thea concentrated on the light, watched it flicker, felt the warmth flood her face.

She closed her eyes. A vision formed in her mind.

Through a haze, a great army marched toward her wearing cloaks that matched the sand beneath their feet. More of Berezan's army riding equox followed. Hundreds. Thousands. An enormous cloud of dust choked the air, filled the sky with darkness.

More men came.

The noise from their march was deafening.

Still they came. Marching. Riding. Closer. Closer.

The terrain changed. Trees surrounded them. Great, mighty specters of green reached high into the sky, so thick they blocked out the heavens.

Still the men came.

Marching. Hacking with enormous swords. Cutting away the undergrowth that hampered their progress.

A huge black equox filled the night. Atop the beast, another, more menacing creature sat, emerald cape swirling in the air, gloved hand raised high.

Lightning bolts sprang from his fingertips. Blood flowed profusely from the equox's nose. Thunder rumbled over the pounding of booted feet.

Marching. Marching.

Thea opened her eyes. She stared into the flame of the candle, no more than a flicker now, and prayed what she'd seen was a dream. A nightmare.

If not, the beast in the emerald cape could only be Berezan.

Did the vision tell of the future, or events currently taking place?

She rose and paced the tower. She tried to consider what her father might have done if he were aware of a threat to the populace of Glacia. There was no way to fight a force of such strength, no way to thwart the attack.

Thea dropped into the chair beneath the window and folded her hands in her lap. Thousands would die needlessly unless something was done immediately. Would the plans she'd discussed with Gustoff work to protect the people of Glacia?

She couldn't meet and defeat a foe many thousands strong alone. One led by a force of evil no average man could even understand.

What if her vision only predicted some future event? Could she risk alarming the people of Glacia unnecessarily? Mass panic would follow information of an invasion. She considered all Gustoff told her about Berezan and realized they never should have trusted him to hold true to his arrival date.

What if Berezan had heard of Erik's demise?

The warrior's face, and everything she'd learned of the Creean race, filled her mind. The Creeans were trained in combat, had been for many decades since Shakara walked Borderland.

The people of Glacia were as lambs led to slaughter.

She closed her eyes and mentally summoned Nola and Elijah to her chamber, then left the tower.

* * * *

Galen opened his eyes to find himself alone atop a pile of pillows. He pushed up to study the chamber. Nothing had changed. When he spread his hand over the pillows where Thea slept, he could still feel her warmth, still smell her scent clinging to the silky fabric so he knew she hadn't been gone long.

He'd made love to her twice, but his need hadn't been sated. Plans to have her again dissolved when she fell asleep and he was too exhausted to wake her.

Cursing the exhaustion that overtook him at the most trying times, he threw his legs over the side and sat up.

He knew Thea would try to escape without waking him. He planned to pretend sleep so he could follow her back to his chamber.

Galen picked up his discarded leggings and dressed. He studied the chamber and found Thea's wet robe at the edge of the pool, the garment she'd brought to wear after her bath gone from the stone floor.

Thoughts of all that beautiful flesh exposed stirred now-familiar longings in his groin. He cursed his inability to control Thea's affect on his body, stood and walked through the archway. He was determined to find out where his enchanting little warden had taken off to, but not before he took time to explore the lower chamber of the Keep.

* * * *

Galen put his shoulder into the ancient door he'd found, hoping to use his strength to push it open. The brittle wood creaked beneath his blow, but didn't give. He stepped back to study the rusty hinges. He tried again, only to knock the breath from his lungs with the force of his shove.

The door held firm.

He leaned against the opposite side of the corridor and looked around. For over an hour he'd explored every cavern and corridor he'd found in the lower chamber. About to give up, he pressed against the stone wall and felt cold air blow over his back. Upon investigation, he discovered what he believed to be a hidden passageway and set about trying to open it.

He pulled from the opposite wall and ran his fingers over the smooth granite stones until he mapped out what appeared to be a doorway enclosed in the rock. He searched for a hidden switch to open it. After several moments and no success, his temper got the better of him and he kicked the stone. He received bruised toes and a crack in the stone wall large enough to place his fingers into as a reward.

When he shoved the door open, he found another dark passageway. He secured a lumalantern from one of the sconces in the outer corridor and wiped years of accumulated cobwebs from his face as he followed the passage, twisting and turning for almost three hundred spans before he reached an ancient wooden door.

With no lock or handle to open the mysterious door, Galen assumed it opened from the other side. Sure he'd finally located a path of escape, he spent the next few moments attempting to open the door.

Frigid air entered through the tiny cracks near the hinges. More flowed in through the inch-wide opening beneath the planks.

Galen shivered and wished he'd thought to find something warmer to wear before he began this venture. His feet were numb. His toes, even the ones he'd bruised, tingled. The leggings from his jungle homeland did little to warm his legs.

Frustration grew. He pulled away from the cold wall and tried once more to break open the door.

He shook his head when the door refused to open and pledged he'd find something to use as a wedge on his next sojourn, bent to pick up the luma he'd left on the floor and walked out of the passageway. He followed the path of disrupted cobwebs back to the secret entrance.

He'd been on his own long enough to be missed, he made his way back to the center station in the hydro-gardens and sat down to wait, determined to put his ruse of blindness in effect somewhere he could warm his cold body.

* * * *

"Thea?"

Nola and Elijah stood in the doorway.

She smiled. "Come in."

"Did you wish our services?" Nola asked as she hurried across the chamber to pause by the chaise where Thea sat.

Thea slid from the chaise and made herself comfortable on the floor near the fire. "Sit with me. I have much to tell you." She waited while Nola and Elijah took a seat beside her, then looked into Nola's eyes.

Sadness tugged at her heart. Nola. Sweet, nervous, Nola. A curious little woman with pale blonde hair and expressive blue eyes, three years older than Thea's own twenty-two winters.

Friend. Confidant. Companion.

Thea smiled. Nola might fidget and fret, but in the end, she'd handle the responsibilities placed upon her like the most steadfast warrior.

She then glanced at Elijah. At fifty-five winters, the slender gray-haired man had been her most avid supporter. He'd come to serve as leader of the servants in the Keep shortly after his mate of twenty winters passed away. His two sons were grown and had families of their own living among the people of the village.

Elijah would need his sons' support to carry out the task she was about to assign him, but Thea had no doubt Elijah would do everything within his power to see his mission succeed.

"You have been my trusted friends my entire life. I don't know what I'd have done without you."

Nola shifted uneasily.

Thea touched her hand. "I must ask you once again to hold a secret for me. One that must be revealed only if the people of Glacia are in danger."

Thea told Nola and Elijah of the vision she'd seen in Gustoff's tower, of the threat Berezan posed to the people of Glacia.

Though his voice trembled, Elijah asked, "What can we do?"

"Gustoff's gone to Borderland to seek an alliance against Berezan with the Creeans. Should his mission fail, the people of Glacia will be left to their own devices to face Berezan's evil."

"But the Sphere of Light--"

"Is the object of Berezan's quest," Thea said, cutting Nola off mid-sentence. She didn't want to hear the rest of Nola's question. "The Ancient Ones have entrusted me with the destiny of protecting world peace. It's my duty to use the Sphere's powers to see that people of Glacia are not placed into danger by Berezan's evil."

"Thea, you can't hope to meet Berezan alone."

She looked into Elijah's eyes. "I'll do whatever I must, my friend."

"But...."

Thea waved away Nola's objections. "Several moonrises ago, Elijah and I set plans into motion to radically change the circumstances at Dekar Facility. We acted in Erik's name, and ordered the fortress refurbished to house the people who live in the settlement. Yet, the majority of the structure is still unoccupied."

Thea walked across the chamber to stare into the fire.

"While I've never walked among the people of Glacia, or spoken to anyone other than those employed in Governing House, you two are trusted by all outside the Keep walls. You have friends and families among the population."

She sat down between Nola and Elijah. "I must ask for your help."

"Whatever we might do to assist you will be our honor, Thea," Elijah said.

Nola agreed.

Thea looked into Elijah's eyes. "We must use the plans we made to evacuate the people to the safety of Dekar."

She then glanced at Nola. "Are you aware of the ancient tunnels hidden in the forest?"

Nola nodded.

"Should something unforeseen happen, I want both of to speak with the people, have them gather their belongings, follow you through the tunnels, down the mountain, and into the Tundra. You will seek refuge at Dekar in Erik's name and remain there until it's safe to return to Glacia."

"What if there's no time?" Nola asked.

"If ample warning is not given to leave Glacia, then pass messages among the people. Advise them not to resist Berezan in any way. I don't believe he'd have a reason to harm anyone if he meets no opposition."

Tears slipped down Nola's face. "I can't leave you, Thea."

Thea reached to hug her dear friend close. "I'll be fine, and so will you."

"What of the warrior?" Elijah asked.

Thea sighed, memories of the last few hours swelling inside her heart. "I wish I knew."

CHAPTER 11

Borderland

Gustoff brushed the heavy fur aside and stepped into yet another empty house. He looked around, noting that, like the others, nothing had been disturbed for quite a while. He backed out and walked to the center of the encampment to pause and study the heavy foliage surrounding the village. Giant iferas hid the sky. Plants with leaves as wide across as a man's arm span hugged the jungle floor. Greens in hues from pale to almost black shadowed the clearing. Flowers of every imaginable size and color sprang from vines wrapped around tree trunks, dangled from limbs, attached to houses, then descended to the ground to disburse in vibrant patches of life.

He studied the construction of the dwellings, each built from granite stone similar to the ones used in Glacia, but cut into smaller blocks and fitted with strange mortar that looked almost black against the glittering stones. The houses were small, perhaps only three or four rooms. Strange, tanned animal furs hung at the windows and covered the doors.

Pens, built of logs cut from the numerous species of trees that thrived in the jungle, sat empty.

No creatures chirped in the foliage. No birds sang from the trees. A deathlike silence crept along with the wind rippling through the leaves.

This was the third such village Gustoff had visited. He took time to study the tools the Creeans used, the weapons left upon the ground. He had believed the people of Borderland to be primitive, had not expected their civilization to be so advanced in some ways, as indicated by the construction of their weapons, yet so backward in others, as evidenced in the tools they used to cultivate their foodstuffs.

He thought about Thea's wish for one world, one people, and how the advancements of the Glacians could benefit the people of Borderland.

A strange premonition crept over him. If there were people of the Borderland.

Gustoff closed his eyes. He tensed every muscle in his body and reached out, seeking a human presence.

He found nothing.

He drew deeply for greater strength and tried again.

Still nothing.

He opened his eyes. There was one more village to search.

* * * *

Gustoff stood before an enormous dwelling three stores high and at least fifty spans wide. He stared at the bronze doors that barred entrance.

A wide stone stairway, guarded by a pair of bronzed beasts Gustoff did not recognize, beckoned. He stepped carefully, honing his senses to be cautious as he ascended, then paused before the bronzed doors. He sensed a place of great reverence, a Temple of some sort, and dared not breach its walls. Instead, he closed his eyes, slipped into a trance, and concentrated on the center of the dwelling.

His essence filled the chamber. He floated above the floor, not desecrating the holy place with his tracks. He paused at an enormous stone altar and studied the bronzed sun suspended above it. He concentrated on the sun, feeling a power foreign to anything he had ever encountered.

He focused all of his energy to answer the plea.

Visions swam before him. Masses murdered. Villages beyond the city of Cree destroyed. The mount of Naro violated by hordes of warriors trespassing through its ancient tunnels. Then, more clearly, hundreds of faces came to him. Young ones. Old ones. Some strong, some weak. All begging for help.

Gustoff opened his eyes to study the two bronzed creatures that guarded the sanctuary. A voice whispered within his mind, telling him to trust his instincts and to go to those people he had sensed, to offer whatever he could to ease their suffering.

"What are you about, old man?"

Gustoff turned to find twelve huge warriors, all similar in appearance to the warrior at Glacia. He studied their clothing, the same as the warrior had worn at Dekar, and noted the length of their hair, ranging in color from deep brown to near white.

"I mean you no harm, warriors of Borderland. I come in peace to offer whatever assistance I can to your people."

A warrior stepped forward. "We trust no one, old man."

"I can understand your hesitation. But, I am old. What possible harm could I do against mighty men such as you?"

The warrior turned to look at those around him. All nodded agreement with Gustoff's statement.

"Who are you?" the warrior before him asked.

Gustoff bowed his head, then raised it to look into the warrior's eyes. "I am Gustoff of Glacia. I traveled far to meet with your leader, Omar Sar. The business I have will be for his ears only."

A series of whispered conversation erupted around him. Gustoff tried to concentrate on the words, but was distracted when a small girl child pushed between the ring of warriors and ran forward to touch his purple robe.

"Pretty."

Gustoff looked into the child's sad eyes, eyes that had witnessed too much tragedy at a young age. He raised his hand to place it upon the girl's blonde head. "What is your name, child?"

The little girl smiled up at him. "I am called Deana, Regis."

Gustoff shook his head. "I am no one's Regis, child. Do not address me so."

The warrior who assumed leadership of the group stepped closer and placed his hand upon the child's shoulder. "Find your mother, little one. Go now."

The girl bowed her head and hurried away.

"I'm Jakar, old man. Omar Sar was murdered. His son taken, we fear also killed, by those who came to destroy Borderland. I'm in charge of the people who remain and look after their welfare. Any business you might have had with Sar will be told to me."

Gustoff tried hard to regain his composure after hearing the warrior's tale, but his heart refused to answer his command and beat furiously in his chest. He recalled the memories he had stolen from the warrior's mind at the Keep and wondered if the warrior might have witnessed the annihilation of his people.

"State your business, Gustoff of Glacia. We prepare to go to battle again and have no time to waste."

Gustoff's thoughts scattered. "Battle again?"

"I've placed lookouts high in the peaks of Naro. We have seen the advancing armies that come from Solarus. We make ready to defeat them."

"How many warriors do you have?"

"Twenty. One hundred or so more will come in from the jungles."

"So few against thousands. Do not be foolish. Hide. Berezan must believe he has already destroyed Borderland. He will not expect resistance. Do not risk yourselves needlessly. Protect your people, Jakar. Do not waste the few lives left."

"You speak strangely, Gustoff of Glacia. Warriors of Shakara must fight. Honor demands it."

Gustoff touched the warrior's arm. "Does your honor call for you to risk the eradication of your entire people, Jakar? Berezan's army will wipe the people of Borderland from the face of the world. He does not care about anyone or anything but his quest. And, that lies in Glacia. Hide yourselves, Jakar. Protect your people by saving them from pointless slaughter. Allow Deana to grow into an old woman and hold her own grand-children to her breasts."

The warrior closed his eyes. "Omar Sar would have been honored to meet you, Gustoff of Glacia. Your words are wise. We will protect our loved ones."

* * * *

The warrior wasn't in the bathing chamber. Someone, perhaps Elijah, must have led him back to his chamber. It was probably for the best, Thea decided. Thoughts of facing him so soon did little to still the emotions raging within her.

Thea picked up her wet robe from the rim of the pool and folded it across her arm. She walked toward the archway as she cast a final glance over her shoulder toward the pool. She pushed away forbidden memories and turned to walk back down the corridor toward the center station.

Instead of going back to her chamber, she climbed the stairs to Gustoff's tower.

"Gustoff?"

"We do not have much time." Gustoff held out his hand.

"What are you doing here, Gus? I thought you were to be gone for six risings?"

"It was necessary that I return with great haste," he said. Gustoff shook his head and smiled. "I could ask you why you are wearing my robe. I am sure the answer would be interesting, but I fear it will have to wait. Sit." He pointed toward the chair beneath the tower window.

Thea immediately did his bidding.

"In Borderland I found destruction beyond your imagination. When Berezan attacked the Borderland mooncycles ago, he killed hundreds of men, women, and children as he searched for the Sphere of Light."

"No."

"I located a small group of survivors. I met warriors similar to the one we rescued from Dekar. Jakar, the warrior left in charge, told me Omar Sar was murdered, his son taken hostage and presumed dead. There are only one hundred and twenty warriors left, Thea."

"Please, Gus. The warrior we--"

"Must have witnessed the massacre of his people. I believe he may be blocking the memories from his mind."

Memories of her own stampeded through her brain. The pain she'd witnessed many times in the warrior's blue eyes haunted her. The strange emotion she'd seen and could not identify became clear. Hatred. Her own scheme to use the warrior to serve her purpose now sickened her. He'd been through so much, and she'd plotted to place him in even more danger.

"Berezan's armies are coming, Thea."

Thea shook her head at Gustoff's words. "I know. I visited the tower a while ago, Gus. I needed to be alone to gather my thoughts." She turned away, unable to look into Gustoff's eyes. She thought about telling him of her intimacy with the warrior, but decided against it.

"I called upon the Ancient Ones to show me the future. I asked them to enlighten me as to what I could expect."

She drew a deep breath. "I saw an army, thousands strong, garbed in cloaks the color of the desert. I also saw men riding equox, carrying weapons.

"In the center of all these forces, a horrible man rode a huge black beast spewing blood from its nostrils. Lightning cracked from the man's fingertips. Thunder, louder than the army's marching boots, shook the ground."

Gustoff placed his hand upon her shoulder. "Thea."

She shook her head. "Berezan comes, Gus. I saw him. Felt him."

"He seeks the Sphere. We must protect it at all costs." Gustoff remembered the vision of his death. He would not be by Thea's side when she faced her brother. Would not be near to watch her wield the talisman that would destroy Berezan's evil.

"Am I ready? Do you feel that I'm strong enough to thwart Berezan's plans for Glacia?"

"Thea, you are strong enough to fulfill your destiny. Only believe in yourself and your sense of good."

Gustoff touched her hand. "The strength of our own will is all we are given, Thea. Although we are all Guardians of the Sphere, the power reacts differently on each of us. The blessing, and curse, of the Sphere is blind faith. I have no way to describe how the Sphere will extend its power through you. You must believe in your own capabilities, rely on the powers nurtured your whole life, and your distinction between good and evil.

"We all have misgivings, anxieties that must be faced. The responsibility we bear is great. It takes courage to face those self-doubts and fears. Courage you will find when you look deep into your heart."

"But, Gus...."

"Go to your bed, Thea. Place yourself into a trance and sleep. Forget all of your troubles until the morrow. Sunrise may bring hope."

Thea turned, kissed Gustoff on the cheek, then left the tower.

Gustoff walked to the window, raised his head, and looked heavenward. Visions of what he had seen haunted him. All of these scnseless tragedies could have been prevented if he had only been strong enough to end Berezan's life years ago.

"Forgive me," he whispered.

* * * *

Thea stared down into the fire. Purple, blue, white, brilliant orange and red blurred before her eyes into wavering lines of heat. She turned from the hearth and made several more sweeps of the chamber before she glanced toward the bed at the center of the room and shook her head.

She hadn't heeded Gustoff's directive. Placing herself into a trance to sleep away the hours until sunrise would accomplish little but wasted time. Time she couldn't afford to lose with destiny so close at hand.

She walked to the thick tapestries that shielded the chamber, parted the fabric and stepped outside. Several inches of new snow from last eve's storm coated the balcony floor. Thea ignored the cold that seeped through her thin slippers. She placed her hands upon the balcony wall, lowered her head, and prayed.

"Give me strength. Bless me as I walk the path chosen for my by the Ancient Ones. Help me to be steady in my beliefs, to hold fast to everything Gustoff has taught me."

Thea opened her eyes and studied the sky. Streaks of silver rose like an aura beyond the cliffs, reaching higher, then higher still, to crown the mountains of Glacia with an ethereal glow. The sun, a brilliant yellow sphere, parted the shadow of the peaks and slipped silently into the bluing of dawn.

Yet, sunrise offered no new hope, no apocalypse that would free Glacia and the whole of their world from the evil that threatened to destroy it.

Thea placed her hand over her breast, felt the steady beat within. She made a decision. The time for deception had passed.

She closed her eyes and reached out to touch Elijah's mind, instilling the need to have the warrior brought to her chamber immediately. She turned and entered the chamber. After closing the tapestries tightly against the new day, she walked to the chaise to await the warrior, determined to set right the one wrong she could control.

* * * *

Galen stretched and turned to his side, sinking into the mound of purple and red pillows that cushioned his weight. He judged he must have slept for at least four hours.

He turned toward the arched doorway. Strange voices and a curious humming noise filled his ears. He sat up, eased his legs over the side of the wall, and dropped his feet to the stone floor. He looked at the luma-lit pool, struggled to commit to memory the wondrous experience he and Thea shared hours before, then stood to stretch his stiff back.

Galen grabbed the jade robe from the peg where Elijah left it, slipped it over his shoulders then pulled on his leggings before walking from the chamber. He paused in the corridor beyond the hydro-gardens and watched numerous servants hustle about, working to gather the fruit of their labors. He realized the whining sound he'd heard came from the conveyors moving along their given paths to deliver each potted plant to the center station.

He considered the drudgery each Creean suffered to provide nourishment for his family. The hours of backbreaking work put into tilling the soil, planting seedlings, nurturing each sprout until it bore its crops. If the sprout survived the hordes of insects that thrived in the jungles, the torrential rains that flooded the streams and valleys, the stampedes of wild animals.

Anger flushed through him. Glacians faced none of these hardships. Walls of solid granite protected their crops. A constant source of light and moisture insured healthy growth.

He glanced around the hydro-gardens. Hours ago he'd sat at the center station, waiting for someone to come and lead him to his chamber. Cold, tired, and hungry, he'd returned to the bathing chamber and had fallen asleep.

The center station now bustled with activity, yet no one seemed to be aware of his presence. Galen stepped out onto the stone walkway suspended above the luma-lit water and walked the path to his left, retracing the journey he'd made earlier that ended at the hidden door.

His mission was twofold. He needed to be certain he could remember the way back once he'd secured warmer clothing and tools to open the portal. He also wanted to judge the servant's reaction when he walked among them to ascertain if they believed him to be Erik.

Galen paused in the hallway. Two copper-robed men walked in his direction. Noting how they bowed their heads when they stopped before him, Galen suspected word of his recovery had reached far and wide.

"May we serve you?" one of the men asked.

Galen inhaled and exhaled deeply. The last thing he needed were two humble servants tagging along while he explored the corridors. "I require nothing except to exercise my stiff muscles. Go on about your tasks."

The two men hurried off and Galen continued down the corridor.

* * * *

"Thea?"

A gentle knock followed the summons.

Thea turned to stare at the door as Elijah's voice announced the arrival of the warrior. The time for confession was upon her. She stood, turned, and walked toward the chamber door. Pulling the planks open slowly, she nodded to Elijah then glanced behind him, expecting to find the warrior's tall form.

"Where is he?"

"I do not know. I entered his chamber. He has not slept in the bed. Thinking perhaps he'd remained in the bathing chamber, I hurried there and found it empty. I do not know where he might be." Elijah gestured nervously with his hands to emphasize his words.

"Perhaps, he's with Gustoff," she said, knowing deep in her heart her words were untrue. Gustoff would have no need to seek the warrior out. "Go to your bed, Elijah. I'm sorry I disturbed your rest."

Elijah nodded and backed away from the doorway. Thea closed the panel and turned to lean against it. Where could he be? How would a blind man find his way around the Keep without assistance? Maybe one of the other servants found him in the bathing chamber and.... And what?

Thea concentrated hard on the warrior, seeking his presence wherever he might be within the Keep. The warrior's image filled her mind. She studied his movements about a darkened hallway.

He appeared lost. Confused.

She left her chamber to find him and assist him back to his chamber.

CHAPTER 12

Thea held her breath as the warrior stepped nearer to her hiding place in the shadows. Fury chased away the feeling of betrayal that clamped around her heart. The warrior's wasn't blind. He probably never had been. All of those moments she'd spent tending him, dressing him, feeding him, he'd watched her every move.

What if he recovered his memory? If he knew from the beginning she had....

Anger overshadowed her sense of caution. Thea stepped into the middle of the corridor, blocking the warrior's path. She placed her hands on her hips and waited.

He moved with a lithe grace, muscles bunching and relaxing just as she'd imagined moonrises ago. His hair, that glorious mass of gold and platinum, swung about his broad shoulders and tickled his collarbone.

Thea felt her heart rate quicken. Her mouth once again filled with fleece. A strong feeling of want, need, flashed along every nerve ending in her body, pooled at the juncture of her thighs, and caused her to quiver.

"Thea?"

He was intimidating, staring down at her from his imposing height.

"Thea, is that you?" He reached out, his fingers pausing less than a hand's span from her cheek.

Thea stepped back. Outrage choked her. Ire, unlike anything she'd ever felt, consumed her. She'd trusted him. Wanted him. Given him her most precious gift and he'd betrayed her.

Just like you intended to betray him, a voice from within cried. Thea ignored it.

She met his intense stare. "You can see me, can't you? You've pretended to be blind from the beginning?"

He broke eye contact and turned his head. "I--"

"Don't lie to me. There are enough lies between us. I brought you to the Keep, helped to restore your strength after your stay at Dekar, and you betray me by pretending to be blind so you could spy on--"

"Enough." He grabbed her arm and pulled her so close she could feel the heat of his body rush over her. "Who betrayed whom, Thea Asvaldr? Do the gentle subjects of Glacia know you brought a stranger into their midst to impersonate your stepbrother? Who are you to find fault? You're the one who connived this scheme to defraud the Elders, the citizens of Glacia, and who knows who else with your wickedness."

Thea gasped. "Wickedness?"

She looked up into his eyes, meeting him stare for stare. "Is it wickedness to try to save my people from an evil they can't fight? To save an imprisoned warrior from his own death by bringing him into my home, offering him nourishment and warmth, healing his body?" She pulled away from the wall to pace.

* * * *

Galen watched the faint light of the luma strike the streaks of gold in her hair. Fury burned bright in her eyes, shadowed her cheeks with a flush, and caused her magnificent breasts to rise and fall rapidly with each gasp of air she drew. He clenched his fists to restrain the need to reach out to her, to bring her into his arms, to smother her fury with another type of passion.

His loins screamed for relief. His heartbeat clamored against his ribs, echoed through his body, slammed into his ears.

He silently recited the reasons for perpetrating the ruse he'd begun moonrises ago. Berezan. Vengeance.

Fury smoldered within him and blocked all other thoughts. He stared into Thea's eyes, willing his temper to calm enough so he could demand answers to the numerous questions he'd struggled with during his stay in Glacia.

"If not wickedness, what other reason would you have to bring me to your Keep and present me to the Messahs as Erik Asvaldr?" he demanded.

She glared at him.

Galen cursed. Even faced with her betrayal, he wanted her still.

"Why should I tell you anything?"

He grabbed her wrist and pulled her closer. He bent until they were almost nose to nose. "Because I'm not weak, Thea. I have never been. Many times, I had the opportunity to hurt you, but I restrained myself. I have played your game, kept your secrets. Now, I demand answers."

She tried to wiggle from his grasp. "Let me go," she demanded as she attempted to pry his fingers from her arm.

"Not until you answer my questions."

"Release me. Please," she said softly. "I'll answer all of your questions."

"How will I know if you speak the truth or not?"

"I swear on my life I won't lie to you, warrior."

Galen nodded. He watched the expression on her face, noting she looked as upset as she had when the Messahs visited Erik's chamber. He considered her actions carefully.

He'd been taught from a young boy never to trust anyone other than his own people. Over the past risings, he'd allowed another being to wiggle under his hide, to touch him more deeply than any Creean female ever had. They'd come together twice as male and female, not as Glacian and Creean, or as enemy against enemy. What they shared had been good. Very good.

Yet, were the truth to be fully out, he'd used Thea Asvaldr in much the same way she'd planned to use him. He'd pretended to be weak, mindless and blind in order to gain knowledge of the people of Glacia, their habitat and defenses, all the while planning to forgo the welfare of these people in order to await and destroy Berezan.

If the reasons she gave for her actions proved truthful, perhaps he'd consider answering the questions she must have about him.

"Could we go somewhere warmer?" She rubbed her forearms briskly to stave off the chill.

"No."

She nodded. "All right. By what name are you called, warrior?"

"Galen."

"Galen," she repeated, then nodded.

"Why did you bring me here?"

* * * *

"What I told you about Erik is mostly true, Galen. He died in an avalanche as he traveled to take his rightful place as heir to the House of Asvaldr. I don't know how familiar you might be with the Articles, but with my father and his heir dead, and me the only survivor of the House of Asvaldr--a female forbidden to take power--Glacia would have been vulnerable."

He loosened his fingers and Thea slipped free. She paced three steps and leaned against the wall. She looked at the stone floor rather than gaze into his eyes as she spoke. "After news reached us of Erik's death, Gustoff and I searched for many moonrisings for an individual to impersonate my stepbrother. When you were found in the dungeon of Dekar, I believed my prayers had been answered."

"Go on."

"Gustoff bribed a guard to allow us to visit your cell." She closed her eyes as memories surfaced. "You were very ill, Galen. They'd drugged you and offered very little by way of nourishment to keep you alive. I feared the trip to Glacia through the extreme cold of the Tundra would kill you."

Thea glanced up to find he'd leaned against the opposite wall and crossed his arms over his chest. He stared at her with cold, calculating eyes.

She lowered her gaze. "We brought you here, placed you in Erik's bed and I nursed you back to health."

"Why?"

Thea looked up to meet his heated stare. "I was told you had no memory of your past. I believed I could convince you that you were my stepbrother long enough to accomplish my goals. When I discovered you couldn't see, I wanted to help you regain your memory, your sight."

"When did you decide I was blind?"

Thea blinked at the hostile tone of his voice. "On the third day after you arrived, you finally awoke from your drug-induced slumber. I watched you for several moments, and although I stood in full view, you gave no sign you saw me. I touched you. You.... You--"

"I what?"

"You grabbed me and tried to hurt me. I told you I meant you no harm, but you wouldn't listen. You ranted and raved about me stealing your memory, your sight. You couldn't see me."

Thea looked up to judge his reaction. He hadn't moved. "I had to restrain you before you killed me." Memories of just how she'd restrained him caused heat to flood her cheeks. Thea tilted her head so he couldn't see her reaction.

"I stunned you then fell asleep. When I woke, I found Gustoff restrained you with ropes to the posts of the bed. I tried to tell him to remove the binds, but he refused."

"By stunned do you mean you somehow knocked me out?"

She bit her bottom lip. "Not exactly. I merely touched you and...."

"Like you healed my wrists?"

She met his gaze. "You saw that? Of course you did. You weren't blind then, were you? How could I have been so foolish? Why didn't I realize your loss of sight might have been only a temporary effect of the drugs?"

Galen closed his eyes. He tried hard to remember the events Thea spoke of, but nothing surfaced beyond waking to find her in bed with him. He wondered what other strange powers Thea might possess besides the ability to stun someone or heal wounds.

Her slow movement captured his attention. The last thing he expected her to do was touch his arm. "Why were you in the Tundra, Galen? Do you remember how you were captured and taken to Dekar?"

He remembered. Vividly. But he did not intend to tell her anything. He dropped his arm to his side to avoid her touch. He closed his mind and heart to the look of rejection on her lovely face. "Why is Berezan coming to Glacia?"

"Everything I've told you about Berezan's arrival is true. I don't know what reason he would have to visit Glacia unless he's heard news of Father's death, and perhaps Erik's, and comes to assume control of Glacia like he took over Solarus."

Liar! Galen clamped his teeth together to keep from uttering the word aloud. Thea knew more about Berezan than she disclosed. If what he suspected was true, she was in alliance with Berezan.

Galen pulled away from the wall and took a step closer to Thea. "You mentioned my impersonating Erik until you accomplished your goals. What goals?"

"Glacians are docile people. We have no armies, no militia of any kind. Decades ago, we gave up the need to defend ourselves, believing in the Articles, and before that, the Ancient Ones to protect us.

"When news arrived of Berezan's visit so soon upon word of Erik's death, Gustoff and I believed we needed help to withstand Berezan's evil. Your impersonation was only to buy time while Gustoff traveled to Borderland to seek an alliance with the Creean people against the threat Berezan posed to both of our worlds."

Memories, stark and graphic, swamped Galen's mind. Visions of his homeland destroyed, his people murdered, caused his hands to tremble. He clenched his hands and drew a deep breath to hide the effect of Thea's words. "What would the docile people of Glacia have offered in a joint defense, Thea? Would you have expected the warriors of Borderland to do all of your fighting while you remained here in your safe ice world?"

"The people of Borderland would have been well compensated, Galen."

He grabbed her arm. "Like you compensated me last eve, Thea?"

Pain, sharp and intense, rushed through Thea's chest. His hateful words took the wonderful things they shared and twisted it into something dark and evil. She felt defiled. Unclean. She'd given him her heart and he crushed it beneath his feet, then threw it back at her like a cheap trinket.

"Release me." The command, followed by a sharp mind probe, made it impossible for him to refuse. He dropped his hands to his sides and stood motionless while she backed away.

She shook with rage as she stared into his eyes, full of disbelief that given all of his physical strength, she could hold him powerless. "You can't move, warrior. I won't allow it. Even with all of your muscle and size, your body cannot function unless your mind commands it.

"And, I control your mind."

She stepped closer. "I don't know why I do this, except I made a vow to confess my transgressions. I believed what we shared to be special. I felt something for you, something very different than I've ever felt for another being. You trample my feelings beneath your feet as if my emotions were nothing but dust." She turned to pace the corridor.

"No male lives to assume leadership of Glacia. Because of this, I would have offered rule to Omar Sar if he agreed to an allegiance with Gustoff. Gustoff has traveled to Borderland to make this offer and found Borderland devastated by Berezan's armies.

"Omar Sar was murdered, his heir captured, and believed dead. Only one hundred and twenty warriors are left to defend the hundreds of survivors of Berezan's invasion."

She turned to stare into his eyes. "Even as we stand here wasting precious time, Berezan's armies are en route to Glacia. He's destroying everything in his path. Everything."

She watched the warrior. His attempt to fight her control caused the tendons to protrude in his neck, sweat to bead on his forehead, and his lips to tremble.

She closed her eyes and released control.

He pulled from the wall, shook his arms, then crossed to the opposite side of the corridor. "Why should I believe anything you tell me, Thea Asvaldr?"

She turned away from his intense stare. The pain of knowing how poorly he valued the love she offered burned too deep to continue looking into his eyes. "I don't care what you believe. I don't have any more time to waste trying to convince you of my needs. I'd thought to request your help in planning strategy against Berezan, but...."

"You've wasted more time than you know. While you sent your man Gustoff on a fruitless search for the leader of Borderland to offer your allegiance, you had the leader of Borderland in your possession. My name, Thea, is Galen Sar."

CHAPTER 13

Borderland

The encampment was less than a league away. The Creean people were in danger. The runner's gaze darted from side to side, searching deep into the thick foliage that covered the jungle floor to avoid detection.

A half league, another quarter. The lush greens of the jungle parted to expose a wide, natural path in the vegetation. Only the towering iferas blocked out sunlight and darkened the mossy ground. After another quarter-league, the hiding place of the people of Cree was in view.

Renewed energy supported his strained muscles, increased the flow of blood from his thundering heart. His fingers shook as he climbed the rock embankment surrounding the caves where his people hid.

Stumbling into the secluded entrance, he fell to his knees, raised his chin high into the cool cave air, and drew deep gulps of air into his lungs.

"Jakar!"

Several warriors rushed toward him, all speaking at once as they attempted to discover his message. He shook his head to clear the fuzziness that engulfed his brain, swallowed hard, and fought the allure of unconsciousness beckoning his exhausted body.

"Jakar."

A tall warrior dropped to his knees on the ground beside him. He placed his hand upon the runner's shoulder and shook him gently. "I'm here. What news has brought you from your station high in the peaks?"

The fatigued warrior turned his head to stare into Jakar's eyes. He drew a deep breath and exhaled. "The armies from Solarus have crossed into Borderland, Jakar. Even now, they forage the jungles in search of a place to camp." He slumped forward, giving in to the hours of exertion he'd expended to bring this warning to his people.

Jakar stood and gazed into the worried eyes of the six warriors standing about the cave entrance. "Take him into the cave and make him comfortable. See that the women give him drink and nourishment. Allow him to recuperate as long as he feels the need. He has served us well."

Three men stepped forward to do Jakar's bidding. They picked up the warrior and carried him deep into the shadows of the cave.

"What are we going to do?"

Thor, Jakar's friend, stepped closer. Jakar looked down at Thor's chest, noted the bloody seepage that spilled through the bandages about his midsection. Only thirty summers, Thor had the look of an old man. His shoulder-length brown hair was caked with mud and debris from his flight through the jungle. His shoulders, wide and strong, slumped from the pain that remained constant, not only from his injuries, but also from his warrior's heart, hurt by what he'd seen and could not avenge.

Berezan's first attack seriously depleted the warriors of Borderland. Of those still within the encampment, most were grievously wounded. Jakar had sent the ones healthy enough to travel into the jungles to gather the warrior force patrolling the boundaries of Borderland, to bring them in to fortify the last hiding place of the Creean race.

No matter how much it went against everything he believed, all he'd learned, the only thing left to do so the people of Borderland could survive was hide.

"The old man from Glacia spoke wisely, Thor. We are too few to meet a force of so many. We must protect our people as Galen or Omar would have done were they here to lead. We will send everyone able into the surrounding jungle, have the warriors gather any evidence of our presence, and bring whatever they find back to the caves.

"We'll hide the sick, the old, the young, and the injured deep in the underground passageways of Naro. Our women will tend them to the best of their abilities while we disburse at strategic locations in and around the mountain to protect what's left of our people."

Thor nodded. "The foodstuffs stored in the hollows will last no longer than a few sunrises. I can send a few warriors deeper into the jungle to forage. There are fruits and nuts aplenty on the western slopes. It would take only a sunrise for a small force to go there and return."

"Go quickly, my friend. See our plans placed into motion. By what we have now learned, we have less than two sunrises to bring all of our people together."

Thor grasped Jakar's shoulder. He squeezed tightly, then dropped his hand. Taking the two warriors who guarded the cave entrance with him, Thor set out to see Jakar's orders done.

* * * *

Berezan reined in his equox and surveyed the humble village around him. The crude, empty houses beckoned his weary bones as if they were luxurious castles. He threw his leg over the horn of his saddle and dismounted, taking time only to pull the black gloves from his hands and release the golden clasp of his cloak before he threw his discarded garments over the saddle, then turned to locate R'han.

His commander, clad in robes of beige to match the desert, stood out glaringly against the lush greens of the tropical region.

"R'han!"

The commander hurried to his side.

"Discard those robes immediately. Have the rest of my army follow suit. I don't care what you do with them. Burn them. Bury them. Just get them gone before I next see your face."

Berezan turned away, slapped at the fur hanging over the doorway of the house closest to him, and entered. His long strides took him across the tiny room in three paces. He kicked aside a three-legged stool before the fire pit, propped his booted foot against the hearth, then leaned down to place his head upon the bent arm he rested on the mantel.

Memories clouded his tired mind. Through a fog he climbed the circular stairway of Governing house, passed by scores of elaborate doorways, carved centuries before by craftsmen of the Ancient Ones. He paused at the rim of the granite railing on each floor, looked up at the chandelier of lumastones that gave light.

The memories faded.

Melancholy grew in his chest. The years he'd missed, the hardships of his youth as he struggled to survive in the harsh desert climate, haunted him. Berezan remembered the thirst that never seemed to be quenched, the feel of flesh that never came clean. He thought about the abrasions on his young skin as the hot desert wind constantly blew sand particles to strip away the resilience of his flesh.

Gustoff cheated him out of a life of abundance and comfort. He'd taken it upon himself to deprive a young heir of the heritage he'd been born to and he'd cast a helpless six-year-old aside to die as heartlessly as one would destroy an ailing animal. For this, the old man would die a slow and agonizing death. But, not before Berezan took possession of the Sphere of Light.

The muscles in Berezan's arm tensed and bunched. His fingernails burrowed into the flesh of his palm. He raised his head and stared at the stone wall above the mantel.

Moments passed. His body trembled. Perspiration broke on his forehead and dripped into his eyes. Berezan did not blink, nor did his concentration waver.

Incantations--strange, foreign--spilled from his lips.

A vision came quickly into his mind and suddenly he was soaring high above the jungle, a huge black bird of prey. He drew a deep breath, expanding his lungs far beyond their normal capacity to accommodate the heady sense of freedom that rushed over him as he swooped nearer to the lush foliage of the dense trees below, coming dangerously close to the treetops before he spiraled upward again, past clouds that threatened rain, until he drew deep, clear breaths of untainted air.

He dove again, spreading his wings to soar through the air. Farther and farther away from the village where his body remained entranced, where his army made camp. Beneath him, the landscape sped by at a harrowing pace. Trees and foliage blended until they appeared no more than a solid blanket of green.

He ascended. Higher. Higher still.

The peaks of Naro jutted up before him. Volcanic smoke and ash sputtered into the air from the crest. Steam blurred his vision as he circled the mountain like a vulture, around and around. Each pass took him lower until again the foliage of the jungle threatened.

Something glittered through the trees and caught his attention. A predator's heart clamored within his chest. He extended his legs, sharp talons exposed, collapsed his wings tight against his body, and dove. The shiny object grew larger.

Trees, each leaf and branch, became visible as he neared the ground.

He salivated, tasting the thrill of capture, experiencing the glory of the kill.

"Master?"

Berezan gritted his teeth against the instinct to kill that bore down upon him. He met his commander's questioning gaze.

"What do you want?"

R'han bowed his head. "All robes have been destroyed as ordered, Master. Camp is established. Your army waits further orders."

Berezan stepped away from the hearth. He looked about the small room, noting for the first time the shabbiness of the interior. Several hand-hewed chairs were placed before a table constructed of a wood foreign to him. A coarse mat of braided straw formed a rug for the stone floor. Several lanterns were scattered about. A cupboard, several other chairs, and a barrel filled the rest of the space.

Berezan thought about his entranced flight, the glittering object he'd seen and had not been able to identify. Elsbar's words came back to plague him.

Was it possible the warriors of Borderland planned an assault?

"Place guards at the perimeter of camp. Elsbar believes the remaining Creean warriors will do all within their power to stop our assault. Execute any Creean found on sight. Have my stallion tended, my belongings placed into this shack, the men fed and bedded down for the moonrise.

"Then see that I am not disturbed again until sunrise."

His commander shuffled his feet before he finally met Berezan's gaze. "But, Master, you have not eaten."

"The hunger that festers in me, R'han, will be assuaged only when I reach Glacia." Berezan turned his back.

"By your wishes," R'han said. He slapped his fist to his chest three times then turned to leave the shack.

"Have more scouts sent out just before dawn. Make sure they scour every inch of the surrounding jungle for any survivors from our last venture into Borderland. Again, anyone from Borderland you discover is to be destroyed immediately."

"Yes, Master." The commander stepped toward the doorway.

"Have my army ready to march at sunrise. I will tolerate no other diversions from our route to Glacia. Is that understood."

"Yes, Master." His commander left the cottage.

Berezan glanced down into the grate and found several logs suitable for burning. He bent, suspended his open hand in the air, and then uttered another incantation.

Arcs of fire sprang from his fingertips to ignite the wood.

He sat down on the floor before the blazing warmth he'd created, crossed his booted feet, and then pulled his ankles close to his body. Resting his hands, palms upon his knees, he closed his eyes and slept.

CHAPTER 14

"Galen of Borderland!"

Galen paused in his furious stride. Chills rippled along his spine as Gustoff's voice permeated every nerve in his body. He forced away the need to strike out in anger, then turned to face the old man in purple who stood in the corridor behind him.

"You know my name, old man?"

Gustoff stroked his long white beard. Galen could feel the path of the old man's gaze as it slipped slowly over his body, head to toe. A strange sense of foreboding tingled in his mind as he wondered if the old man had witnessed his encounter with Thea.

Purple robes swished in the silence of the corridor as Gustoff took a step closer. "I overheard your argument with Thea, Galen of Borderland."

Gustoff's words renewed the frenzied cadence of Galen's heartbeat. Galen clenched his fists to fight the tremors that flowed through his body. For sunrise after sunrise, he'd been away from his people. A prisoner within walls of stone, held captive because he'd tried to avenge the deaths of his mother and father and the countless other murders committed by the very one that now threatened Glacia.

Revenge was at hand. He could feel it to the marrow of his bones. He had no more time to waste with the old man. "My identity has been established, Gustoff. I see no need to remain here. By Thea's words, the people of Borderland are in danger. I must go to them."

"You cannot."

The old man's words were soft, but the finality in his statement gave Galen pause. "Are you going to stop me, old man?"

Gustoff took another step closer and bowed his head. "If I must."

Galen smiled. His stay in Glacia's Keep had replenished the strength he'd lost during his incarceration at Dekar Facility. Gustoff's bones were old and brittle. One well-positioned blow and the man in purple would crumple to the floor, helpless.

Galen drew a deep breath and stepped forward.

Gustoff raised his withered hand, uttered several strange words, and Galen froze, unable to do more than breathe and stare in disbelief at the man before him. He strained against a mysterious force holding him immobile. His arms ached at the force he exerted to reach forward.

"I have many powers to hold you, warrior of Borderland. To struggle against my will is useless. Until I wish to release you, you will remain as you are. Paralyzed." Gustoff stepped closer.

Galen could only follow his steps with his eyes.

Gustoff continued to stroke his beard as he spoke, "I wish you no harm. Nor does Thea. You were brought here to delay the discovery of Erik's death long enough for me to go to Borderland and seek your father's aid against the evil that threatens us all."

Galen closed his eyes and strained once more against the invisible bonds the old man used to hold him.

"I will release you if you pledge to hear me out as I tell you all Thea has been forbidden to disclose."

Galen swallowed in an attempt to release Gustoff's grasp on his throat muscles. He opened his eyes and stared intently into the old man's face.

Gustoff waved his hand.

Galen collapsed against the stone wall.

"I have no wish to use my power against you, Galen. I think it would be wise if you listened to the words I have to say. I have been to Cree, witnessed the plight of your people firsthand. I can tell you how they fare. But, before it do, you must agree to hear all I will tell you."

Galen stared into Gustoff's eyes, searching for the deceit he expected to find. There was nothing. He considered what other powers the old man might use to restrain him if he refused, then nodded.

"I must tell you first of Thea's heritage. To understand her destiny will enable you to comprehend why such drastic measures as the ones we undertook were necessary." Gustoff waited while Galen digested his words.

"I must ask for your trust, Galen. The words I speak will be strange to your limited knowledge of the Ancient Ones, but you must believe each thing I say is truthful."

Galen nodded.

Gustoff explained in detail the history of the Ancient Ones. He told of the formation of the Elders, the Articles, and the bloody wars that forced the separation of their world into three regions. He touched on the part Galen's ancestor, Shakara, played in the development of the Articles then told Galen of the evil that once again threatened their world. He spoke briefly about the Sphere of Light.

Questions raced around inside Galen's head. "Berezan killed my people to possess this Sphere of Light, Gustoff. What is this Sphere you speak of, and why would he believe the people of Borderland might possess it?"

"The Sphere of Light is the last magical talisman of the Ancient Ones that protects our world from destruction. The person who wields the Sphere will have almost unlimited power over life and death. I have no idea why Berezan would think the Sphere was in Borderland, unless he believes I would not be foolish enough to hide it within Glacia."

"You?"

"I am one of the remaining descendants of the Ancient Ones, Galen. Berezan also carries their blood in his veins."

"Who else?"

"Thea."

"Thea?"

Gustoff ceased stroking his beard and crossed his arms over his chest. "Yes, warrior. Thea. Long before Thea was old enough to understand the strange powers she carries within her, I foresaw her destiny. Throughout the years of the life, I have tutored her, helped her understand the many powers she holds. Some of those powers you have experienced firsthand."

Galen thought about Thea's power to heal, then recalled the strange magic she'd used earlier to restrain him, much like the force Gustoff exerted. He pulled away from the stone wall and paced, trying to understand what Thea and her curious powers had to do with him.

"Thea and the Sphere of Light she must wield are all there is left to protect our world from Berezan's evil, Galen."

Galen turned to stare into the old man's eyes. A quick vision of Thea flashed before his mind's eye. Thea-- beautiful and seductive. The way she touched his body, his heart, his soul. Auburn hair and sensual brown eyes. The pout of her lips, the softness of her body....

Fierce protectiveness welled within him. "The warriors of Borderland are mighty and strong, Gustoff. We were not powerful enough to destroy Berezan. How could you expect a lone woman to accomplish what we were unable to do?"

Gustoff raised his hand and pointed a crooked finger at Galen. "As long as Thea does not doubt the powers within her, she will be successful."

"Doubt? Within her? Old man, what foolishness have you filled her head with?" Galen charged forward, only to stumble when the old man raised his hand in a fashion that threatened to immobilize him again. "I won't allow you to use Thea in schemes to destroy Berezan, old man. I won't allow it."

"I have seen the future, Galen. I know what trials and triumphs lie ahead for Thea. To face Berezan is her destiny. Neither you nor I can change that. All things in life have a purpose. Thea's objective is clear. Yours also."

"My purpose is to save my people."

"Your function is to stand by Thea's side, to help her see her destiny through."

Galen shook his head. "No, old man. I have to avenge the lives of my parents, to protect those entrusted to me when I became Regis of Borderland. Many lives already depend upon me. You can't expect me to stand by Thea's side and see her killed because of some foolishness you believe in.

"I'll take Thea away, hide her in the caves of my homeland. She'll be safe from Berezan--and from you."

Gustoff studied the warrior carefully. He noted the massive muscles that bunched and coiled across the warrior's chest, the confidence in his stance, the proud cock of his blond head.

Galen Sar of Borderland was trained in the arts of combat. He believed wholeheartedly in his ability to protect Thea and his people from evil. But the warrior knew only of such skills as one acquires by practice with swords, knives, and clubs. His physical stamina and prowess honed by many cycles of physical exertion.

He had never understood, nor would he ever understand until he came face to face with such powers, that evil and the power to wield it did not need any of the skills the warrior had so laboriously acquired.

"What say you when I tell you all the physical prowess you possess will be useless when faced by Berezan, warrior? Will you throw spears against arcs of flame? Use swords to cut flesh, when the power Berezan possesses can melt the flesh from your bones?"

Gustoff placed his hand upon Galen's arm. "I sense deep affection within you for Thea. In your need to protect the one you care for, you will make serious mistakes and place Thea into even more danger."

"Stand aside, old man. Let me pass. I'll take Thea to safety."

"There are but one hundred and twenty or so warriors of Borderland left, Galen. Many of those warriors are seriously wounded. Hundreds of the survivors of Berezan's attack are in need of medical attention. As each day passes, more may die from lack of care. Berezan polluted some of Borderland's rivers. With Berezan's army encamped in the Borderland, there is no way for your men to forage for food. Your people will starve if you interfere in something you cannot control."

Galen's stomach churned at Gustoff's words, but he could do little more than clench his fists.

"Food grows aplenty here in Glacia, Galen. Enough to feed your people and ours. If you take Thea away from her destiny, Glacia will fall into Berezan's hands and there will be no hope of any of us. You must believe me. Thea has the power to destroy Berezan. She must be in Glacia to wield that power."

Galen stared furiously into Gustoff's eyes. "And what of you, old man? What will you be doing while you send Thea to meet Berezan? What part do you play in the massacre you plan?"

"My life path is short, Galen. I cannot foresee how much longer I will be alive to guide Thea on her chosen path. For this, I need your strength, your sense of right and wrong.

Thea needs you, warrior. She requires your support to fulfill her destiny.

"But she loves you. If you attempt to convince her to leave Glacia and escape into the jungles with you, she will go and forsake her destiny. Then all will be lost."

A hard knot twisted in Galen's chest. Warmth flowed to every nerve in his body. Anger followed. He clenched his hands tighter, longing to strike out at something. Anything.

He closed his eyes and tried to still the rage churning within him. The memory of Thea's hands gliding over his flesh, the sweet smell of her permeating his every pore, the feel of her woman's warmth engulfing him, cradling him....

"No."

"You cannot defy destiny, Galen. There is no way to change what is predestined. Berezan's armies are within twelve moonrises of Glacia. The threat is real and very near. Thea must wield the Sphere of Light against Berezan and destroy the evil that threatens to overtake us."

CHAPTER 15

Thea sat up slowly. She blinked at the bright sunshine that filtered in through the open tapestries at the balcony. She wondered about the time, swiped her palms against her eyes, then dropped her feet to the floor.

Feeling she wasn't alone in the chamber, she glanced over her shoulder to find Galen standing in a stream of sunlight. The golden glow emphasized every muscle and plane of his tall body. He wore the leggings he arrived in and one of the bronze wool tunics the seamstresses had worked so hard to complete.

The tunic hung to mid-thigh, but did little to hide his magnificent torso. The neckline plunged into a deep V and exposed more than an abundance of golden chest. Long sleeves fit tight to his wrist, outlined his muscular arms as he stood before her.

"Thea," he whispered.

Pain knifed its way to the middle of her chest. She'd given this man more of herself than she'd ever afforded another being.

Thea turned away and walked to the open tapestries to stare out over the snow-covered mountainside. She listened to his footsteps as he crossed the chamber. Felt his breath on her neck when he paused behind her.

She closed her eyes. "Berezan will arrive within a few moonrisings, Galen." She shivered when the pressure of his hand warmed her shoulder. Drawing a deep breath, she continued, "I understand your need to be with the people of Cree and will have Elijah gather the supplies needed for your journey."

Heat seeped from the point of his contact with her shoulder to penetrate her body. Thea inhaled and exhaled three times to fight the mysterious magic the warrior cast over her. She shrugged away from his touch and stepped out onto the balcony. Cold air prickled her body, erasing the effect of his touch.

"I've spoken with Gustoff, Thea. He verified the words you spoke in the corridor.

"Gustoff told me he's spent years filling your head with foolish ideas that you alone can defeat Berezan."

"Foolish?" Thea shook her arm free and continued across the chamber. She paused before the fire, her back toward Galen as she stared into the flames. "I know not what convictions you honor, nor do I denounce your beliefs. Yet, you are quick to say nay to what I hold as truth without understanding all there is to know."

"Gustoff informed me of the powers of the Ancient Ones. He also explained the part my ancestor, Shakara, played in the shaping of history. Much of this I learned from my father."

Thea heard his footsteps approach and tensed to withstand the emotions he created.

"Even I, fool that I've been, can't deny the strange powers you possess. Will these powers protect you from Berezan while you attempt to defeat him?"

Thea turned to stare up into his eyes. "Yes."

Galen trembled from the intensity of the emotions running rampant through his body. He took a deep breath then wrapped his hands across her shoulders. He fought the instinct to shake some sense into her. He released her shoulders.

She was so small, yet so desirable. She fit perfectly into his arms, against the planes and valleys of his body. Her hair, those glorious flaming tresses he liked to wrap around his hands, sparkled in the sunlight filtering in through the open tapestries. The lush swell of her breasts, the narrowness of her waist, the length of her legs were highlighted in tones of sunlight and shadow.

The memory of touching her, exploring every inch of her tender flesh caused his heart to ache with the knowledge of what she believed she must do. What he knew his own responsibilities were. Images, vivid and devastating streaked through his mind. Galen fought to resist the memories that caused his heart to race, his body to quake.

Blood. So much blood. So much death and destruction.

* * * *

Thea watched, mesmerized, as the color of Galen's eyes changed from light blue to the darker shade of midnight.

She had the inexplicable urge to touch his mind, read his thoughts, until she realized she'd seen that same expression days ago and named it hatred.

She knew and understood the memories that haunted him. She wanted nothing more than to wrap her arms around him and kiss away the nightmare that made his body tremble. He had his own battles to fight, his own responsibilities. As leader of Borderland, his people needed Galen Sar.

The protection of Glacia was her Fate.

"Galen." She glanced up to find his gaze firmly fixed on her face. "I must go," she said. "There's much to do. Elijah will have your supplies readied and provide an equox for your transportation." She lowered her head so the warrior wouldn't witness the pain in her eyes.

She stepped around him and walked away. Without looking back, she said, "Good journey, Galen of Borderland. I'm sorry."

"What of my needs, Thea?"

She turned to meet his gaze. "What of your needs, Galen? You're free to leave Glacia. I've promised adequate supplies and transportation." She lowered her lashes. "Go to your people. See to their safety."

He grasped her shoulders and applied enough pressure to pull her toward him.

Thea melted into the safety of his embrace and cast aside all doubts, fears, and hurts. Her lips quivered as she stepped closer to his muscular length. When he bent his head, her lips parted in eager anticipation of the magic spell his kisses could cast.

As they stumbled toward the bed in a wild tangle of arms and legs, Thea groped for his tunic and struggled to remove the wool from his body.

Galen ripped at the sash on her robe, knotting it in his haste. He released her long enough to slide his hands around her back and tore the sash in two. The slippery cloth dropped from her shoulders when he lifted her in his arms, then fluttered to the floor in a pool of lavender.

He laid her gently on the heavy fur and stepped away to remove his own clothing. Urgency threatened to destroy his control, but he stood mesmerized by the sight of Thea's loveliness as the sunlight poured in and enveloped her in a golden blanket. Her fiery hair was in disarray, longs strands flowed out to cover the fur and formed a burning halo around her body. One strand fell across her shoulder, kissed her taut pink nipple, then cascaded over the soft white indentation of her stomach to tangle with the matching nest that shielded her women's heat.

Galen's heart pounded. His groin screamed in agony, but he couldn't move. Couldn't take his eyes from the perfection before him. A radiant glow covered her cheeks, flushed her breasts. The lushness of her lashes almost hid the soft brown of her eyes.

The spell was broken when she lifted her hand to beckon him closer.

Galen tugged at the wool tunic, jerked it over his head, and dropped it to the floor in one movement. He bent, peeled the tight leather leggings from his body and stepped free.

Thea studied every inch of the warrior she could see from her prone position. Long locks of gorgeous hair fell forward over his shoulders to graze his chest, each ripple of muscle creasing his abdomen. She studied the dark whorl of hair that grew about his navel, then dropped into a thick thatch that silhouetted the engorged evidence of his desire.

He raised his knee to the side of the bed and climbed in.

There was no hesitation in her touch as she reached out to him, placing her palm against the warmth of his stomach, sliding upward across his breastbone to tangle her fingers in his hair and tug his head close enough to kiss his lips.

He opened for her. Devoured her. Possessed her.

She moaned, demanded, and received.

Thea ignored Galen's grunt of displeasure when she tore her lips free. She smiled at his sigh of contentment when she kissed his brow, his cheek, the tiny cleft in his chin. The warmth of his skin, the scent of his body, tempted her beyond her limited knowledge of sexual pleasure toward new horizons. She needed to feel, experience, all the marvelous adventures he offered, for there would never be another time.

She sensed Galen's tenseness, heard his ragged breath echo in the silence of the chamber, felt his hand at her waist tremble, and understood his hunger. Each touch, each caress, brought her burning fever to a higher level. When his nipple hardened, hers responded. Each flutter of her tongue against his flesh brought a strange and exciting quiver to the apex of her thighs.

She forced away the pain of denial she would eventually face and continued, determined to etch the very essence of Galen Sar, warrior of Borderland, into her mind for all time. Thea trailed her fingers lightly over his body, around and around the swirl of dark blond hair that arrowed downward. She followed the growth, fascinated and in awe of his maleness. She brushed her fingers up and down his engorged length, gasped when it shuddered beneath her touch.

Galen's reaction was too quick to anticipate. She offered little more than a startled gasp when he rolled her over, pinned her to the mattress. For each swipe she'd made with her tongue, the gesture was repeated threefold. Each kiss, each soft bite, turned into a profusion of exquisite little moments in kind, until she writhed beneath his onslaught.

She cried out in relief when he eased between her thighs and thrust forward. She arched to meet every advance, each withdrawal and she matched his rhythm. She kissed every inch of his accessible flesh as she fought to prolong the rapture and stave off the inevitable peak that would break the epitome they achieved.

All sense of reality evaporated. All awareness of time and space vanished. Nothing but bright, blissful light filled her universe.

Galen reached the same pinnacle seconds later.

Thea had no idea how long they lay entwined, limp, replete. Galen shifted to lie beside her. She turned until she could see his face, noted his uneven breathing. She touched his chest. A smile split his lips.

He turned slowly, planted a soft kiss on her palm, and drew her closer to his side.

Thea wanted to say something. Needed to say something. No words formed that could adequately relate her feelings. She couldn't ask him to forsake his duty, his people, any more than she could abandon her own destiny. Yet, were they both to undertake their chosen paths, she'd never see him again, never experience the wonderful way she felt in his presence.

She loved him. No matter how confused her emotions or how deep her commitments, she loved Galen Sar and would love him for the rest of her life.

Thea closed her eyes to the tumultuous thoughts and succumbed to exhaustion.

* * * *

Galen forced his body to remain still longer than his protesting muscles would have allowed, waiting for Thea's even breathing to signal she slept. He sat up slowly and eased from the bed. He watched her sleep and wondered how in such a few short sunrises he'd gone from planning to use this lovely woman to aid in his revenge against Berezan to needing her as he needed air.

What was it about this tiny woman that drew him like no other? Numerous times over the last few summers his father had urged him to take a mate, to beget his own heir.

None of the females among his people has been able to reach into that sheltered part he kept closely guarded. None had stirred his lust so quickly, then equaled his appetite, urgency, and passion.

Perhaps it was Thea's confidence, stolid and unwavering at times, easily destroyed at others. Or the way she bravely prepared to meet a foe she knew she had no means of defeating.

In the moments after their mating, he'd decided to place Thea before his hunger for Berezan. To postpone his own destiny and take her away from Glacia to the safety of Naro.

CHAPTER 16

Gustoff closed his eyes and ran the tips of his fingers slowly over the outline of the ancient doorway the warrior found. Cold air penetrated the sleeve of his robe and raised the hair on his arm. He fought past the discomfort and concentrated on the task ahead. A faint line of light glowed along the path he traced, grew brighter as the old wood began to creak and moan. Moments later, he stepped back to appraise his work. The door had seemingly disappeared. In its place was a solid rock wall.

Praying his illusion would hold, Gustoff left the corridor. Later, he stood in his tower reassessing all the plans he had made since Galen left him hours before.

Berezan's army had to cross the Tundra before they reached Glacia, leaving less than ten moonrises for strategies to be drawn. Had Gustoff an army to command, he would send his forces to meet their foe in the center of the frozen wasteland, because the soldiers of the desert would be ill-equipped to withstand the sub-zero temperatures.

A withered old man, an untried female, and a reluctant Creean warrior did not make an army, no matter how powerful the magic they might create.

Gustoff wondered at the conviction of the Solarus army. Were the soldier's beliefs stronger than Berezan's will could command? Or, did they fear the evil that might befall them if they exercised their own free will?

Gustoff walked slowly around the tower. If Berezan met his demise, would his followers carry on a siege against Glacia or retreat to Solarus with the promise of everlasting peace?

More troubled thoughts invaded his mind. Questions he had been unable to answer for a number of years resurfaced. What force drove Berezan? Someone, for some reason, had to have instructed the young heir in the ways of the Ancient Ones. He could never have learned the evil magic he possessed on his own. But who? And why?

Gustoff thought back over the many years of his life, of the persons he had encountered as he rose through the ranks of the Ancient Ones. Because their numbers were few, the competition had been great between the younger members to prove themselves worthy of the task as Guardian to the Sphere of Light. Many equally worthy as he had been passed over.

Of those not selected, Gustoff remembered two who turned their disappointment into hostility and challenged his nomination with physical force. Meridian of the Peaks and Elsbar of Solarus. The Ancient Ones had dealt severely with their behavior and dishonored each with banishment from their studies, sending them home in shame, never to be heard from again.

Gustoff gazed down at his withered hands and considered the sixty-eight winters that had passed since he became Guardian of the Sphere. Had he made another mistake? Could he have neglected to consider the animosity that might have grown over the decades into a need for revenge so great it fueled Berezan's evil?

Gustoff closed his eyes and drew several deep breaths. The hour of reckoning fast approached. With a resolute shake of his head, Gustoff left the tower, and ordered another equox prepared for a long journey.

* * * *

Thea opened her eyes abruptly and drew several deep breaths to still the rapid pounding of her heart. Chills raced over the length of her body, forcing her limbs to tremble within the warrior's embrace. Strange emotions whirled around in her mind, all fighting to gain supremacy. The feeling was unlike anything she'd ever felt.

Something was wrong. Very wrong.

Wiggling from the confines of Galen's arms, she sat up and looked around the chamber. Everything was as it should be. Nothing had changed, except sunlight no longer poured in through the tapestries and the air in the chamber had grown very cold. She guessed she'd slept for several hours and the sun had long ago set behind the mountains of Glacia.

All seemed quiet and still, yet she couldn't shake the feeling something important happened while she and Galen slept.

Thea closed her eyes. She concentrated on the Keep, seeking a disturbance in the natural order. Nothing appeared out of the ordinary. She mentally searched for Gustoff. She needed to discuss her feelings and seek his guidance.

She probed Gustoff's tower room, the steam bath, the meeting chambers, then broadened her sweep when she could detect no trace of Gustoff's essence.

Alarm raced through every nerve in her body. She threw back the thick fur covering and slid to the side of the bed.

"Thea?"

Galen's husky voice reached out to halt her flight. She turned to meet his sleepy smile with one of her own. Warmth infused her when he pushed up on his elbows, causing the covering to fall away and the golden expanse of his chest to be exposed. Memories, vivid and wonderful, of the hours she'd spent in his arms flushed her cheeks and warmed the very core of her being. Familiar tingles rushed to every nerve ending in her body.

Guilt for the time she'd spend enjoying Galen's embrace chase those memories away and dissolved the strong want that threatened to override her determination. She had too much to do. No matter how much it meant to spend these last few hours with the only man she'd ever love, her attention should be elsewhere.

* * * *

Galen sensed Thea's anxiety as she slipped from his side. Shadows clouded her beautiful eyes. Something happened to upset her. He searched for memories of the last few hours and felt his body harden in response. Thea enjoyed their lovemaking as much as he did, and Galen couldn't guess what put the strange apprehension in her eyes.

"What's wrong, Thea?" He twisted until he could free his left elbow and reached across the bed to touch her cheek. Her flesh was cold to his touch.

"Something's not as it should be. I've the strangest premonition that things have gone dreadfully wrong. I've searched the Keep for Gustoff, but he's not here. I can't imagine why he'd leave when the time for Berezan's arrival is so near."

Galen could. He remembered the old man's face when he'd challenged his reasons for sending Thea to do his own work. Galen witnessed sadness in the old man's eyes he'd not seen before. He wondered if the words he'd hurled at Gustoff in anger struck some hidden cord. Could it be Gustoff left Glacia to meet Berezan himself?

"I must find him." Thea scrambled from the high bed and grabbed her lavender robe from the floor. She wrapped the silky material around her and groped for the sash, only to find it severed in two. She threw the cord to the floor.

"Summon Elijah," Galen said.

"Why?"

"I believe Elijah might have information on Gustoff's whereabouts."

She stared at him in confusion then raised her hands to her temples and closed her eyes. When she opened her eyes, she stared at Galen's body. "You'd better dress. I don't think it would be wise for Elijah to find you in my bed."

Galen bit his lip to keep from saying he didn't give a damn what the servant thought, but reconsidered when he realized Thea's nervousness worsened by the moment. He threw the fur back, dropped his feet to the floor, and pulled his leggings on.

"Galen, I'm so--"

Whatever she was about to say was lost when a soft knock came at the chamber door. She hurried across the chamber to throw back the bolt.

Elijah walked into the chamber.

Galen noted the servant never looked into Thea's eyes, but kept his gaze downcast, almost as if he were hiding something.

"Elijah, I need Gustoff. Do you know where he might be?"

The older man reached into the pocket of his robe and withdrew a piece of parchment. "I have no idea where he has gone, Thea, but he bade me to give you this." Elijah's hand shook as he handed the paper to Thea.

I have left Glacia to correct a great wrong committed many years ago. Should I not return, know I have always loved you and believe completely in your abilities. Be strong in your convictions, Thea Asvaldr, last of the Ancient Ones. Hold true to your feelings and see your destiny through.

Convinced his assumptions were correct, Galen placed grasped Thea's hand and drew her toward the chaise. He turned back to Elijah. The servant shook his head, revealing he knew no more than what the letter stated.

Galen nodded and dismissed the servant. He watched Elijah close the chamber door softly behind him.

"Where would he have gone?" she asked. "Why would he leave Glacia at a time like this?"

Galen gathered Thea into his arms. He wondered if he should tell her he suspected Gustoff had gone to do battle with Berezan in her place.

Undecided on the course of action he should take, he held her for many moments, waiting for Thea to regain the composure he suspected she rarely lost.

"This isn't like Gustoff. He'd never abandon me. Now, in my hour of greatest need, he's not by my side to guide me. I don't know how to proceed from this point."

Galen placed his hand beneath her chin and raised her face. He looked into her eyes, trying to determine what her reaction to his theory would be. The temptation to kiss her lips, ate at him. He sensed Thea needed his support more than ever to see her through the next few hours.

He pulled her closer to his chest, stroked the length of her auburn hair, and placed his chin atop her head.

"Gustoff's never gone off without giving me some sort of an explanation."

Thea stiffened within his grasp and pulled away to pace the floor. "Tell me you don't believe Gustoff would be foolish enough to go to Berezan's camp. Make me see how silly I am to even give credence to such thoughts."

She stood before him, looking into his eyes. The temptation was there to turn away from her gaze, but Galen resisted. Her untied robe hung open, giving him a full view of her abundant charms.

Galen felt his erection grow as she strode around before him, not considering the state of her undress. He cursed the weakness in his loins where this female was concerned.

She turned and advanced upon him. "Do you know something of Gustoff's disappearance, Galen? Did you come to my chamber to detain me while Gustoff slipped away? Did Gustoff solicit your aid, knowing I would do everything possible to stop him from leaving the Keep?"

Each question brought a sharp poke to his chest. Galen reached to grasp her wrist. "Is that what you believe? Do you think the time we spent over the last few hours was nothing more than a diversionary tactic?" He pulled her closer until he could feel every breath she drew. He stared into her eyes, challenging her to take what they'd shared and turn it into nothing more than a ploy to detain her.

She stared back, meeting his gaze with a stubborn battle of wills.

He held her wrist with one hand and slipped his other hand inside her robe. He slid his fingers up her side to settle over the fullness of her breast. He caressed her, rolled the pebble-hard nipple between his fingertips. "What do you think, Thea?"

She buried her forehead against his neck. "I don't have any idea what to think anymore," she whispered.

"I've not spoken to Gustoff since meeting him in the corridor last eve. At that time, he told me nothing of his plans, but I suspect I know where he's gone and why."

"He--"

Galen placed his finger over her lips. "Listen to me, Thea. Promise you won't interrupt until I've finished explaining."

She nodded.

"I believe as you do. Gustoff may have left Glacia to meet Berezan in an attempt to thwart his invasion.

"I think Gustoff is trying to protect you in the only way he knows how. If he can meet and destroy Berezan before he ever reaches Glacia, there will be no need for you to--"

"I won't let him do this!" Thea jerked away and hurried across the chamber to the wardrobe. She threw open the doors and dug through the contents, scattering discarded items all over the floor in her haste.

Galen realized Thea was looking for warm clothing so she could follow Gustoff into the Tundra. He rose from the chaise to stop her.

"You can't go to him, Thea. If Berezan discovers you, all you've worked for over the past years will be in vain. Gustoff obviously doesn't want Berezan to know you exist. Why else would he have gone off alone?"

"I must go to him. You can't stop me."

Galen understood her threat well. There was really no way he could prevent her from leaving Glacia, but he could make sure she didn't go unprotected."

"If you insist on going to Gustoff, I intend to go with you."

"No."

"You can't stop me either, Thea."

"You have your own responsibilities. Your people need you. You can't risk your life needlessly."

Galen folded his arms over his chest. He refused to debate the wisdom of his choice to accompany her. His heart had spoken for his mind, and there was no turning back.

"I'm going, Thea. If you choose to leave me, I'll find my way somehow. Berezan is also my enemy. You can't deny me the opportunity to avenge my people and to protect you."

Warmth flowed through Thea's heart to engulf her entire body. Her love for Galen grew tenfold when she realized though he'd never said the words to confirm his returned love, he'd just pledged himself to her safety.

It was her duty to protect him.

She reached forward to touch his cheek. "You can't go with me, Galen. I can't take a chance you'll be harmed in some way."

"Call Elijah."

* * * *

She watched as Galen turned to the ancient wardrobe to search for garments large enough to wear. He secured the heavy cape and gloves Gustoff had used as a disguise at Dekar, then walked across the room to pull on the woolen tunic he'd removed hours before.

Thea watched, fascinated, as Galen clothed himself in garments suitable to withstand the cold beyond the Keep walls. She wondered how he'd known there were men's clothing in the wardrobe, and guessed he'd done some nocturnal snooping.

She hurried across the chamber and opened the door so Elijah could enter. She turned to find Galen standing in the center of the floor.

"Have two equox prepared for a long journey, Elijah," he said. "Make sure to pack plenty of blankets and food. Thea and I might be away from the Keep for a lengthy period."

Thea glanced from Galen to Elijah and witnessed the servant's acquiescence to the warrior's orders. Elijah never questioned Galen or looked at her for confirmation. He turned and set about to handle his task, not bothering to shut the chamber door behind him.

Thea had time only to thrust out her arms as Galen shoved several items of heavy clothing in her direction.

"Put these on. We leave as soon as Elijah has readied our supplies."

Indignation rose at his assumed command. Thea opened her mouth to protest, but shut it quickly at the determination burning in his blue eyes.

"The choice is yours, Thea. Either we ride together, or I follow you."

CHAPTER 17

Solarus
Five days later

Elsbar raised his crippled hands to wipe at his eyes. "Berezan?"

"No, not Berezan."

The old man squinted, attempting to focus his eyes on the purple robe before him. "Who are you?"

"I am surprised you do not recognize me, Elsbar."

"Gustoff?"

Gustoff glanced around the tower to discover a structure similar to his own in Glacia. He noted the lone tower window, the hot sunlight that poured in through the opening, the swirls of dust floating in the furrows of light. He then studied the old man hunched over behind the center of the table, the parchment beneath his ink-stained hands.

"I thought you dead many decades ago, Elsbar."

The old man tapped his fingers upon the table. "Not dead, Gustoff, only banished from the Ancient Ones, and finally exiled by the devout Solarians because I refused to give up my practice of the ancient arts."

Gustoff stroked his beard. "I have made many mistakes since I removed Berezan from Glacia. My most serious is never taking time to discover who was behind the evil Berezan embraced."

Gustoff stepped closer to the table and studied Elsbar's parchment. "Sixty-eight winters have passed since our last meeting, Elsbar, but I remember it well. You believed you would be selected by the Ancient Ones to guard the Sphere of Light. When rejected, you attempted to end my life, then fled Glacia in bitter defeat. Now, I find you have turned Berezan into an instrument to gain revenge."

"You have always been too soft-hearted, Gustoff. You could not destroy me when you had the opportunity, and you could not kill Berezan. Because of your strong belief in the laws of the Ancient Ones, and their forbidden code that none of us who carried their bloodlines could harm another, you exiled a young boy because you did not believe you had the strength or the wisdom to alter his destiny.

"Fortunately, I did not share those beliefs." Elsbar dropped his quill to the table and pointed a crooked finger at Gustoff. "The woman you paid to leave the young child in the desert was useful, old friend. When touched by my probe, she revealed the truth about young Berezan before she died.

"Berezan knows of his heritage. He will claim Glacia, and the Sphere."

"I have suffered much because of my weakness, Elsbar. Our world has suffered, too."

"Where is the Sphere?"

Gustoff stared into Elsbar's eyes and saw the greed, the hatred that had too many years to fester and grow. "Do you believe I would be foolish enough to bring it with me?"

The old man shrugged his shoulders. "One could only hope. Why did you come? Could you not sense that Berezan was not here?"

"I did not come for Berezan."

"Certainly, you have not--"

"I have come to right one of the many great wrongs I have committed in my lifetime, old man." Gustoff raised his hands, spread his fingers wide. Incantations recognized by the old man before him spilled from his lips. Blue fire erupted on Gustoff's fingertips, growing in intensity until the glow filled the chamber.

Elsbar countered Gustoff's threat. Red fire spread between his arthritic fingers. "The right of challenge is mine, Gustoff. You are in my abode." Elsbar rose slowly to his feet.

Gustoff moved quickly, avoiding the first flames of red fire that streaked past his shoulder. He quickly returned the volley, issuing a bolt of blue that singed the sleeve of Elsbar's robe.

Elsbar laughed. "We are getting too old for this foolishness, Gustoff. Our reflexes have slowed," he said as another flash of red light burst from his fingertips.

"I don't consider the evil you have spawned foolishness, Elsbar. Numerous persons have died because of your teachings to Berezan. Without your wisdom, he never could have attained the Ancient Ones full powers. The evil within you has fueled his passion for the Sphere of Light, but he will never possess it as long as there is life yet in my old body."

"That might be arranged sooner than you think," Elsbar said as darker red flames danced over his hands, down his arms, across his body. He launched another red volley toward his foe and laughed as the fire barely missed Gustoff's head.

Gustoff raised his arms above his head and placed his palms together. After several softly spoken words, he pointed his joined hands at Elsbar. A shimmering aura of dark blue surrounded the old man, freezing the look of horror forever on his face seconds before he drew his last breath and crumpled to the tower floor.

Gustoff curled his fingers into his palms, extinguishing the blue fire, then walked to the table. He picked up the quill his old enemy had dropped, dipped it into the ink. He scribed a message across the face of the parchment Elsbar had been working on and stepped around the table to place the quill in the old man's gnarled fingers.

* * * *

Borderland

Every nerve in Berezan's body quaked, jarring him awake. He gazed around the shabby room, unsure where he was. Deep shadows created by the sunlight pouring in past the hides covering the hut windows cast most of the room in darkness.

Berezan uncrossed his legs and rose to his feet. He filled his lungs with smoky air, and then shook his head in an attempt to ward off the annoying ringing in his ears. He scanned the room again, looking a reason for his abrupt awakening, but found nothing disturbed. He paid close attention to the sounds outside the hut. Again, nothing explained his odd behavior.

He focused within, concentrating on the noise that appeared to reverberate inside his head.

Berezan closed his eyes.

Berezan. The hour has finally come for our meeting, but I will set the time and choose the place. For more than two decades I have regretted I did not destroy you when I had the opportunity. Because of my weakness, many people have suffered.

But no more. No one else will feel the burden of my error. I alone will right the great wrong I wrought upon mankind.

The object you seek is in my possession. To obtain it, you must meet me at the appearance of the fourth sunrise in the great valley of the Tundra.

CHAPTER 18

The equox of the north are magnificent creatures. Bred to withstand the frigid weather, the beasts stood more than seventeen spans high and weighed over a ton each. Their backs were several spans wide, capable of carrying great weights. The massive muscles in their legs enabled them to tread with little effort through deep snow, their cloven hooves picking their way carefully over slick ice, and their long, shaggy coats protecting them from the elements.

Thea gazed down at the beast beneath her. Though they had traveled throughout the night and the sun now rode high overhead, the beast showed little sign of tiring. She wished she felt as little discomfort. Her hands, even gloved in thick fur, were frozen to the point she could no longer feel her fingers. Her toes long ago simply ceased to exist. Only the chattering of her teeth kept her from falling sleep.

Pushing aside the fur mask that covered her face, leaving only her eyes exposed to the elements, she glanced at Galen. She wished there was something she could do to ease his discomfort. She'd lived in the north all of her life, and her tolerance for cold was above normal. A product of the humid jungles, Galen was on the verge of freezing to death.

At the beginning of their journey, he'd sat erect on the back of the beast, shoulders squared, constantly turning in all directions as he searched for any sign of danger. Now, many hours later, he slumped over the beast, fighting exhaustion and the bitter effects of the cold wind and sub-zero temperatures.

Thea wished he'd allowed her to come alone. Instead, in trying to protect her, he'd subjected himself to this torture. She felt deeply sorry for his condition. However, she couldn't change what she started, couldn't forget her journey to assist Gustoff in whatever undertaking he'd initiated.

Nor would she leave Galen alone to fend for himself in the frozen wasteland.

To fight the cold, Thea concentrated on Gustoff's essence, pleased to find it stronger and stronger with each step the equox took. She also sensed great peace, a cleansing calm, and knew he was in no immediate danger.

Thea closed her eyes and wondered again why Gustoff left without discussing his plans with her. He had to know she'd not remain in Glacia if she believed he might face danger. Was this another part of her training? She shook her head. Whatever it was, it didn't make any sense.

Looking up into the bright sky, she estimated they would have to travel at least four more hours before they could rest in the cover of darkness. She sighed when she realized how much she looked forward to the warm tent Elijah packed in their supplies. A break from the constant wind that blew over the Tundra would allow a few hours of rest.

Night fell quickly in the vast emptiness. Since there were no trees or rocks to produce shadows, the full moon created a wondrous white sheen over the ice and set aglow the particles of loose snow whipped high by the wind.

Thea glanced over her shoulder when she realized Galen's equox stopped moving. Galen pointed to what appeared to be a huge snowdrift that would offer shelter. Turning her beast, Thea followed Galen and waited patiently while he dismounted, then walked to her side to assist her down.

Working quickly, they erected the small tent and bed down the equox for a for a few hours rest.

Thea watched Galen feed the beasts from his saddle pouch, then scrape up small piles of snow for the animals to consume for moisture. Remembering her own duties, she filled a kettle with clean snow and carried it into the tent. By the light of several small lumastones, she built a fire with the dried boughs they carried and heated the kettle of snow, mixing in portions of special herbs and spices to form a strong tea.

Thea shielded the fire from the blast of wind that flooded the tent when Galen pushed the flap aside and entered. He thrust a small pouch into her hands before removing his heavy gloves. She opened the pouch, took out two large chunks of bread, some cheese, and several pears, then placed them on the plate she'd set over the fire to warm.

The thick fabric of the tent not only kept the cold air out but after a while, held the heat of the fire in. Thea slipped the fur from her shoulders and turned it inside out to use for a bed, allowing what little warmth remained from her body to heat inside the tent. She watched as Galen did likewise, and noted he positioned his bed on the side of the fire near hers.

When he finally looked at her, Thea noticed the redness around his eyes where his skin was exposed by the fur mask, the strange pallor of his flesh, the purple stiffness of his fingers.

"Give me your hands, Galen."

He looked at her strangely then complied.

Thea called forward a warmth from deep inside, felt it slip slowly down her arms to the tips of her fingers. She took one of Galen's large hands into the protection of hers and, as the heat flowed from her fingers to his, felt something inside her quiver, almost as if a part of her was being joined with him. She reluctantly broke the bond and captured his other hand.

Again, the strange closeness enveloped her. She didn't resist the urge to raise his hand to her lips, to kiss each finger warmed by her touch. He repaid her homage with a like gesture then released her fingers.

Thea raised her hands to touch his face. Within seconds, the flesh around his eyes healed and his skin glowed in the warmth of the fire. She handed him a cup of herb tea she'd prepared, and almost laughed when he took a moment to sniff it before he brought the cup to his lips.

"You've had this tea before, Galen," She chuckled, remembering the day that seemed so long ago.

He winked at her then drained the cup and held it out for more.

Thea ate the remainder of her meal in silence. After packing their supplies, she turned in for a few hours' sleep, cuddling close to Galen to share the warmth of his body, too exhausted to think about more than the comfort of his arms.

* * * *

Galen shifted against the thick fur. He arched away from Thea's side to stretch his back and relieve a cramp in his side. His actions did little to appease the discomfort caused by a long, sleepless night.

He'd spent hours listening to the wind howl beyond the tent, watching the fire dim and almost die. He'd gone over everything he'd experienced since waking bound to the bed a few sunrises ago.

Galen shifted until he could look down upon the woman in his arms. What he'd first believed to be deceit was the desperate act of a woman, a leader, attempting to protect her people. He suspected even without her strange powers or the Sphere of Light, Thea would do everything possible to protect the subjects of Glacia if she knew they were in danger.

He remembered Gustoff's words from the corridor. Though the teachings of the Elders were banned in Borderland, Galen understood the Articles devised centuries past. Shakara had created an assumed need for such scriptures because of the bloody wars she'd led against Glacia and Solarus.

The Articles specifically stated that never again could a female rule any region of the world.

Erik's demise placed the House of Asvaldr, and Glacia, in the vulnerable position of having no male heir to rule, thereby making it accessible to Berezan.

The inequities of the Articles plagued him. Thea was as capable as any male to lead the people of Glacia, but she was judged unfairly by his ancestor's deed. Thankfully, the Creean race chose their disciplined lifestyles, separate and apart from the rest of the world. Words, no matter how honorable, were useless if they could not be enforced.

The time had come for great changes in their world. The Council of Elders and the Messahs effectiveness had passed, and along with them, that of the Articles. In order to lead a people, you had to be able to protect those within your charge, not stand idly by preaching peace and harmony, then bowing out sheepishly at the first threat of rebellion.

Galen thought of Gustoff. The people of Borderland lived a great number of years. His grandsire had been one hundred and ten summers when he passed. Galen couldn't guess Gustoff's age. The old man appeared to float rather than walk, his every movement slow and smooth, as if he calculated each action before it was taken. His eyes were almost colorless, yet in his gaze, Galen detected great wisdom and power. A sample of which he'd also encountered in the corridor.

During the Messahs' visit, they hinted Erik Asvaldr was associated with Berezan. Could the heir to Glacia have been Berezan's accomplice in a quest to rule the world?

Galen rubbed his temples to ease the ache in his head caused by more questions with no answers. He pulled Thea tighter into his embrace, determined to do all he could to keep her safe from whatever they might face on the morrow, and beyond.

At the first noise from the equox outside the cozy boundaries of their tent signaling the coming of dawn, Thea helped Galen break camp.

Several hours later, they crested a huge snow mound just as the sun broke above the horizon. They stared down at a horrifying, yet unbelievable sight.

* * * *

Gustoff, clad only in his purple robe, stood at the bottom of a deep snow valley. Perhaps one hundred spans away, another tall, imposing figure cloaked in emerald stood facing him. Thea could not hear their conversation from her vantage point, but it was apparent from the angry waving of each man's arms that they were in the middle of a heated confrontation.

"Berezan." The word slipped from Galen's tongue like a curse. Thea shivered in response. She couldn't see Berezan's face, but she could tell from his stance, his posture, he was a much younger man. He also projected a confidence that caused Thea's heart to flutter.

Unfair! The word echoed inside her head. Gustoff was no match for Berezan. Age alone would be his downfall. They always knew Berezan was a much younger man. It had never been their purpose for Gustoff to meet him. Thea had been trained to pit her strength against Berezan's, defeating him with the same advantage his youth gave over Gustoff's age. She couldn't allow this travesty to continue. She had to assist Gustoff in some way.

Thea slid down from her equox. She ran to the edge of the precipice that dipped into the deep valley. She threw her heavy gloves to the ground and began to scramble over the edge.

A strong hand pulled her back.

"Don't be foolish, Thea," Galen whispered in her ear. "Gustoff needs all of his concentration to defeat that bastard. He can't commit himself fully to combat if he has you to worry about."

Thea turned and stared into Galen's concerned gaze. The need to be at Gustoff's side clawed at her heart. "There must be something I can do." Thea looked around. "Berezan's alone, Galen. This is my opportunity to face him without endangering the people of Glacia."

Galen glanced around the Tundra. "Something's not right. Berezan isn't the type of man to come unprotected into combat. Nor is Gustoff, for that matter.

"Don't act hastily, Thea. I don't believe--"

The frozen ground beneath their feet began to shake. Ominous black clouds suddenly appeared in the sky. Darkness covered the Tundra. Great claps of thunder filled the morning air. The tremors of the earth shook harder, almost throwing Galen to the ground. Thunder continued to boom directly overhead, each blast louder than the one before.

Thea scrambled away.

Another strong quake caused her to fall to the ground. Something drew her to the edge, called to her as if it was necessary she see what happened in the valley below. Unable to regain her feet, she crawled to the edge and gasped.

Gustoff and Berezan had finished their argument. Apparently, they settled nothing. Now, instead of hurling angry words across the space that separated them, arcs of fire similar to lightning, blue from Gustoff, red from Berezan, flashed back and forth over the valley floor.

Thea attempted to go to Gustoff's aid again, but Galen's arms tightened around her, holding her away from the edge. Another blast of thunder echoed off the valley walls. Thea watched in horror as Berezan pointed to the heavens and a bolt of lightning streaked down from the sky toward Gustoff.

Gustoff raised his arm, hand spread, and issued a bolt of fire of his own that deflected Berezan's volley and sent it ricocheting to the ground where it melted a black hole ten spans wide in the ice.

Another bolt. Another deflection. The frozen ground around the combatants became pockmarked with deep black craters.

Smoke filled the valley. Arcs of blue and red light flashed back and forth. Thunder grew louder. The earth began to shake violently. A huge ridge of snow broke free from the peak behind Berezan's back, sending an avalanche plummeting toward the valley floor.

Thea pulled from Galen's grasp. "Gustoff is weakening. His return volleys slowing."

A bolt of red fire struck the ground near Gustoff's feet. Something inside Thea snapped. "I can't watch this any longer. I must do something."

He shook his head.

"Can't you see Gustoff's tiring?"

Galen placed his lips near her ear. "You'll destroy all Gustoff has given if you make your presence known, Thea. Don't you see? Gustoff gave Glacia two barriers of defense by meeting Berezan here in the open. If he succeeds in destroying Berezan, Glacia will never know what danger it faced."

And if he doesn't? "He needs my help."

Thea ignored Galen's warning and scrambled over the edge of the snow bank to slide down the slick walls. Thankful that her cape was white and shielded her presence against the snow, she eased to the bottom of the snow bank and made her way cautiously closer to Gustoff.

She mentally reached for Gustoff's mind. "I am here, Gustoff. Tell me what I can do to assist you."

Stay away, Thea. This is not your fight. Berezan must not know of your existence. If he discovers you here, all of our people are doomed."

"But you are tiring, Gus. Berezan is much younger and--

A loud, evil laugh echoed over the Tundra, drawing every nerve in Thea's body tighter and tighter. Then all was silent. Deadly silent.

Thea glanced around.

Hundreds of craters blackened the snow, still steaming in the aftermath of battle. But no trace of Berezan. Or Gustoff.

A tiny spark of hope sprang forth in Thea's breast until her mind cried out that Gustoff would never have voiced such a dreadful cry of victory. Uneasiness filled her. She searched frantically over the valley floor for Gustoff.

A scrap of purple flapped over the rim of one of the craters caught her attention. Thea hurried to the spot where her mentor lay.

* * * *

Galen, stunned by the destruction below, didn't realize Thea had left his side until he saw her on the valley floor, picking her way carefully around the deep craters. He crawled over the edge and slipped carefully to the bottom.

Galen heard Thea's mournful cries long before he reached her position. When he neared the crater, he saw Thea sitting in the charred, wet snow, holding Gustoff's body to her chest. She gazed up at him, and Galen knew he'd never forget the look of anguish on her beautiful face. She eased to the side, positioning Gustoff's body on the crater floor, then closed her eyes and touched him, willing all of her strength to heal the old man.

"Thea."

She ignored him.

Galen called out to her several more times, but Thea shook her head and continued to work over Gustoff. Thea was irrational in her grief. She didn't see what he saw when she looked at the old man. Where she saw a soul in need of healing, he stared into the empty eyes of the dead, saw the wound that mutilated his entire torso, leaving nothing but shreds of bone and flesh. Yet, Thea would not give up.

Galen watched helplessly as Thea poured every ounce of her being into reviving the old man. Finally, her wails of anguish echoed across the valley.

* * * *

"No. I won't leave him. I can't."

"There's nothing more we can do for Gustoff, Thea."

"I can't just leave him. I must see that his body is taken back to Glacia," she said as she wiped tears from her eyes. "He was all I had left."

"Berezan will now believe nothing stands in his way as he marches to conquer Glacia." Galen remembered the battle he'd witnessed and guessed Berezan would be correct in his assumption. Swords, knives and clubs would be no match for Berezan's magic. No warrior he'd ever known could compare to one who spit lightning from his fingertips.

How could Thea Asvaldr expect to be such a warrior? Galen didn't believe the gentle female he knew and loved would take a life instead of attempting to heal it. However, if she continued to persist in the same foolishness that cost Gustoff his life, she would eventually meet a similar fate.

One he could not, would not allow.

Well aware he was powerless to prevent Thea from doing what she wanted, Galen prayed she'd remain with him until his own plans reach fruition.

"Can you use some of your gifts to locate Berezan and his army?"

"I can't truly touch his mind without him knowing of my presence. I can, at least, sense his location and his physical state."

Galen watched as she closed her eyes.

* * * *

Thea inhaled deeply and sent a seeking trance over the Tundra. She mentally searched for any hint of a malevolent mind that would match what she'd witnessed hours before.

It didn't take long to discover Berezan's presence many leagues from the valley where he'd taken Gustoff's life. She could tell that he, too, was exhausted.

To have expended as much power as he had used in the valley, he had to have tapped into reserves that he couldn't afford to use. He was definitely weakening. And, his weakness could work to her advantage.

As she had learned early in her training, magic and the effort it took to use it, was debilitating. She had been fortunate to be able to rely on the Sphere of Light for her powers, but Berezan used only the powers he must have acquired directly from the Ancient Ones.

Knowing this, she understood Berezan would not have the physical stamina to make a march upon Glacia within the very near future. And, if he had sustained any injury, his travels would be delayed further.

This new development would give her time to prepare her own defense.

Pulling quickly away from the malevolence within his mind and thoughts, Thea drew a deep breath and opened her eyes to find Galen awaiting her response.

"He's exhausted from the powers he extended to fight Gustoff. He doesn't have the Sphere to rely on for his power and must use only the Ancient Ones gifts that are obviously hidden within him. It will probably be a long while before he builds up his reserves and can march upon Glacia."

"Good. That gives us time to go to Borderland."

"I can't go to Borderland with you. I must return to Glacia to protect my people."

"You said Berezan would not have the physical strength to lead his armies to Glacia in the near future. The people of Glacia have been given a brief reprieve. But, I must know the Fate of my people."

"Berezan is not the only one who is exhausted, Galen. I also feel the need to seek a few hours of sleep to restore my stamina. I can't do this if I have to ride that equox for any length of time."

"You can sleep as we travel."

"And how might I accomplish that?"

"You can rest in my arms as we travel the leagues we will cross to reach my home."

* * * *

Galen made sure Thea was covered in her fur cloak as he settled her more securely into his lap. He used the fullness of his own cloak to wrap them both in a cocoon of warmth and kicked the equox firmly to spur him into motion. He looked up, checked the position of the moon, and headed toward it.

Galen remembered nothing of his flight from Borderland mooncycles ago, yet he knew from Thea's earlier directions, that by traveling south until he neared the melting snow, then west, he should arrive in Borderland before the sun rose twice. He looked over his shoulder to the place they'd left. New snows would eventually create a grave for Gustoff he'd not had time to make.

Galen grieved for the old man. He grieved for Thea. He knew the deep anguish that ate away at one's soul when a loved one was lost. Galen pulled Thea tighter into his embrace, wanting to do anything in his power to shelter her from such agony.

CHAPTER 19

Just before the second sunrise, Galen rode into the foothills of Naro. He purposely bypassed villages in order to avoid the devastation he couldn't yet face. He studied the foliage they passed, the deep greens, the multicolored flowers that grew in no particular pattern.

Hours before, he'd shed his heavy cloak and tunic. The warmth of the sun felt marvelous against the bare flesh of his back.

A rustling sound drew his attention. Galen pulled back on the reins, bringing the equox to a halt. With all senses of preservation fully charged, he stared into the foliage, listened for any abnormal sounds, and waited. He had no weapons to defend the woman cradled in his arms, no skills other than his own abilities to fight whatever threatened their passage.

"Who trespasses in the land of the Cree?" a gruff voice shouted.

Every muscle in Galen's body relaxed. "Who would ask such a question of a weary traveler?" he responded. "Come forth and show yourself."

Three Creean warriors, swords poised for a fight, stepped out of the foliage to block his path. Galen knew he'd been away many sunrises and presumed dead by his people. But these young warriors were known to him. He'd seen them many times before, yet he could not recall their names.

"Stand down, warriors. I have business with your leader, Jakar. I wish to speak with him immediately."

"Who travels with you?" one of the warriors asked.

Galen glanced at Thea riding behind him, then returned the warrior's stare. "My woman. Take us to Jakar."

The three young warriors huddled for a moment of frantic whispering. One warrior, the tallest of the three, came forward. Galen watched his eyes and guessed the man to be in his eighteenth summer. A streak of pain flashed through Galen's chest. Before Berezan's raid, warriors such as these would be in training, not yet expected to defend their homeland. He considered the circumstances these young warriors were faced with, and knew they presented themselves well.

"We will take you to Jakar."

Galen nodded. The warriors positioned themselves around his steed and Thea's mount, one before, two behind. They led him into the hidden passageways of Naro.

As they rounded a camouflaged bend in the rock, three large warriors stepped out from cover. The older warriors recognized Galen immediately, but he shook his head as a silent command for them not to give his identity away. Each warrior nodded in turn.

"This stranger wants to see Jakar," the young warrior who led them said. One of the older warriors nodded, turned, and entered the cave.

Moments later, Galen's old friend ran to his side. "Galen! We believed you were dead."

Galen shifted his gaze from his friend's face to those of the younger warriors before him. He noted the flushness of their cheeks and understood their mortification. "You have served Borderland well, warriors. I commend your actions, and I would speak to each of you on the morrow."

The young warriors bowed in unison and backed quickly away.

"Who is she?" Jakar whispered, almost as if he were afraid to approach the beautiful woman on the beast behind him.

"Mine," was Galen's only answer.

Jakar gave him a curious glance, which Galen ignored. "I'll explain everything later. Right now, I require rest, nourishment, and a place for my female to sleep. We have traveled for five suns across the Tundra."

Galen dismounted.

Jakar nodded, sending the two warriors standing near the cave entrance inside to carry out Galen's orders.

"These are curious beasts, Galen."

"They are creatures of the north as you can see by their thick coats. See if you can find them a cool place to rest. They've served me well."

One of the warriors who'd gone to prepare for Galen's arrival stepped from the cave and paused beside him. "Your bed and food have been prepared, Regis. Please follow me."

Galen followed Jakar and the warrior inside the cave. He led Thea to a secluded alcove jutting deep into the rock and watched as she sat down to rest comfortably on a thick pallet of furs. "Are you hungry?" he asked.

Thea shook her head. "Tired and sore."

"Rest here while I speak with my friend," Galen offered. "I will return shortly."

* * * *

"Where have you been for the past five mooncycles, Galen?"

Galen took a chunk of meat from the platter before him. He savored the flavor of a staple in his diet he'd been without too long. After washing it down with alsa wine, he wiped his mouth on his hand and met his friend's gaze.

"I followed Berezan's mercenaries for several sunrises through the jungle. On my third waking, I discovered they'd changed the direction of their flight and, instead of heading south, turned north. I didn't expect their trap." Galen closed his eyes and struggled to remember what happened after he was captured.

"Why would Berezan's army turn north?"

"They must have thought the warriors of Cree would follow them once they left the city. I believe they were disappointed when their ambush netted only me. Until they learned who I was."

"You told them?"

"No. They took me to a cave deep in the northernmost section of Borderland. One I never new existed. I don't recall how long I was shackled, but I remember thinking about my need to escape."

Galen closed his eyes. "Berezan came to me when my strength was almost at an end. He did little more than touch my flesh, but he learned everything he wanted to know."

"How?"

"All I remember is excruciating pain."

Jakar paled.

"I escaped and, knowing I couldn't lead Berezan's army back to our hiding place in Naro, I headed toward the Tundra. I don't remember anything else until I awoke in a strange chamber with a beautiful woman hovering over me." Galen glanced at Thea's sleeping form.

Jakar grasped Galen's arm. "You are home now, my friend. I can see you are exhausted. Rest. We'll talk more tomorrow." Jakar rose and left the alcove.

Galen finished his wine, then climbed into the furs beside Thea and fell promptly to sleep.

* * * *

Thea blinked at the strange light that danced on walls of rough granite and sparkled in the silver flecks. She wondered about the walls. They were similar to those in Glacia, yet somehow different, almost as if they were unpolished.

Thea struggled into a sitting position. She studied her surroundings. She was in some type of cave. The walls were high, almost thirty spans above her head, and the floor solid rock. There was only one entrance, and no hole in the ceiling for the smoke from the fire that burned in the center to escape, yet the air was not tainted.

The cave wasn't furnished. Several mats made of some type of animal fur covered areas of the floor. She looked down. Similar furs piled several spans deep beneath her formed a bed.

Thea glanced over her shoulder to watch Galen as he slept on the mat beside her. She studied the firelight as it flickered on his bare shoulders for a moment until horrible memories flooded back, filling her mind and tearing at her heart.

Tears rolled down her cheeks as she relived the battle between Gustoff and Berezan. She had wanted desperately to help Gustoff in his battle to destroy Berezan, but she had arrived in the valley too late. She had allowed Gustoff's mental words to cause her to hesitate, which, in the end, had cost his life.

Thea drew a quick breath and reached deep inside for something she felt missing. A strange emptiness in the area of her heart felt as if a piece of the organ had been torn away.

She glanced at Galen. He'd turned over on his back. The fur slipped until it exposed his chest. Warmth stirred to life in the pit of her stomach.

She reached to glide her fingers along the line of his cheek.

She'd given everything to revive Gus, but, in the end, she'd failed. Deep inside a tiny voice offered her efforts were doomed from the beginning, but she brushed the thoughts away and remembered holding Gustoff in her arms, seeing the life leave his kind eyes, knowing he'd died in her place.

Her entire life had been torn asunder and, with Gustoff's death, she had become the sole source remaining to destroy Berezan.

Frustrated, Thea closed her eyes and concentrated on her bedchamber in Glacia. She imagined every wardrobe, the poster bed, the lavender-covered chaise where she'd spent many hours relaxing, and even the heavy tapestries that shielded her balcony.

Many moonrises from her home, her energy drained, she could only pray Nola and Elijah would be successful in evacuating the people of Glacia to safety.

Thea laid back against the thick fur pallet and buried her forehead against Galen's arms as he slept.

* * * *

The fire in the pit at the center of the alcove had dimmed until all that remained were hot coals and ash. Shadows climbed high on the stone walls, darkening every imperfection in the granite and causing the silver flecks to peer back at him like tiny red eyes.

Galen arched his shoulders, shifting Thea's weight until the pinpricks that raced up and down his arms subsided. He rolled his buttocks, easing the cramps that tightened his left thigh, then looked down at the woman asleep in his arms.

He tried to close his mind to the memories of the hurt he'd seen in her beautiful eyes. He wasn't strong enough. Each moment replayed itself over and over, bringing another twist to the knife of pain that tore through his heart.

He'd witnessed her anguish, her grief. And, there had been nothing he could have done to ease her pain or relieve the sense of failure and guilt he knew she felt.

Galen closed his eyes and leaned back until his head rested against the stone wall. For well over an hour, he'd held her. Thinking. Planning. Hoping for a miracle, when all around them seemed doomed.

Much, and little, had changed over the past five sunrises. Gustoff was gone. Thea's, grief over the death of her mentor, saddened him until he wished there were some way he could ease her pain, but he knew only time would ease the emptiness in her heart.

He'd finally returned to his people, but Berezan represented the same threat he had before they began their journey away from Glacia.

Galen opened his eyes and glanced at Thea. No words of love or commitment had ever been spoken between them. Now it might be too late.

"Galen."

Galen turned to find Jakar standing in the opening of the alcove. He studied his friend for several moments, remembering the times they'd shared as children. Love and laughter filled their days. He recalled how confident they each had been in their training, invincible warriors, the strongest and the best of the best. Neither would have ever believed a future filled with bitterness and defeat.

"I see she is still sleeping." Jakar walked to the center of the cave and stirred the embers of the fire until a bright glow lit the darkness. He added several branches from the pile against the cave wall, and took a seat on the fur mat directly across from Galen's.

"I never thought I'd see you again. After so much time passed, I'd all but given up." Jakar shook his head. "The people are asking for you. News of your return spread fast. So, too, are rumors of the woman you carried into the cave."

Galen laughed. "Rumors?"

"Our society has always encouraged our people to speak our minds. Young warriors, old warriors for that matter, converse freely when their leader brings a stranger into our midst, Galen. Especially a female."

"I didn't think you'd be satisfied with my earlier answers to your question, old friend."

"Much has happened since you left our village to seek revenge against Berezan, Galen. I gathered all of the survivors together as ordered and brought them to hide in the caves.

"We are a crippled people. Our numbers are few. Sickness is rampant. Hiding here like animals, we've been unable to forage for herbs and medicines or nourishing food to take care of our people. Our warriors have wounds that fester and steal their strength." Jakar dropped his forehead into his hands.

"Now, with rumors Berezan has once again traveled into our land..." Jakar shook his head. "Several sunrises ago, the sense of helplessness began to eat away at me to the point I felt I had to do something. In frustration, I led a small band of warriors through the jungle to search for any evidence of a new invasion and stumbled upon a mysterious man in the clearing of Cree."

"Gustoff," Galen whispered.

"You know this man?"

"Yes."

"Then you can tell me if he spoke the truth when he said he was from Glacia."

Several seconds passed. Galen closed his eyes and remembered Gustoff's tale of what he'd discovered when he visited Cree to seek his father's aid. He opened his eyes and met Jakar's gaze. "The old man spoke the truth."

Jakar nodded toward Thea's sleeping form. "And this female?"

Galen lifted Thea from his lap and laid her down on the bedding. He covered her with the furs then rose to his feet.

"Come, old friend. Walk with me through the caves of Naro. There's much for you to know and even more to be done."

* * * *

R'han raised his hand to shield his eyes from the brilliant flare of sunlight. He blinked then lowered his hand to watch Berezan, emerald cloak covered with ash, pacing before him.

All had been ready to begin their invasion of Glacia three sunrises ago. When he'd come to advise Berezan of their readiness and found the hut he occupied empty, R'han ordered the army of Solarus to stand down. Now, he was still confused by his master's strange disappearance.

R'han stood silently and watched Berezan, not daring to speak until spoken to.

Berezan stalked before him like a madman, taking three strides, pausing, turning, then stomping back to his original position. Then he would laugh his evil laugh that always brought the hair at R'han's neck to attention and caused chills to ripple over every inch of his flesh.

R'han wondered why Fate had taken the turn that placed him into the service of this evil man. His life had once been peaceful, but he now lived in constant fear. That same fear caused him to carry out every order Berezan gave to the minutest detail.

R'han now wondered if whatever horrible torture Berezan could manufacture to cause his death might not be better than waking each sunrise and wondering if some of the evil that drove Berezan might be invading his soul.

* * * *

Berezan reveled in the accelerated beat of his heart that pumped blood through his veins like raging floodwaters. Every cell tingled with the thrill of victory.

"Fool!"

Shedding anything that encumbered his movement, Berezan ripped his cloak free and tossed it on the ground. He raised his fingertips to touch his temples and closed his eyes, seeking a vision of his mentor leagues away in Solarus. His sense of self-power grew twofold when the old man's conjured image appeared in his mind's eye.

"Arrogant, old fool. All these years you've cautioned me that Gustoff would prove a worthy adversary. Well, you were wrong, Elsbar. Wrong!" Berezan shouted. "You should have been in the valley with me, old man. You would have seen for yourself how useless your teachings of the past twenty-five summers have been.

"I have conquered the last obstacle that stands in my path. Nothing can stop me now. Nothing! The Sphere of Light will be mine. Glacia, and the whole of our world will answer to my call. Nothing, no one, can ever take away what rightfully belongs to me again."

Dismissing Elsbar's effigy, Berezan opened his eyes, spun, and stared in the opposite direction. He noticed R'han and halted. "Why are you standing there gaping at me?"

"I thought we were to have marched three sunrises ago, Master. All has been ready."

"The enemy has been conquered. Have someone fetch my clean cloak. I wish to be presented as befits my station when I arrive in Glacia."

"Yes, Master."

"I shall precede my army into Glacia, R'han. Have my men ready to move immediately. I will await you...." Berezan passed his fingers through his hair. "No. I shall ride at the front of my army in the fashion I have earned. Send a messenger ahead to advise the Elders their time has passed and I expect to find all assembled when I secure the position denied me for so long."

R'han nodded and hurried away.

Berezan raised his hands to the afternoon skies. Spreading his fingers wide, he uttered words that sent streaks of red fire from his fingertips to soar high into the heavens until they brought thunder down from the clouds.

CHAPTER 20

The aroma was delightful, unlike anything Thea ever smelled. Inhaling deeply to capture the heavenly fragrance, she willed her eyes to remain shut and allowed her senses to appreciate the softness and warmth surrounding her.

The rumble deep in her belly destroyed her pretense.

Thea opened her eyes and sat up to find she was alone in the cave.

Searching for the source of the aroma, she discovered someone had left a pot full of something warming on a spit above the fire. The escaping steam hovered in the still air.

Thea climbed to her knees in the middle of the furs and, unable to locate her missing clothing, wrapped the fur around her body and scrambled to her feet.

She dragged the fur behind her as she made her way to the entrance of the cave and peeked out. Another stone cavern filled her vision. To her left, a tunnel ran for about one hundred spans before bearing off to the right.

All was quiet. No one appeared to be about.

She considered following the tunnel to discover where it led, but discarded the idea in favor of the pleasant aroma that tantalized taste buds that hadn't tasted nourishment for more hours than she cared to remember. She made her way back to the fire.

The mysterious someone who'd left the food also provided a wooden bowl filled with fruit of strange shapes and colors beside the fire pit. She couldn't resist plucking a palm-sized orange object from the bowl, bringing it to her nose. Another pleasant aroma filled her senses.

Unsure how to eat the unusual fruit, she pried it open with her fingernails and devoured the juicy pulp. After wiping her mouth with the back of her hand, she tried another.

The pot on the spit drew her attention. She discovered a wooden spoon on the floor, picked it up, and dipped it into the pot to sample whatever awaited to appease her hunger.

The tasty vegetables that made up the body of the stew were foreign but filling. Each bite renewed a little more of her strength. She sat back on her calves to survey the cave.

"Renia?"

Thea turned toward the opening of the cave.

Shadows partially hid the tall, thin woman holding a bundle against her hip.

"I'm sorry to disturb you, but Galen bade me to return your garments."

The woman stepped into the light of the fire. Thea stared in awe at a being almost two hand spans taller than she was. She studied the woman's strange clothing, or lack thereof. For her entire life, she'd been clothed in layer upon layer of fabric for warmth. This woman wore a whisper-thin garment of light blue that hung from her bare shoulders, clung to her abundant breasts, then belted in at her waist by a braided cord of the same fabric.

Thea stared at the woman, but she couldn't help herself. All this woman had recently experienced was depicted in the condition of her gown. At one time, the soft creation must have been lovely. It now hung in tatters from the woman's frame. A great number of holes were burned into the fabric, exposing bare skin. Dirt accumulated on the skirt until the light blue appeared gray in several places. A dark stain ended in a long tear that capped the woman's left knee. Glancing down, Thea saw a partially healed wound on her leg, and assumed the stain was the woman's blood.

Chills passed over Thea's body.

"I'm sorry. I don't mean to stare at you, but I didn't expect anyone." Thea stepped forward to greet the woman and held out her hand. The woman draped Thea's heavy woolen robe over her forearm.

"You will need something lighter to wear in our climate, Renia. The other women are searching their belongings for something small enough to fit you."

The sadness in the woman's voice spoke volumes. Everything the people of Cree once possessed was destroyed in Berezan's raid. Thea had a mental flash of all Gustoff told her of the condition of the Borderland villages he'd visited.

With so little of their own, the women of Borderland would share their belongings with her.

Thea felt humbled.

"I'm sorry I've disturbed you for so long." The woman turned to walk away.

"Please wait." Thea held her hand out to the woman. "Are you responsible for the fine meal prepared for me?"

The woman glanced toward the pot on the spit and nodded.

"Thank you. It's delicious. I appreciate your kindness."

The woman smiled and attempted to leave the chamber.

"I have eaten my fill. I hate to think such food would spoil. Won't you please share it with me?"

The woman cast a long gaze over her shoulder toward the pot, then shook her head. "My son is restless, Renia. I would not have him disturb you."

"Your son? You have a baby in that bundle?" Thea stared in amazement at the bundle the woman held against her hip. It was small, but as she studied it more carefully, she could see the definition of tiny legs and a back outlined under the cloth that covered it head to toe.

Emptiness welled within her. Her sheltered life had not afforded her the opportunity to hold a baby in her arms, to touch its tiny body, to see its chubby fingers and toes. With the exception of the Keep staff, the people of Glacia were glimpsed from afar, their laughter and sorrows diluted by distance.

The woman suddenly reminded her of Nola, of times when they were younger and sat outside the Keep on sunny days to watch Nola's younger brother play on the ice. But, at that time, Nola's sibling had seen eight winters.

"Please, stay," she whispered. She pointed toward the pallet near the fire. "Make yourself comfortable. Your son will not disturb me." Thea watched the woman gaze cautiously around the alcove and then make her way to the pallet. She placed the child down beside her and waited while Thea seated herself.

"My name is Thea. Will you tell me yours?"

The woman finally met her gaze. Thea was taken aback by the striking resemblance the female had to Galen. Blue eyes, blond hair. Was this a trait of the Creean people? A coincidence?

A strange feeling crawled over her flesh. Who was this woman? Why had Galen sent her to the cave? Galen had never discussed his family. Other than the fact his father and mother were murdered by Berezan, she knew little about him.

Could this woman be....

Her chest tightened. Her heart skipped a beat. Was this woman Galen's sister? His mate? Could this child be Galen's?

"Mya."

"Mya," Thea repeated.

"Yes." Tears glossed the woman's blue eyes, spilled over her lashes, and dripped down her cheeks. "The women of Cree gave me the task of tending you. They think to take my mind away from the sorrow." Mya wiped her face with the back of her hand then turned to retrieve the baby from the furs. "I cannot bring my troubles to you. Deja and I will leave you to your rest."

Thea felt a desperate need to touch this woman's mind, to offer whatever comfort she could to ease her way. "Please, don't leave me, Mya." She reached across the space separating them and touched the woman's hand. "I'm a stranger in a strange place. I need a friend."

Mya cuddled her son against her chest, sniffed, then met Thea's gaze. "You are a beautiful woman inside and out. Galen has chosen well."

Thea tried hard to ignore the woman's words. She had to fight down the urge to scream that Galen had chosen nothing. He'd taken her love, betrayed her, left her with a pain inside nothing would ever take away.

However, this woman had enough problems of her own.

"Call me Thea, Mya." Thea squeezed Mya's hand. "I come from a place far different from Borderland. I have never seen caves such as this one, or felt strong sunshine on my face. My home's covered with ice and snow for all seasons. Other than the granite boulders that protrude above the snow line, I've never seen the earth or walked around barefoot."

Mya looked down at her feet. A bewildered expression crossed her face.

Thea smiled. To take this woman's mind off of her troubles for a few minutes was worth the time she'd lose in returning to her own home, her own problems. "Help yourself to what is left of my meal, Mya."

Mya placed her tiny burden back down on the fur beside her then reached for the fruit bowl. She devoured several pieces before pausing to look at Thea.

Thea's heart ached as she remembered the abundance of good, nourishing food grown in the hydro-gardens of Glacia. Gustoff had told her the Creean's gardens and livestock were destroyed. "Do all of your people live in these caves?"

Mya swallowed. "We were forced to flee here after ... after...." Tears filled the woman's eyes again. She looked away.

Thea leaned forward. She placed her fingers along side Mya's temples. "Mya, look at me," she whispered. Mya turned her head slowly, but Thea did not release her touch. "Close your eyes, my new friend. Relax and allow me to ease some of your burdens."

Mya closed her eyes.

Thea watched for signs of even, shallow breathing. She shoved aside the tiny flare of guilt she felt for touching this woman's mind without permission then closed her own eyes.

"Tell me what happened to you, Mya. Let me share your pain."

Mya nodded slowly. "Deja is crying. A loud noise has disturbed his rest."

"Go on."

"People are running. Screaming. Smoke is so thick I can hardly find my way across the hut." Mya swayed gently back and forth.

"I cannot breathe!" Mya gasped for air, choking.

"Relax, Mya. You can breathe. Inhale slowly. Draw the air deep into your lungs then allow it to escape."

"My eyes burn. I can't find my son. He's crying louder. I can't get to him. I can't see him." Mya rubbed her hands against her closed eyes. "Deja! Deja!"

Thea could feel the blood rushing through Mya's veins, the thundering of her heart.

"Fire! There's fire everywhere. I can't get through. It's hot. My son!"

Mya began to sob. "My knees.... My hands burn so badly I can hardly place them to the floor. I must get to my son. I must. Oh, Deja!"

Thea probed further into Mya's memory. The baby's cries are louder. He's terrified. He's in pain. Bits of burning wood are falling from the ceiling, charring Mya's back, burning her hair.

She's coughing. Crying. Crawling.

Great booming sounds erupt beyond the hut walls. People are still running. More and more pass the hut. The stone walls begin to pop and hiss with the heat. A great timber rafter engulfed in flames falls to the floor with a loud thump and an eerie hiss.

The baby is silent.

Mya reaches his pallet. She uses his blanket to wrap him up, not knowing the blanket is full of burning bits of wood. She crawls to the doorway, stumbles to her feet, and joins the fleeing multitudes.

Thea wiped at the tears streaming down her own cheeks. Every detail of this woman's anguish washed over her, but she forged on, past the gory details of the invasion to the aftermath.

She sees through Mya's eyes as the woman, babe in arms, stumbles numbly over what is left of her village.

Blood. So much blood. Dismembered bodies with the horror of what they experienced etched into their faces.

Her mother. Her father. Her sister and three small children.

Blood. So much blood.

So little hope.

Warriors bodies. Strange. Garbed in cloaks the color of sand.

She passes people with grief-stricken faces so much like her own shifting through the ashes of their lives.

Searching.

Desperately searching for her mate, Nortu. Praying he didn't return from the hunt with the other warriors of Cree.

Thea gently withdrew her touch. She didn't need to experience any more of Mya's memories to know Nortu did not survive Berezan's attack on Borderland.

Thea considered her own grief at Gustoff's passing. She realized such misery was the way of coping with things they could not change, accepting the hurt, and in time, allowing the fond memories to surface.

"Mya, there are things you have experienced you should remember, for these memories will make you wiser as you pass through your life. The pain you have suffered and recall so clearly will lessen in time. I can't make that go away. But, I promise you, I will do what I can for those who remain."

Thea touched Mya's forehead. "Wake up now, Mya."

Mya's lashes fluttered open. She stared blankly at Thea for several seconds.

"May I?"

Mya shook her head. I'm sorry. I--"

"May I hold your son?"

Mya looked down to the infant at her side. "He's so sick. Trapped here in the caves as we are, we can't forage for necessary herbs and roots. We are lucky to have sufficient food." Mya reached down and brought the baby into her arms.

Thea studied the child's blanket. No evidence of fabric burns remained. She supposed Mya had disposed of the infant's charred wrapping in order to help her forget. "Please."

Mya looked at Thea then slowly handed her precious bundle into Thea's open arms.

The child was so light, so tiny. But it was also hot, almost as if she held a burning log. Thea cast a questioning gaze to Mya.

"His fever is much worse. He has taken no nourishment in two days," Mya sobbed. "He's all I have left. Now, he's being taken away."

The tiny infant squirmed in Thea's arms. "There is life left in his body, Mya, so there is hope," she whispered.

Very carefully, she placed the infant on the pallet beside her, praying she wouldn't find what she expected when she pulled the blanket away and exposed the tiny body within. She couldn't hold back the cry of anguish she made when she folded the fabric back to look at the baby.

Its tiny arms were so weak the baby could hardly move them. Burns that had partially healed, then festered, covered his legs, his chest and neck, and completely engulfed one side of the baby's face.

"He was burned in the fire that destroyed our home. I tried to get to him. I tried to save him."

"Shhh, Mya. Your child senses your anxiety. He's very sick, and your grief is only making him worse."

Mya scrambled to her knees and crawled to the pallet beside Thea. She lovingly touched her infant's face, cooed to him, and leaned to kiss his unburned cheek. "Deja, my sweet. This should have been me. Why do you have to suffer so?"

Thea touched Mya's shoulder.

"My people have done all they can for him," Mya said. "I know it's only a matter of time before he joins my mate in the hereafter, but I cling desperately to him. I don't know what will happen to me when there is nothing left, no one to care for, and no one to need me. I feel so helpless watching him slip away from me. There are times I wish I could die in his place."

"Your son will not die, Mya." Thea reached down and wrapped her hands around the child's naked body. She lifted him carefully to her chest, cuddled him in her arms. Should her powers ever fail, she prayed it would not be at this moment, not when this tiny creature needed her so.

She bent her cheek to the top of the infant's head, closed her eyes, and rocked him back and forth. She drew three long breaths, holding each until her lungs burned, then exhaled. Each time reaching deeper to touch the part of her that had the power to heal.

The baby cried out. Thea's skin suddenly seemed to be burning, melting away from her bones, exposing all her nerve endings to the air, and causing excruciating pain. She held on, forged past her own discomfort, absorbed the child's agony.

From a distance Thea could hear Mya crying, but her entire concentration was caught up in a blinding white light, a light that nurtured her, healed her. The light began to fade, leaving in its place a sense of peace and calm.

Thea opened her eyes slowly to discover Mya had fainted and lay on the cave floor before her. She looked down to find a tiny pink infant, free from all blemish, gurgling softly and tugging on a strand of her auburn hair.

Thea cried.

CHAPTER 21

"Mya."

Thea shook the woman gently. The infant in her arms regained strength rapidly, exercising its lungs to display his need as he fretted against her breast, hungry for the nourishment he'd refused for the past two sunrises.

"Mya, please, wake up." The sensation the tiny creature created when he clutched handfuls of her woolen robe, and rubbed his mouth against the heaviness of her breast, caused a strange warmth to flare in Thea's chest, a deep yearning for something missing from her life. The acknowledgement that this was another of those emotional experiences Gustoff never explained pulled hard on her heart.

The nagging feeling she was never meant to experience the same emotions other females felt twisted deep, reminding her of the course of her life decided many moonrises ago.

She was the daughter of destiny, fated for a purpose far beyond that of other mortals. Gustoff and the Ancient Ones must have deemed the joys of love and motherhood would interfere with her life path.

Thea closed her eyes to distance her thoughts from the feelings rapidly crumbling her composure. She remembered everything Mya's memories had disclosed, the horror the people of Borderland had witnessed, the grief they must still carry.

Images of Nola, Elijah, and the numerous other servants of Glacia sharpened in her mind. If Berezan succeeded in his evil, each man, woman, and child of Glacia would experience a fate similar to that of the people of Borderland.

Time closed in around her.

Thea opened her eyes to glance about the cave, the woman waking on the mat across from her, the baby in her arms. She could do much to assist the people of Borderland in their struggle for survival.

* * * *

"Take this."

Galen turned to find Jakar holding the emblem of the bronzed sun he'd taken from his father's neck. The same emblem Galen rejected when he allowed his emotions to override common sense and set out after Berezan many sunrises ago.

Galen held out his hand. Jakar dropped the golden-linked chain across his palm. Clutching it firmly, Galen felt the warmth of the metal sear his flesh. It was his destiny to lead the people of Borderland. His duty to keep them safe, provide ample nourishment, medicine, shelter. Responsibilities he'd forsaken in his hour of grief.

He closed his eyes against the memories that tormented him, the bitter and the sweet. He thought about what had befallen his people, what could still befall his people, and that there was little he could do to stop it.

He'd witnessed Berezan's power firsthand. Stood high above and watched as two men possessed with abilities he'd never considered possible attempted to destroy each other. Abilities he nor his few remaining warriors could conquer or imitate.

For the last two hours, he and Jakar had walked through the many winding tunnels of Naro. He'd told Jakar of all he'd experienced since leaving Cree. Jakar told Galen of all the events that took place in Cree since his departure.

Strategies were discussed. Tactics reviewed. Until it became evident they had no way to defeat Berezan.

Much talk. No solutions.

Now, his best friend stood beside him, demanding he take his place as heir to Borderland, Regis of a desperate race of people with little hope for the future.

Galen's hands shook as he placed the medallion around his neck and felt the heavy disk against his chest. Strange warmth flowed through his body, renewed his spirit, and lifted him from the clutches of defeat that ridged his shoulders.

The blood of Shakara ran through his veins. A warrior's heart beat within his chest. The warrior's creed, something he'd forsaken many sunrises ago, echoed in his mind. 'Death with honor in defense of our own, no matter the foe, had been the war song he'd lived by, would go on living by until the last breath left his body.

"There must be a way to separate Berezan from his army," he said. "From what we've experienced, his men fight as we do, with weapons we can defeat."

Jakar shook his head. "We are only a little more than a hundred strong, Galen. Our scouts report Berezan's army numbers in the thousands."

Galen paced before his friend. Hundreds of different strategies bounced around in his mind. He rubbed his chin, tried to place himself into Berezan's position. What if the men who made up Berezan's army were reluctant participants? Suppose there were those among the vast numbers who didn't want to create the havoc on which Berezan seemed to thrive?

The warriors of Borderland had trained their entire lives to reach their state of physical accomplishment. To his knowledge, the men of Solarus had never been warriors. By all the accounts he'd heard the people of Solarus were farmers and herdsmen who eked out a meager living from the hot desert sands.

Berezan obviously used the threat of his evil to turn docile men into a militia. Men who killed rather than be killed.

Would this work to his advantage? Offer some firm ground on which they could fight?

"What do you know of this mysterious Sphere of Light, Galen? Why would it be so important Berezan would kill everyone in his path to attain it?"

Galen glanced at Jakar. His friend leaned against the stone wall, crossed his arms over his chest, and stood watching as he waited patiently for an answer.

"I learned from Gustoff of Glacia that the Sphere is an ancient talisman, handed down through the generations by a people the Glacians refer to as the Ancient Ones. This Sphere is supposed to protect the world from evil."

"Some protection," Jakar grunted. "If this magical talisman was supposed to be in Gustoff's possession at Glacia, why did Berezan invade Borderland? From what we were told by the survivors, Berezan spent numerous sunrises searching for it among the destruction created by his army. Nothing fits."

Galen agreed. The more he thought about what Gustoff told him in the corridor of Glacia, the less sense his words made. If Gustoff truly possessed some magical force that would destroy Berezan, why had he allowed the demon to wreak such havoc over the world? Why had Gustoff himself perished?

Jakar pulled from the wall to pace. "If this Sphere is to protect from evil, why would Berezan want it? Seems to me something that destroys the type of magic Berezan creates would be the last item he'd wish to possess."

Galen studied Jakar's face and wished he had some way to ease his torment. He'd asked himself that same question numerous times over the past few sunrises. He had no answer.

"This Glacian woman you brought home with you is also supposed to be able to control the Sphere and use it to destroy Berezan?" Jakar asked, confused.

Galen sighed. "Thea has been taught the whole of her life to believe she carries special powers. Gustoff proclaimed it to be her destiny to wield the Sphere against Berezan and destroy him."

"Do you believe this tiny woman capable of such deeds?"

Galen closed his eyes and ran his fingers through his hair. He remembered the battle he'd witnessed in the Tundra, the desperate effort Thea had made to restore her mentor's life, the horrible aftermath that left huge charred pits in the snow.

Unbidden, Gustoff's words echoed through his mind. *All things in life have a purpose. Yours is to stand by Thea's side, to help her see her destiny through.*

Other memories followed. He saw Thea as she'd been in the steam bath, beautiful, curious, and willing to share herself completely. Innocent, yet seductive. As clearly as if she were standing beside him, he felt her touch on his body. The effects of that remembered touch almost staggered him.

Galen recalled Thea as she'd been in the alcove only hours ago. Her attempts to use her powers to save her Gustoff had depleted her strength, leaving her in a state of exhaustion.

To face Berezan is her destiny. Gustoff's words filled his mind. *She must be in Glacia to wield that power.*

Sharp pain jabbed Galen's heart. Was it possible the old man spoke the truth? Had he made a serious mistake in his attempt to protect the woman he loved? By taking Thea from her homeland, had he doomed them all?

"Well, do you?"

"I don't know. I've experienced some of her strange powers, Jakar. She immobilized me with the slightest touch of her fingers. I've seen her heal wounds, leaving no evidence the wound ever existed. No matter how hard I try, I can't envision Thea striking another being to death with an arc of fire."

"Then you believe the tale told to you by the old man?"

Galen shook his head. "There's so little left to believe, Jakar. All we know has been taken from us by powers we never knew existed before Berezan invaded our world. Who's to say whether Thea, diminutive as she may be, might accomplish what the warriors of Cree could not."

"Maybe we should do everything in our power to assist her toward that goal."

"A part of me says yes, another part no. I've fought all my life to protect the women left in my charge. If we allow Thea to proceed with what she believes to be her destiny, she'll be protecting us."

Jakar placed his hand upon Galen's shoulder. "This woman, is she your chosen mate?"

"She is to me what no other can ever be, my friend. I've made her mine."

Galen reached down to grasp the bronzed medallion against his chest. He lifted it until the polished metal glistened in the sun. "Gustoff came to Borderland to seek my father's aid in forming an alliance to protect both Cree and Glacia from Berezan's wrath. In my pain, when he approached me with the same request, I adamantly refused him.

"But, as I finally accept the responsibilities attached to this medallion, I acknowledge the old man's heart was true when he proposed a joint effort. The people of Borderland and the people of Glacia must unite to protect what they possess."

Galen closed his eyes and cursed Berezan's soul to burn in eternal damnation.

"Thea's a very stubborn woman, my friend. Over the past few sunrises, she's experienced more pain and frustration than many suffer their entire life. She's exhausted, but she'll do everything in her power to get home. In her present condition, a hasty act will mean certain death."

Galen opened his eyes and stared into his friend's face.

"Nothing will be gained by making an unplanned march on Glacia. By the time we arrive, Berezan will have already committed all the mayhem he's capable of. The only thing we will accomplish is to warn him of our retaliation."

Galen thought about the hidden doorway he'd found on the lower level of Glacia's Keep. Still convinced the cold air that seeped in around the door meant the entrance led outside the Keep. An entrance that could be used to their advantage.

"There are secret entrances into the Governing House of Glacia. Ones I pray Berezan knows nothing about. A force as few as ours could sneak into the Keep under the cover of darkness.

"I've had the opportunity to explore Glacia's Governing House over the last moonrises. I know where the best areas of defense lie.

"A rational, structured invasion would allow us to seriously deplete Berezan's warriors and increase our chances of victory. But our plans must be carefully drawn."

Jakar agreed. "We also need time to mass our warriors and instruct them as to what they might expect when the warriors of Borderland finally come face to face with Berezan's wrath."

"I pray our warriors never come within a thousand spans of Berezan, Jakar," Galen whispered.

"Are you prepared to believe what you've been told about your woman?"

"Do I have another choice? All that's left is to convince Thea that alone she has no chance against Berezan and his army. But first, Thea must be given time to recuperate from her past ordeals."

Galen slapped Jakar on the shoulder. "Come, my friend. It's time you met the woman who's captured my heart."

CHAPTER 23

Glacia

Thousands of men, women, and children lined the ice-covered roadway that wound through the center of Glacia and approached the Keep, but the silence was deafening. Even the wind, which blew constantly through the high mountain passages, was calm.

Nothing moved.

Berezan looked up. Thick gray clouds hung heavy in the air, obscuring the jutting peaks of the mountains surrounding the city, blocking out the sun.

The eerie creak of Berezan's saddle as he stood in his stirrups to survey all around him pierced the quiet like the shriek of a wild creature. Berezan looked into the faces of the people standing near, saw the terror he knew would be there, and smiled.

He'd withstood two moonrises of unnecessary frozen travel for this moment, but every discomfort had been worth it. Glacia was his. Yet, his victory was incomplete.

Spurring his stallion into motion, Berezan rode slowly through the winding streets, passing hundreds more frightened faces. He gazed about, taking in all he commanded. The houses, constructed from the silver-flecked granite so abundant in these mountains, were as he remembered them. Tiny, no more than four rooms each. The roofs were several spans thick and woven from boughs of the mighty trees that thrived in the snow-filled valleys below the city to the north. Windows, covered with wooden shutters, kept out the blinding light of the sun reflected off the snow and the howling winds usually present.

His party passed an intersecting roadway. Berezan stared at the huge metal vats that burned constantly on the corners.

The closer he came to the Keep, the more familiar his surroundings became. As a young boy, he remembered running through the ironsmith's shop, watching in awe as the fires that burned in the pits turned heavy chunks of black ore into flaming spears of red. He remembered the hissing of steam created when the smith plunged the hot rods into the vat of cold water, the way it burned his eyes, his fingers if he got too close.

He closed his eyes. Vivid pictures came to his mind, images he'd recreated repeatedly for twenty-five cycles. There had been a time when he was a normal boy, able to run and slide along the icy passages with the other children of Glacia. He'd been the cherished heir to all around him, loved by a mother whose face he couldn't remember, a father for whom he now felt only deep hatred.

Bitter memories churned the fire in Berezan's blood. Lars Asvaldr. The name burned deep in Berezan's chest. His father, the one who'd forsaken him. A man who had never searched for him, had forgotten he even existed.

Berezan opened his eyes and, this time, saw Glacia in a different light. He pushed memories of the past far back into a hidden corner of his mind.

Glacia was his. His! On the eve of his thirty-second winter, all that had been taken away had been returned. Anyone who thought to oppose his destiny would perish.

"R'han!"

Berezan turned to face the columns of men who stood at attention behind him. His army. Thousands strong in flanks that lined the icy streets six deep and five hundred spans in length. Men who would carry out his orders without question. They had no choice. Just as the people of Glacia had no choice.

Peasants, all of them. Men who aspired no higher in life than to dredge out a meager existence. He cared little that his army had been unequipped to traverse the leagues of frozen wasteland, that their clothing, suited for warmer climates, had caused more than one death.

Berezan's purpose had been met.

He looked down from his position high atop his stallion to stare into R'han's face. "Disburse this crowd immediately. Send these people to their homes and post guards along the streets to see that they remain there. Anyone caught disobeying my orders will be executed."

Moments later, the streets stood deserted, except for the guards his commander posted along the slippery walkways.

Berezan spurred his mount, listening to the clopping of his beast's hoofbeats echo off the mountainside. The wind reappeared, whipping through the passages, stinging his face. Snowflakes fell from the clouds. Berezan drew his emerald cloak around his body.

"Master?"

Berezan looked ahead to find his commander standing on the street corner, back toward the fire in the vat. Berezan pulled back on the reins.

"Master, your army freezes."

"Do you question my orders?"

R'han shook his head. "No, Master. It's just that so many have already died from the cold, I fear our numbers will be weakened."

Startled by R'han's comment, when in the past he'd offered no voice, Berezan looked around and studied the men posted along the roadway. Each man hugged himself to ward off the cold, and attempted to brush away the snow that fast accumulated on his clothing. "Send a party to search each house. Have them confiscate all warm clothing found and distribute it to my men."

"Thank you, Master." R'han nodded and quickly set about his task.

Berezan spurred his mount and rounded the last bend that would take him home. He never tried to see beyond the blinding snow or look up at the sight he knew would be just as he'd left it so many years ago. The Keep, positioned a hundred spans above the roadway, appeared as a natural formation in the mountainside.

Berezan knew better.

He remembered each stone, carved to fit perfectly together to create the rounded surface of Glacia's Governing House. He could see in his mind each of the balconies that jutted away from the mountain, the deep crevice cut into the stone that formed a tunnel almost fifty spans deep, a tunnel lit by thousands of tiny lumastones. He could envision the ornate wooden doors at the end of that tunnel and what lay beyond.

He closed his eyes as his stallion picked its way carefully over the icy bridge across the deep crevice that separated Glacia's primary mountain from the rest. He allowed his mount free rein, knowing the beast would seek shelter from the cold and snow deep within the tunnel.

His mind conjured up the vision of the first place he intended to visit. His flesh tingled in anticipation of a warm steam bath that would wash away years of sandy residue from his flesh.

* * * *

"Nola! Here!"

Nola turned in a circle, seeking the source of the voice that reached her above the howling wind. She pushed her fur-lined hood closer to her ears, covering all of her face except her eyes.

"Here, Nola!"

Nola squinted to make out a dark figure huddling behind one of the houses that lined the avenue. Trusting her instincts to know it was Elijah, she hurried in his direction, careful to look over her shoulder to avoid the horrible soldiers who were moving from house to house, ordering everyone inside.

As if the people of Glacia needed to be told to stay inside when the wind and snow reached blizzard proportions!

Nola blew out a disgusted sigh. "Elijah?"

"Come here, girl. You'll catch your death." Elijah grasped her around the arm and pulled her through a back doorway. He shoved the panel shut against the wind and cold, then ushered her over to a fire pit burning brightly in the center of the room.

"I'd all but given up hope for you, girl. What took you so long?"

Nola shrugged out of her wrap and handed it to a woman standing near. She nodded thanks then bent to warm her hands before the fire. "It wasn't easy sneaking out of the Keep with all those hideous soldiers rambling around. As it was, I had to use the exit we led Thea and the warrior to when they left the Keep." She raised her warm hands to cup her cheeks.

Elijah tugged impatiently on her arm. "Were you successful?"

"The Keep's empty. The foodstuffs harvested over the past four moonrises were distributed among the households of Glacia. All members of the staff were able to get out before that demon's men got in." Nola turned to look Elijah in the eye. "I hope he finds it lonely in that big stone monster all by his evil self."

"Here, dear. You need something warm inside you."

Nola looked over Elijah's shoulder to find a very pregnant blonde woman holding a cup of something that steamed delightfully. Outwardly Nola smiled, but inside she hoped the woman didn't decide to give birth while they were confined to these tiny quarters.

Elijah stepped to the woman's side. "I'm sorry, Nola. This is my oldest son's wife, Willa. That's my only grandchild, Lemont, and my son, Julian."

A little blond boy Nola guessed to be no more than six winters huddled into the arms of Elijah's son. Nola placed her cup on the table, then walked across the room and dropped to her knees before the child. She reached out, attempting to touch the boy's face, but the boy turned and buried his head beneath his father's arm.

"Lemont is still upset over seeing all of those strange men in the streets of Glacia," Julian said.

"Aren't we all," Nola replied. She bowed her head then rose. "I'm please to meet all of you."

She retrieved her cup and turned back to Elijah. "How about you, Elijah? Were you able to get Thea's message to the people outside of the Keep?"

Elijah nodded. "Julian and my other son Tomas helped me pass the word. I'm just sorry we didn't have time to flee into the mountains and go to Dekar."

"Do you think everyone will cooperate?" Nola brought the steaming cup of herb tea to her lips and drained the contents. She handed the empty cup back to Willa. "Thank you."

"I believe any doubts the people of Glacia had were set aside when Berezan and his army entered the city. I don't think anyone will want any part of him or his evil doings."

"Good. Now, all we have to do is wait for Thea and Gustoff to return and--"

Thump! Thump! Thump!

All eyes in the room turned toward the door.

Julian eased his son into his mother's arms and stood. He walked to the door, threw back the bolt, and opened it. A soldier stood huddled before the door for shelter from the blast of cold air and snow.

"The Master has ordered that you relinquish all warm clothing to his army. You will do so immediately or we will search your home and take what we need."

Indignation swelled within Nola. She hurried around the room, gathered up all the cloaks, then walked to the door.

"Here. Take these. The citizens of Glacia know better than to stand outside in weather like this. Now, leave this house!" She slammed the door in the soldier's face.

"Nola!"

Nola, realizing what she'd done, turned sheepishly and stared into Elijah's eyes. "I'm sorry. I just--"

Willa hurried across the room and placed her arm about Nola's shoulder. "We understand, dear. Come. Make yourself comfortable. We are liable to be here for many moonrises to come."

Nola sighed. I wish Thea and Gustoff were here."

"We all do, Nola," Elijah whispered. "We all do."

* * * *

Berezan closed his eyes and drew a deep breath. He had spent the last two moonrises searching every inch of the Keep for the Sphere of Light. Gustoff had not brought the Sphere with him when he met his death, and Berezan knew there was no place left to shield its powers.

Anticipation stirred within him, but Berezan fought it. He took each step slowly, pausing after five to draw another deep breath. He listened to the sound of the wind that whirled around the outside tower walls and seeped through the cracks in the ancient stones. He inhaled the scent of musk, the aroma of stale smoke and ash.

Chills peppered his flesh, but he shook away the eerie feeling and continued, faster and faster, until he reached the last step. He stood for several seconds in the darkness, watching the faint moonlight through the lone tower window. He closed his senses to everything around him, searching instead for any trace of power, no matter how weak, within the tower.

Cold air, nothing more, rippled along his spine.

Berezan held his hand in the air, fingers spread, and called forth a spark of fire to each fingertip to light his way. He touched a candle he found on the table and watched the flame flicker. Shadows crawled over an old cauldron at the room's center. He walked to the cauldron and looked down into the liquid that lay smooth as glass.

His reflection stared back.

Casting a glance over his shoulder, Berezan found a lumalantern on the shelf and walked toward it. He slid the lid open and a shaft of light touched his face. He stared into the light, looking even deeper, searching for the source of its power.

He opened the lid completely and bright light flooded the tower to reveal a room about thirty spans in diameter and another thirty spans high.

Along the wall on the opposite side from the window, bookshelves climbed to the ceiling. Hundreds of scrolls and ancient texts lined each shelf. Hundreds more had fallen to the floor.

He walked toward the shelves, bent and picked up one of the scrolls. The scroll crumbled into bits and fell to the floor.

Soon several more scrolls and a number of books littered the center of the tower. He'd found nothing to lead him to the Sphere.

Berezan vented his anger by setting the worthless pile of parchment afire.

He then turned slowly in the center of the tower, and concentrated on every crack between the stones, each chink that might give him a clue to the whereabouts of the Sphere. He cursed Elsbar, Gustoff, his father, and all of those who had gone before.

Arcs of fire streaked from his fingertips to fill the room. He raised his hands higher. The red arcs of fire shot toward the ceiling of the tower. A great rumble occurred, and then the ceiling disintegrated, leaving nothing but smoking timber exposed to the cold night sky.

He then turned his wrath to the bookshelves, the volumes lining the shelves, those on the floor.

Seconds later, all were destroyed. The cauldron, the chair, the table and candle were next to feel his fury, but Berezan still wasn't satisfied.

When the contents of the tower were no more smoldering ash, he drew a deep breath and left the tower moments before the stone walls tumbled down the mountainside.

CHAPTER 24

Galen watched Thea sleep.

He bent to kiss her pale forehead nestled against his breastbone. "Gustoff said it's my destiny to stand at your side, not before you as a shield, but beside you as your strength." He shook his head. "I doubt when you wake you'll accept any assistance I might offer."

Galen inhaled, drawing the fragrance that was Thea's alone deeply into his mind. Many times in the sunrises he'd know her, he'd doubted her, believed her to be Berezan's pawn. He'd once spent a great deal of time trying to decide if Thea Asvaldr was truly as innocent as she seemed when she touched him.

Gustoff's words haunted him. He didn't want to believe Thea was all Gustoff claimed her to be, but with each unselfish act of kindness she preformed, evidence of the power within her he witnessed, the old man's words seemed more accurate.

Tenderness, foreign to his warrior's nature, grew. Galen longed to tell Thea of his affection. To explain what she'd believed to be his betrayal had actually been the act of a desperate man attempting to protect the woman he loved.

But, he couldn't tell her. Too much still stood between them.

He stroked her shoulder. Buried his hand in her hair and caressed the back of her neck. He thought about the battle ahead. His people. Glacia's subjects, and Thea.

How many more would die?

* * * *

Thea opened her eyes to find her head pillowed against Galen's chest, her body stretched over the mounds of furs that made up his bed. She stifled a moan as his large, callused hand glided over the exposed area of her arm, her shoulder to rekindle the fire deep inside she'd fought to douse.

She couldn't remain any longer in Borderland. She had to return to Glacia. Galen would not be able to return with her because he had his one people to protect.

She'd miss the feel of his arms around her, the heat of his flesh against her own. His mouth. His hands.

She swallowed hard.

"Thea?"

The sound of his voice rippled over her flesh, causing her heart to sputter. She drew a deep breath, raised her hand to touch his abdomen and pushed away.

Galen picked up her robe from the floor.

She snatched it out of his hand and pulled it over her shoulders. She drew three determined breaths before she rose to her feet.

She glanced over her shoulder to find he remained seated on the fur pallet. He wore the same taut leggings and tall leather boots all of the warriors of Cree wore. The dim glow of the fire glistened off the fine sheen of perspiration on his bare chest.

Something different had been added.

A thick gold chain hugged the cords of his neck and dropped to his breastbone. Suspended from that chain was a bronze-colored object she couldn't identify. Curiosity almost caused her to ask what the object was, but she suppressed the urge. Since he'd not worn it in Glacia, it apparently was some symbol of authority here in Cree. A symbol that brought their different destines into sharp focus.

Galen displayed the powers bestowed upon him by his ancestors proudly on his chest. Hers hidden deep within, but were no less binding, no less restricting to any wishes she might have otherwise. Fate chose a path for her life to follow. She couldn't forsake her duty.

"I must return to Glacia immediately."

"You can't."

She met his intense gaze. "I'll do what I must, Galen." Before he could offer further argument, she hurried to the cave entrance.

"Thea."

She didn't hear Galen rise or walk across the cave. The whisper of his breath over the side of her face caused her to shiver before he stepped away. She bowed her head and fought the familiar longings that, no matter how hard she tried, would not be conquered.

Thea turned to find Galen by the fire, looking down into the flames.

She studied his tall body. The flickers of fire sent patches of light dancing over his muscular chest, defining the tension in his arms, the enlarged veins that protruded from the top of his hands as he clenched his fists.

"I can't allow you to leave Borderland without me, Thea."

His words were soft. Final.

All they had shared finally came to this. "Am I now your prisoner, Galen? Have you brought me to Borderland to hold me against my will?"

Galen's bark of laughter sent another chill along her spine. "How could I possibly hold you if you're determined to leave?"

You could tell me you love me, Galen. Make me believe all that has gone on between us is real. Ask me to stay by your side. Say no matter what happens in the future, we will face it together.

Thea betrayed none of her inner turmoil as she stepped to his side. "Each of us has responsibilities." She reached up to touch the bronze medallion. "Your people need you. Mine need me. Just as your duties as the new Regis of Borderland demand your attention, my destiny is also about to be fulfilled. I must meet Berezan in Glacia. I must do everything I can to see his rein of terror ended. I have no choice."

He turned and looked down to meet her gaze. His features were distorted by firelight and shadow, but his eyes blazed with another unnamed emotion.

Thea swallowed. "I must leave," she said softly. Before he could offer another objection that might chip away at her resolve, Thea dropped her hand to her side, turned, and walked toward the cave opening.

"Go. I can't stop you."

* * * *

Galen closed his eyes to the sight of Thea walking away from him. His tense muscles ached, but he continued to hold firm, knowing if he weakened, if he gave into the tremendous fury burning deep in his gut, he'd be lost. His emotions ran rampant. Churning with the intensity of the storms that raged through Borderland when the monsoons came.

He drew a deep breath and held it. Listened to the pounding of his heart as it echoed against his ribs.

"Thea?"

She stopped walking but didn't turn around. He shook his head and crossed the space that separated them, pausing so close he could smell her soft fragrance. His hand trembled as he laid it upon her shoulder.

"Thea."

"Please, Galen. Don't do this."

He released her shoulder to place his hand beneath her jaw and lift her face. When he saw the tears in her eyes, his anger disappeared. "Thea, look at me."

Thea bit her lip and tried to think of what lay ahead, but she couldn't concentrate, couldn't get past the anticipation twisting through her body. Circling, swirling, racing through every nerve until her flesh tingled.

His hands slipped from her jaw to her neck, drawing her closer as he bent his head. His mouth, less than a breath away, stole her willpower, replaced it with want, need, far deeper than any mystical force that might lie within her. He gazed into her eyes, cast his own arduous spell, held her in a sensuous web she had no desire to escape.

All sense of reality fled when his mouth touched hers and began the motion so familiar, gently shaping her lips to his. His tongue probed for entrance, found no resistance, and challenged hers to the same erotic dance they'd shared many times before.

She slid her hands up the muscled planes of his chest, past the medallion that built the final wall between them. She wound her fingers in his golden hair. When his hand slipped beneath the folds of her woolen robe to caress her aching breast, she leaned against his body for support.

She moaned in protest when his hand slid away. In response, he deepened his kiss, asking, begging for her surrender. His hands slipped lower to the juncture of her thighs.

Thea welcomed his exquisite touch, arching her body so he might ease the ache within her.

She cried out when he pulled his mouth from hers, abandoning her lips to kiss the soft flesh of her neck and lower to the wool-covered tautness of her breast. She clasped both hands, fingers entwined, behind his head and held him to task.

Galen slid his hand beneath the rounded fullness of her buttocks to raise her from the floor, then silently cursed his own hunger when he heard Thea draw a startled gasp and grow still in his arms.

He tightened his embrace, holding her against him, breast to chest, her feet dangling above the floor. He buried his face into the hollow of her neck, inhaled her sweetness, and tried to still the raging force inside him, to conquer the urgency in his loins.

He loosened his embrace. Thea slid slowly down the length of his body, torturing him with the warmth he desperately needed to ease his aches of denial.

"Galen," she whispered, clutching at him for support. She panted for breath, needing a fresh supply of oxygen to restore the self-control Galen fast stripped away. She looked up into his eyes, saw the deep blue, and recognized the passion that burned just within the barriers of his control. She dropped her gaze to his chest. She couldn't look at him, couldn't witness the same desperate need within him that she carried.

Her memories were already too vivid, two raw. She needed to leave Borderland. Leave him. Destiny called her. She had to use all of her powers of concentration to meet the challenges the future would hold.

"We--"

He placed his finger over her lips. Thea tried to slip away, but he refused to release her. The safety of his arms was like a balm to her soul, a comfortable haven in a world of strife and turmoil.

"Spare me a few minutes before you leave, Thea. Walk with me."

She looked up as he released her and stepped back.

"Come." He held out his hand.

Thea watched for several heartbeats, waging a silent war. One part of her demanding she take his hand, hold it to her heart. The other arguing this was her chance to sever the bond between them, to refuse and turn away from the ties that secured her eternally to him.

She placed her hand in his.

Without another word, Galen led her from the cave, down the long corridor of stone that ended in the great cave. Beyond, through another set of winding, hot tunnels deeper and deeper into the mountain.

Thea followed in silence, listening only to their soft footsteps as they trod through yet another tunnel. They passed several people. Galen stopped to speak with each one. She ignored his words to study the look of adoration on each Creean's face, the forthright manner in which they spoke to their Regis, the way Galen absorbed their every word before continuing.

She looked ahead, beyond Galen's tall body, and found they traveled toward a bright light. As they grew nearer the light, Thea realized the source was an opening in the cave a hundred spans ahead.

Beyond the cave opening, Thea shielded her eyes with her free hand until her sight adjusted to the brilliance of the jungle sun.

She stood on a small plateau overlooking a clear pool of water shimmering in the dapples of sunlight that filtered down through the tree--trees unlike any Thea had ever imagined. Mammoth trunks, dark brown in color, reached to touch the heavens before displaying a profusion of leaves bent toward the ground longer than she was tall. Greens in shades ranging from almost black to a softer hue of green rustled softly in the breeze that floated around her.

She followed the trunk of the tree closest to her, down its magnificent length to the base, to find yet another profusion of color. Leaves, hundreds of different shapes and sizes, in as many shades of brown, yellow, and green as there were species, hugged the jungle floor. Through this tangle of greenery, a multitude of tiny flowers grew, displaying a full rainbow of color. The breeze mixed the fragrances, filling her with a scent more enticing than anything she'd ever smelled.

Humid air swirled around her, warmed her flesh, and relaxed her muscles.

"This pool feeds an underground spring that flows through the middle of Naro. The fresh water you saw in the main cave begins here."

Galen's words shattered the spell. Thea looked up to find he'd leaned against the side of the stone walkway, arms crossed over his chest, watching her as if he were judging her impression of his homeland.

"It's beautiful, Galen. I never imagined such a display of nature could exist. Often, I've thought of the magnitude of the snow-covered mountains of Glacia, of the piceas with boughs bending to earth beneath their burden of snow and ice and believed nothing on our world could equal the sight. I see I've been wrong."

Galen pulled away from the wall and walked to the patch of greenery and flowers she'd studied. He pulled up a small bouquet and placed it in her hand. Thea couldn't resist bringing the tiny blossoms to her nose and inhaling several times to capture their fragrance, closing it tightly in her memory.

She looked up at Galen. Watched his face. She saw his blue eyes shimmer in the sunlight.

He was in his element here. The warmth of the sun, the light wind that ruffled his golden hair magnified his personality. His muscular chest seemed a bit larger, swelled, she guessed, with pride in his homeland, his people. His handsome face bore none of the telltale signs of his recent stay at Dekar and the horrors that had gone before.

"Come. I have something else to show you." He held out his hand.

Thea accepted it.

She couldn't imagine where he might be taking her, but they were climbing higher. Each bend in the stone walkway they passed seemed steeper, the trees less tall. She became aware of a roaring sound that grew louder the higher they climbed.

Galen paused and looked back at her. "Are you all right?"

"I'm fine. My curiosity is about to get the best of me."

Galen laughed then tightened his grasp on her hand.

When they rounded another bend, Thea almost cried out in awe. They stood on a rock balcony projecting about ten spans from the stone walkway. The pool was beneath her, and above was a spectacle the likes of which she would never have imagined.

A great wall of falling water flowed over the side of the mountain, pouring down hundreds of spans to splash into the pool. Curtains of vibrant flowers grew on each side of the falling water, clinging to the base she knew to be solid rock. Looking higher, she saw the sky, unobstructed by the tall trees. Aqua, unblemished by a wisp of cloud.

Acutely aware her heart beat too fast, her breath seemed to whistle past her teeth, Thea looked down to the pool. Its color mimicked the sky, yet was so clear, so pure, she could see a bottom as white as the new-fallen snow that covered her homeland. She scanned the shore, the blankets of vivid color that grew to the water's edge, then up again past the towering trees and sheer rock cliffs that cut this beautiful retreat away from the trouble beyond its walls.

Galen was forgotten by her side as she stood mesmerized by the spray that flew when the tumbling water hit the rocks below, sending cascades of water high into the air. Bright sunlight filtered through the sprays, causing prisms of light to rival a rainbow.

* * * *

Galen leaned against the stone wall rimming the balcony and watched Thea. He couldn't force his gaze from her face as she absorbed a world so different from the frozen plains and valleys of her ice-covered home. He thought about how he would like to keep her here, safe within the walls of Naro, to take her as his mate, to bear his children. To grow old with her, to lie eternally at her side when their lives ended.

"It's breathtaking. Thank you for bringing me here."

"There are many such sights in Borderland and beyond, Thea. Our world is as multifaceted as what you see before you. To the south, Solarus offers its own beauty, if you like leagues and leagues of hot, dry sand."

"I've often wondered about the world beyond Glacia. For as long as I can remember, I've dreamed of one world, one people. A place where one could travel freely from one region to another, experience the different cultures, learn new things." She slid slowly to the stone, wrapped her arms around her knees, and pillowed her cheek against her forearm. "Gustoff never discouraged my imagination. He saw it as a part of my training. He persuaded me to test the limits of my imagination beyond the knowledge I could acquire in Glacia.

"There are great scrolls and huge leather-bound books in Gustoff's tower that were passed on from the Ancient

Ones. I spent every available hour studying those treasures. Though I read about such spectacles as I witness here, nothing compares to seeing them with my own eyes."

She closed her eyes. "Do you know that before I touched Mya's child, I'd never held an infant in my arms?

"My mother died giving me birth. I don't remember too much of my early childhood, except Nola's mother was there for me, and Gustoff was always at my side. Teaching me. Guiding me. Sheltering me. I don't recall when I realized I was gifted with powers beyond those of my servants.

"Each day Gustoff would take me to his tower. For hours, he'd teach me of those who had gone before, telling me of their abilities, their beliefs. Each time we'd leave the tower, he cautioned me to hold silent, never tell anyone of the things we discussed. I trusted him completely and never thought to question his words.

"When I reached my second and tenth winter, Gustoff performed the ritual that would transfer the Sphere of Light into my care. Over the years that have passed since, I learned there are those who would destroy me to possess the secret I hold."

Galen cursed Gustoff and her ancestors, those mystical people who'd stolen away Thea's soul and replaced it with a sense of purpose that wouldn't give her peace until her destiny was fulfilled or her life forfeited.

He thought about this own life, how vastly different his childhood had been. He was heir to Borderland, but there had always been laugher, companionship, and love. He'd had a loving mother to dote upon him, a father to guide and teach him right from wrong, to ready him to one day lead his people.

Gustoff's sole purpose in teaching Thea had been to meet and defeat any evil threatening the Sphere of Light. Beyond that, he'd given her no insight to a normal life, to function as a complete person, separate from her Guardianship.

Thoughts of Gustoff rekindled the quilt Galen hid. He knew he had already had time to recuperate and Berezan had probably left Borderland, and, perhaps he had already reached Glacia. By this time, Thea would have realized it, too.

Galen prayed he could convince Thea to wait for the Creean warriors to go with her, for the plans he and Jakar had discussed to be placed into action.

Galen walked to her side and dropped to his haunches. "We must go back, Thea. After you've had nourishment, we have much to discuss."

She looked up at him. Galen saw the fatigue that dulled her eyes and darkened the circles beneath. He wanted to take her into his arms, shelter her from all that would happen over the next few sunrisings, but he knew he couldn't.

He stood and held out his hand. She placed her fingers in his hand, and he helped her to her feet.

CHAPTER 25

Thea looked around the central cave and studied each face, every smile. She touched the head of a small blonde girl sitting beside her. The little girl looked up, casting a grin that exposed two missing front teeth, the back down to the tasty domini par she'd all but devoured.

She bent her head to study the sleeping form of Mya's boy child cuddled against her breast, and felt her face warm when she sensed Galen's eyes upon her. Thea raised her head slowly, meeting his gaze from across the fire that burned between them. A thin smile creased his lips. Her heart skipped a beat, and another deep ache like the one she'd experienced when this same child nuzzled her breast bore through her chest. She turned away from Galen's eyes.

"Renia Thea."

The warrior Thor eased in between her and the little girl. Thea looked into his smiling face. "Thor."

"How are you feeling, Renia? You scared me when you collapsed. I thought Galen was going to--"

"Thor."

Galen's sharp voice cut off whatever Thor was about to say. Thea wondered what that something might be. Instead of asking him to continue, sure later the warrior would feel Galen's temper, she looked deeply into Thor's eyes. "I'm much better, Thor. Thank you for asking."

"Renia?"

"Yes?"

"I wonder if you'd share with us something of your homeland. Few people of Borderland have seen snow. Please tell us of Glacia."

Thea cast a quick glance over the thirty or so people seated in the circle around the fire sharing their meal. Curiosity beamed from their faces. She looked at Galen. He nodded his agreement that the people of Borderland should hear of Glacia.

"Well, Thor, today I witnessed such beauty in your homeland. I hope my descriptions of Glacia don't disappoint you."

Several people murmured at once.

"The Governing House of Glacia sits high in the mountains on a plateau about four leagues above the Tundra. To reach the city you have to travel by equox or cart up a winding road that cuts through the beautiful picea forests. The road itself is steep, and during a blizzard it can be treacherous, but our animals are bred to withstand the climate and terrain."

Thea watched the eyes of the people as they listened to her tale. She saw them struggle for understanding. She knew unless one had felt cold, had snowflakes touch one's cheek, seen the wind whip piles of fluffy white high into the night sky, one could never understand or form a mental picture of Glacia's beauty.

She thought about something Gustoff taught her as a child that she'd not used in a number of winters. She looked down at the babe sleeping against her breast, crossed her ankles beneath her robe, and made a cradle in the opening of her legs for the infant before laying him down.

"I'm going to ask each of you around this circle to join hands." She reached for Thor's hand and felt his callused palm, then his strong fingers close around hers. She touched Mya's hand, squeezed it for reassurance, and then looked across the fire to see Galen smile. Thea returned his smile, nodding for him to join hands with those on each side of him. He complied when Thea nodded. "Now, please close your eyes and trust me. I want you to concentrate on my voice."

Thea looked toward the little blonde girl whose hand was hidden in Thor's much larger one. She noted the girl squeezed her eyes so tightly lines appeared on her forehead. She glanced around the circle, pausing only to lock gazes with Galen before he closed his eyes.

Thea closed her own eyes.

She concentrated hard on Glacia, described each detail as she saw the snow piled in drifts twenty spans high, the piceas, heavy with snow and ice, bowed in the afternoon sun. She mentally traveled up the steep roadway to the city, pausing several times to touch an icicle, concentrating on the cold upon her fingers. The sentry mountains of Glacia came into view, each reaching thousands of spans into the sky with snow-capped peaks sparkling in the sunlight. The houses, the people who walked the streets, even the cauldrons on every street corner filled her mind.

She stood on the frozen bridge, looking up at the Keep, past each balcony to the icicles that hung from the roof hundreds of spans overhead. She then saw shadows fall, the sun pass beyond the peaks.

Night followed, bringing with it a sky full of stars and a full moon to light the snow and turn Glacia into a fairyland.

Several ooohs and ahhs broke her concentration. The images disappeared. She opened her eyes. Her spell had been broken, but she could tell from the fascinated expression on each participant's face that they had seen what she saw, felt what she felt.

"It's beautiful," one woman whispered. Several others agreed.

"I want to go to your home," the little blonde girl announced.

Thea smiled. "I would love to take you to Glacia, little one." She looked around. "All of you would be welcome in my home, just as you have made me welcome in yours."

"Does the snow ever go away?" someone across the circle asked.

Thea had no idea who'd asked the question so she addressed the group. "I have never seen the ground in my twenty-two winters. I have never seen grass, or water outside of the Keep that wasn't frozen into ice."

"How do you grow your food?"

Thea smiled. She glanced at Galen.

"I've seen the gardens of Glacia, my friend," Galen answered. "It's hard to describe to someone who has never witnessed such strange methods of cultivation, and I don't have Thea's gift of sharing what is in my mind." He winked at her, then went on to tell his people about the hydro-gardens beneath the Keep.

Thor squeezed her hand. "You have no hordes of insects to destroy your crops?"

Thea thought about Thor's question. "We have no insects I can recall. I guess they don't survive in our climate," she whispered, realizing she'd never given any thought to the tiny creatures.

"As Galen told you, our crops are well protected within our mountains. Nothing threatens our food supply," she said, not adding that Berezan threatened not only Glacia's food supply, but its very existence.

Thea gazed about at the faces of those around her, noting their expressions had changed dramatically. She felt her eyes burn at the terrible ordeal these people had gone through, but she blinked the wetness away. These were a proud people, a race of warriors and strong females who would eventually rebuild their way of life. Their jungle homes would again be filled with children's laughter. They would survive.

But, if Nola and Elijah failed in their mission, the people of Glacia were as helpless as innocent animals under Berezan's hand.

"Renia Thea." The small voice pulled Thea from her pain-filled thoughts.

Thea smiled at the little blonde girl who'd scrambled across Thor and now knelt beside her. She released Thor's hand and placed her fingers alongside the girl's cheek.

"Take me home with you," the little girl pleaded. "I want to see snow. I'm tired of living in this old cave."

"I must leave Borderland very soon, little one. My people need me as desperately as you and your people need Galen." She looked to Galen then back at the child. "The same mean men that came to your home and caused you to live in this cave threaten Glacia. I must go and use the strange powers I possess to fight this evil and make all right with the world again."

The little girl started to cry.

Thea wiped away her tears. "When I was only a little older than you, my greatest friend helped me to understand why I could do things others could not."

The little girl nodded.

"The ability to heal is but one of my gifts, just like the way I made you see my home."

A bright smile lit the child's face.

"Do you know what destiny is, little one?"

The child looked toward her mother then back at Thea. After a moment she said, "They teach us that each person has a path to follow in life. Is that destiny?"

"Yes. My path was chosen for me just as your life path has been chosen for you. Some of us go through life not knowing where our destiny will lead. Mine has been clearly drawn. Because of this, I must return to Glacia and do whatever I can for the people I know as family."

"I'll miss you," the little girl whispered.

Thea leaned forward to kiss the child's forehead. "I shall miss you, too."

Thea rose and walked away from the gathering.

"Thea, wait."

She turned to find Galen had followed her from the main cave. Thor stood by his side. "Come with us, Thea." Galen held out his hand but Thea was reluctant to take it. She'd stayed too long with Galen's people, learned to love each one as she'd never had the opportunity to love the people of Glacia.

"Please, Thea. This is very important."

She met Galen's gaze and witnessed a strange emotion she couldn't identify. She placed her hand in his. She followed him through another set of tunnels. Thor walked behind them.

Galen entered a cave, smaller than the main cave but larger than the opening she'd slept in earlier. Thea noticed over a hundred warriors seated around a center fire. They each bowed their heads.

"Join us," Galen said, holding out his hand to indicate several empty spaces. She walked across the floor and joined the group by the fire. Galen sat next to her. Thor next to the man she'd learned earlier was Galen's second in command, Jakar.

"We welcome you to our meeting," Jakar said.

"Thank you."

Galen grabbed her hand and held it. "Thea, these men are what's left of the Warrior Council of Cree. I've called this meeting to discuss something that involves you as well as the people of Borderland. I hope you will bear with us for a moment."

Thea nodded.

Jakar addressed the group. "It's the proposal of Galen, and me, that we band our remaining warriors together and accompany Thea back to Glacia."

Thea felt Galen's hand tighten on hers. She concentrated instead on the loud murmuring going on around her. It appeared the warrior's of Borderland did not agree with Galen and Jakar's proposal, and rightly so.

"No." The word fell from her lips before she realized it. All eyes turned toward her. "I can't allow you to do this. Your people have suffered enough by Berezan's hand."

"Our people will continue to suffer Berezan's wrath if we don't destroy him, Thea," Galen said. "What happens if you fail in your mission? Do you think Berezan will be satisfied knowing the Creean people exist and, after his attack, are still not under his control?"

Thea glared at him. "I have no intention of failing."

"Even if you're successful in defeating Berezan, what about his army?"

Thea shook her head. "No, Galen, I can't let you do this. I cannot allow--"

"Thea," Galen said, then turned away to look at the other warriors about the fire. "We have no other choice. We can't fight Berezan. We can't use our weapons against his fire, but his army fights as we do with swords, clubs, and spears. We can destroy the backbone of Berezan's strength."

Thea chewed her lip, trying to find the words that would dissuade Galen's course. "There are so few of your people left, Galen. I can't let you sacrifice more lives for the people of Glacia."

"True, there are few of us left to carry on as our ancestors, but should Berezan decide to bring his wrath down upon us again, we will cease to exist. Our only hope of survival lies in destroying Berezan's evil before it destroys us."

"I agree." Several other voices echoed the same statement.

Thea turned to look into the faces of the warriors of Cree. All but a few were young men. She considered the women and children in the caves, the life they would lead if these men were killed. She shook her head.

"It's not possible."

Galen addressed the warriors seated around the fire. "Do I have a unanimous vote?"

All voiced their approval.

"We march with you or we march alone, Thea."

"Oh, Galen, no," she said as Galen rose to stand before her.

He dropped to one knee and took her hands into his. "I'm only a man, Thea," he insisted quietly. "I have no special powers other than those I have acquired by years of hard training. I can offer only my sword, my life, in your protection, but all I have is yours, all that I am is yours."

A hearty round of cheers erupted in the cave.

Thea could only stare into Galen's eyes, at the emotion she believed she saw there. She couldn't be sure of Creean customs, but from the tone of his words and the response those words created among his peers, she guessed he'd just done something she'd never though he'd do.

She touched his cheek. He took her into his arms.

"I have just declared myself to be yours, Thea. Do I get no words in return?"

She touched his brow, his cheek, the tiny cleft she loved in his chin. "I love you, warrior. I don't know what else to say."

Galen scooped her into his arms and twirled her around the cave. Cheers and laughter echoed off the stone walls.

"You have just said all there is to say, love, except...."

He kissed her cheeks, her eyelids, then her mouth. "Be my mate, Thea. Bear my children. Love me the way I do you until my dying breath leaves my body, and beyond to whatever eternity brings."

"Children? Oh, Galen, I'd love to have your children, to hold a little one like Mya's against my breast, but--"

Galen silenced her with another kiss.

Thea broke away. "Please, you're embarrassing me."

Galen laughed. "The warriors of Borderland honor their females. We have no inhibitions about showing our affection to the one we have chosen."

A chorus of agreement followed Galen's words, then the chant: "Thea! Thea! Thea!"

Thea shook her head. "This isn't right, Galen. We can't celebrate our happiness when so much lies ahead. There may be no tomorrows."

"That's right. There may be no tomorrows, so today we rejoice and draw strategies needed to meet and defeat our mutual enemy." Galen took her hand and led her back to her place before the fire.

Thea had a hard time concentrating on the words that passed around the circle, until Galen's voice rang clear in her mind.

"There's a hidden entrance to Glacia's Keep. I found it while exploring the hydro-gardens. We could slip into the Keep and remain hidden in the numerous corridors that intersect below the main floor until the time is right to strike."

Thea looked at the warriors. Each was clad in the same leggings and fur vests Galen wore. She studied their size, the muscles that crossed their chests and rippled down their arms.

"Galen." She touched his arm, drawing his immediate attention. "How long will it take an army afoot to reach Glacia?"

"Five sunrises."

"Then this is all impossible. I must return to Glacia immediately."

"Berezan can't do more harm than he's already done in a matter of sunrises, Thea. Besides, you need rest before you meet your destiny."

She looked into Galen's eyes and saw his determination. He'd given her little choice. To leave for Glacia now would be placing the warriors of Borderland into danger.

"Look at these men," she said. "Each one is as large as you. We can't possibly find suitable clothing warm enough for them to wear across the Tundra. They would become sick and die in a matter of days."

"We could have the women and children forage through the remains of the villages, bring back all of the furs and hides that are not damaged. With everyone working together, we could find suitable clothing," Thor responded.

Several others agreed.

Thea shook her head. Agreeing to have the warriors of Borderland accompany her to Glacia was like sentencing them to death.

"Please, listen to me," she shouted. "I can't tell you how much I appreciate all you are offering, but you can't do this. You can't place yourselves in danger for me."

Every man present denounced her statement.

Thea swallowed hard. "If you are insistent upon doing this, you should know all." She looked at Galen, saw the expression on his face, and realized he thought she was about to disclose something he should've known long before.

Perhaps he should have.

"Before Galen and I left Glacia, I gave instructions to my most trusted friends to deploy in the event Berezan arrived before I returned. Nola and Elijah will have organized an evacuation of the village into Dekar Facility. If there wasn't enough time for an evacuation, they were told to instruct the people against any resistance to Berezan's will. If they are docile subjects, and no threat to his takeover, I don't believe Berezan will harm them."

"The people of Cree posed no threat to Berezan but he murdered innocent men, women, and children," a warrior across the fire challenged.

"Berezan invaded Borderland because he believed the mountain Naro shielded the Sphere of Light. Your people were massacred because of something I hold inside me, something that was placed there by the man some of you met many days ago, Gustoff."

Jakar and several of the other warriors nodded.

She went on to explain about the Sphere, its origin, her destiny. Each warrior listened in silence to her tale. When she'd finished, many moments passed before anyone spoke.

"Do you believe you will be able to create the arcs of fire like Berezan used to kill Gustoff in the Tundra?"

"I don't know, Thor. I've never used any of my powers to do harm. The Sphere of Light releases its power differently through each Guardian. Gustoff could not tell me what path my strength would take, but did all he could to prepare me for my destiny before he died."

"Do you feel this Sphere inside you?"

Thea looked first to Galen, then to the warrior who asked the question. "No."

"Then how can you be sure it truly exists?" another warrior asked.

"I have to have faith. I must believe that the strange powers I learned about and use are but a fraction of the force that lies within me. I have to trust in my destiny, see it through, no matter what happens to me." She looked into each man's face, pausing on Galen's. She spoke directly to him, needing to hear his answer above all others.

"Can you follow me into a battle knowing when the time comes to meet Berezan, I might fail?"

Galen captured her hand, brought it to his lips, and kissed her fingers. "Many sunrises ago Gustoff told me that my place, my destiny, was by your side, no matter what that future might be.

"I believe in my destiny as strongly as you believe in yours."

CHAPTER 26

Forays into the jungle to bring back necessary supplies became a celebration. People were divided into groups. Women and children large enough to help set out into the jungle at sunrise with three warriors to a group. Those children too young to be away from the caves were brought into the center cave, and women carrying unborn children did their part by taking care of the young.

As the hours passed, the piles of furs and hides grew, as did the stack of discarded weapons left by Berezan's army. Warriors formed hunting parties, and the food gathered also grew. Another group of women prepared the food, saving out enough to feed the people left behind and preserving a vast quantity for the warriors to consume on their trek through the Tundra.

At each meal, Thea and Galen were toasted before the huge fire that lit the jungle through the darkness and light for two sunrises. As each party returned, Galen supervised the refurbishing of the Solarian weapons. Thea directed yet another group of women as they prepared the clothing for use by the warriors of Cree. Using the supplies and clothing Thea and Galen had worn to travel through the Tundra as examples, hides were stretched, measured, and cut into long rectangles, then sewn together with heavy thread to make tents. Each warrior was carefully measured, then thick animal fur was cut to each man's size and sewn into warm clothing that would keep out the cold but not restrict movement.

At the twilight hour, when the exhausted children were placed upon their pallets for the night, Thea walked among them, touching each one's head, placing kisses on their foreheads, and wishing them a good sleep. She then sat with the women around the fire, sewing as they sewed, before she fell into Galen's bed too exhausted to think about what might lie ahead.

An hour before sunrise, she woke to find Galen had joined her on the furs sometime during her sleep. She kissed him tenderly and began another day.

On her fourth rising, Thea looked over her shoulder, expecting to find Galen sprawled out beside her. But, he wasn't there. She sat up slowly to stretch her stiff muscles then rubbed the blisters on her hands. She clasped her hands together and concentrated on healing the abrasions just as she had for the last three risings.

She eased unsteadily from the mounds of fur and groped for the silky gown she'd borrowed from Mya. She took a moment to experience the luxurious softness of the homespun cloth against her bare flesh, then belted the sash about her waist before she walked to the cave entrance.

Galen met her as she stepped into the corridor.

"We're not going to the central cave today," he said.

She glanced at the pouch in his hand.

"I've had food prepared for us. We'll not return until sundown."

Thea didn't question him as he captured her hand and led her down yet another tunnel that wound and twisted through Naro.

She was mildly disappointed when they stepped out of the tunnel. She'd looked forward to visiting the waterfall again and hoped that was where Galen led her. Instead, their path appeared blocked by towering trees and dense shrub. When Galen didn't pause, curiosity got the better of her. He continued to lead, shortening his strides to match hers, down a path she'd not seen before.

Thea took advantage of their trek to study the many different species of plants and flowers that grew in abundance. She listened to the sharp cries of the multicolored birds that perched in the trees, the humming of insects, and tucked each sound into her memory for the mooncycles ahead, for she might never pass this way again.

Galen paused.

Thea was so intent on her surroundings she almost bumped into him.

"Behold before you lies the city of Cree." He swept his hand wide.

Thea stood in an area devoid of vegetation and surrounded by skeletal trees. To her left for about a thousand spans, the remains of tall stone houses captured her attention. Huge gaping holes where windows used to be absorbed the sunlight. The stone, the familiar gray granite she'd seen all of her life, was marred by soot and ash. Not an inch of any wooden structure left unscathed.

Multicolored flowerbeds that lined the avenues between the houses wilted from neglect. The vines and crawlers that crept down from the trees in the jungle nearby were blackened by the heat from the fires that destroyed this glorious city.

Thea looked at the ground to find the terrain swept clean, all evidence of those who had died here cleared away.

"Cree is many times larger than the other villages." Galen pointed to an open area ahead of them. "The farmers from the outlying villages used to bring their wares here to be sold."

Thea studied the area. If she concentrated hard, she could visualize marketplace stalls where piles of burned wood and rubble now stood. Broken pieces of pottery, small portions of woven baskets that escaped the fire, several old unturned carts, and pieces of metal for which she could fathom a use, littered the ground. Neither plant nor weed grew up through the ashes.

Galen touched her hand. "Since we have but two defined seasons, one hot and dry, the other hot and wet, the farmers and craftsmen of Borderland would bring their goods to market on the full moon of each month. The Creeans are people who seize any opportunity for a festival, and marketing day became just such an occasion."

He closed his eyes. "It was such a day when our hunting party left Cree to go into the jungle."

Thea placed her hand on his arm. "Sometimes it's best to put the things you can't change behind you and concentrate on those matters within your control."

He opened his eyes and met her gaze. "There is much you should know before we leave Cree, Thea. Come with me." He placed his arm around her shoulder and led her away from the marketplace.

"This is the Temple of Cree."

Thea looked up at a structure miraculously untouched by the destruction around it. She recalled Gustoff describing this building to her. A moment's grief twisted in her chest as she studied the same three-story dwelling at least fifty spans wide.

She mentally climbed each of the stone steps that led up to an enormous pair of bronze doors embossed with an emblem that matched the medallion on Galen's chest. She stared at two huge beasts that stood sentry, wondering what they were, and more important, if they were modeled after a beast that roamed the jungle where she now stood.

"This temple was built in the time of Shakara. Those beasts, the Tighra, which guard the doors, are said to have been my ancestor's pets. We see them as symbols of Shakara's great power."

"They're terrifying."

"You can rest at ease. No longer do the great beasts of Shakara roam these jungles." He hugged her close and placed a kiss on her forehead.

"Join me."

Thea sat by his side. Galen opened the pouch he'd carried, handed her a small section of bread, a chunk of cheese, and two domini pears. They ate in silence, washed down the food with water from his flask, then soaked up the sun for several moments until he captured her hand.

"There is much you should know about the events that took place before you found me in Dekar."

Thea watched his eyes.

"When you brought me to Glacia and prepared to use me as an imposter for your stepbrother, I could have been more forthright with you and explained even if I did resemble Erik, I could never have portrayed him." He met her gaze.

"Berezan has seen my face, Thea. He would have known me the moment he stepped into the same chamber with me."

"How?"

Galen leaned against the steps and closed his eyes. He told her of returning to Cree, finding his village in ruin, his people murdered. He described the agony that tore him apart when he found his father dead, witnessed his mother's death.

"I allowed rage to consume commonsense. Jakar tried to tell me I shouldn't leave Cree alone, but vengeance drove me. I refused the symbol of the station I suddenly held." He reached down and grasped the medallion. "Even now, I don't feel worthy to wear this badge of leadership," he said quietly.

"Nonsense, Galen. This is your heritage. You've trained all of your life to lead. No one is more worthy."

"In my anger, I didn't place my people above my own needs for revenge, Thea. I left them to fend for themselves and set out to destroy Berezan. At the time, I had no idea what I might face. Then, to me, Berezan was only a man. I didn't know about--"

Thea touched his lips. "There was no way you could have known. Stop berating yourself for something over which you had no control."

"I should have had control," he argued.

"Think back, Galen. Consider the words spoken to you by Gustoff moonrises ago. Gustoff's vision foretold of your part in my destiny. Can you say with certainty that our paths were never meant to cross? That what we've found was never meant to be?"

"I don't know, Thea. I just don't know."

She grasped his hand. "Tell me about your meeting with Berezan."

Galen squeezed her fingers. "I don't remember everything that happened before I was taken captive, but running through the jungle, hearing men shouting and equox hooves thundering closer and closer still creep into my dreams. The thing I remember most vividly is being held in Berezan's camp, secured by metal chains like an animal, subjected to painful torture.

"I don't know how long I was held captive. Pain obliterated all sense of reality. After a time, it became harder to breathe, hard to remain conscious. Lucid time escaped me, yet with each clear thought, I plotted a way to escape and to extract my own brand of revenge."

"There were no marks on your body when I found you in Dekar," Thea whispered.

"Berezan has ways of inflicting pain that leave no scars. Just as you touched me to heal my wrists, Berezan touched me to set every nerve in my body on fire."

"No."

"My escape is something that fades in and out of memory. I know I overpowered my guard. I remember running and running, going nowhere. I recall the cold, the sting of the wind against my flesh. I also have vivid memories of feeling my skin catch fire, of heat so intense it seemed to melt the flesh from my bones, and the relief I felt when I stumbled and fell into something that blanketed my hot body in cold.

"My last coherent thought was I would die and there wasn't anything I could do to prevent it."

Thea touched his cheek, his lips, and the cleft in his chin. "But, you didn't," she whispered.

Galen stroked her arms, the contours of her back. When she arched into his embrace, he reached forward to run his fingers through her fiery hair, then placed his fingers beneath her chin and raised her face higher for a kiss.

Desire rode hard on his body. Need burned deep into his very being, but thoughts of what lay ahead, of what the beautiful woman in his arms would face over the next few sunrises, ate away at him like a festering sore. He'd faced Berezan's wrath, knew the pain he could inflict. Thoughts of Berezan administering such agony upon Thea twisted like snakes in his mind, drawing him away from the beauty around him.

He raised his hands and pushed Thea gently away. The soft moan that slipped from her lips tore open a piece of his heart. "We must leave this place, Thea. Darkness fast approaches. On the sunrise our journey will begin."

Thea swallowed hard to relieve the lump that clogged her throat. The day she'd trained for all her life fast approached, but she was reluctant to leave the safety of Galen's arms. She clung to him, needing his strength, for hers failed fast.

"Galen," she whispered as she snuggled closer.

"We can't stay here. We're a great distance from Naro."

Thea's heart turned a slow somersault in her chest. The many times she'd pledged never to lie with Galen again, not to experience the deep, binding emotions his lovemaking evoked, melted away like ice upon fire. "Take me to the waterfall again. Give me one more chance to experience the magic of that place before I leave Borderland. Allow me to witness the unspoiled beauty of Cree before I face my destiny." She kissed him, wanting him to understand the need she couldn't express in words.

* * * *

The sun slipped below the tree line, casting long shadows in the dense jungle and cooling the air. Galen walked a path taken many times in his life. By the time he reached his destination with Thea in his arms, twilight had come, bringing with it a strange gray glow that radiated from the frothing pool of water at the fall's base. Vapor caused by the rapidly cooling air and the warmth of the water rose like a specter from the surface, lending an ethereal quality to the beauty of the pool.

He placed Thea upon the bank at a spot where the flowers ended and a mossy green carpet grew down to the waterline. He welcomed one deeper kiss before he pulled from her arms and stood to look down at a vision more beautiful than their surroundings.

Flowers of pale pink and lavender tangled in long tendrils of her auburn hair that spread over the moss like a silken blanket. The blue gown she'd worn for three sunrises when her own woolen clothing became too warm to bear in the jungle heat molded sensually to every soft curve of her body.

Her face, pale and pure as the vapor around them, highlighted by liquid brown eyes and feathery lashes that dusted the flushness across her cheeks. Her lips, still puffy from the kisses they'd shared, were moist, enticing. His heart skipped a beat when she whisked the tip of her tongue over the fullness of her bottom lip.

Galen yanked at the laces on his leggings. He pushed the leather down over his thighs, then discarded them along with his boots. He dropped to his knees beside her.

Thea watched each muscle in Galen's body stretch and relax. His hair, silver in the mist, swayed as he bent over her. She listened to her heartbeat, accelerating until each thump overshadowed the steady roar of the nearby waterfall. A quivering began in her belly, radiating outward to her entire body. She twisted her fingers into the soft moss beneath her instead of following her heart's command to reach out, to hurry the ecstasy too long denied.

When she thought she'd scream from anticipation, she met his gaze, witnessed the dark passion in his eyes, and understood that he too fought to prolong their union, to draw out the few moments of privacy they would have for many tomorrows and beyond.

She reached out, entwined her fingers in his, and held his hand. She watched his eyes. Felt his gaze slide slowly over her like the touch of a feather. She dropped her hand to the moss when he slipped his fingers from hers and reached to untie the silky cord that belted her waist.

The bronzed expanse of his chest filled her gaze, drawing her fingers like magnets to the harden planes. She raised her arms, splayed her palms against his hot flesh, then grasped the chain of his medallion.

"Please, remove this," she whispered. "I want nothing between us to dredge up memories of what lies ahead."

He looked down at his medallion in her hand then met her gaze. He nodded, removed the chain and dropped it atop his leggings.

"Please remove this," he countered, tugging on the hemline of her gown.

Thea smiled. She rose slowly from the moss to stand before her warrior. Her fingers deliberate and slow as she loosened the laces that held the neckline of the blue gown closed. When enough of an opening appeared to slip the gown over her head, she bent, grabbed the hem, and lifted the silky material gradually, exposing her flesh inch by inch to his view.

Galen swallowed hard to dislodge the knot that threatened to choke him. The ache in his groin screamed for release, but he held fast, using every ounce of willpower to stay there on his knees, watching as Thea enticed him with her disrobing. His hands twitched with the effort it took not to reach across the scant span separating them, grab the cloth, and tear it into scraps.

The light wind that rippled the leaves overhead joined forces with Thea to increase his torment by lifting the thin garment gently and flapping it around her, silhouetting her lush curves in the moon-drenched mist. His heart slammed against the walls of his chest when her thighs, then the auburn curls that shielded her woman's heat, were exposed. He swallowed again as the garment slipped higher, until the edge caught against the fullness of her breasts.

He wanted to trace that path. Explore every inch of her flesh. He almost lost control when Thea discarded the silky gown to flutter to the ground like a fallen leaf.

He dropped to his knees before her and looked up into her eyes. Nearer still, until the heat radiating from her flesh drew him closer, teased him with promises of things to come.

She kept her hands clenched at her sides, and Galen fought to keep his in the same position. He wanted to touch her, but didn't dare to break the magic that surrounded them, didn't want to destroy the calm that fused their souls as they remained less than a breath apart locked in each other's gaze.

The splashing of the water, the roar of the falls, the night creatures that came awake in symphony, were overpowered by the thundering of his heart. Swirls of mist thickened as the air grew cooler, closed in around them as the moonlight filtered through the mist to illuminate the pool.

Thea had no idea who moved first. She was aware only of the moment she tumbled to the moss, buffeted by Galen's strong arms. She moaned in satisfaction as he took her mouth, opened her lips to his tongue, and touched her soul. She clung to him, digging her nails into the hard, sculptured contours of his shoulders, arching her body when his callused hand closed over her breast, spreading her thighs wide to accommodate him as he bore deep inside her.

He slipped his hands beneath her hips and raised her higher. Thea felt the tiny muscles within her quiver. Blood pumped furiously through her veins, and breath, when she thought to draw it, burned her throat.

She thrashed her head back and forth against the moss, tangling bits of greenery into her hair. Lightheadedness made the world around her move in slow motion. An eternity passed before her hand reached his hair and her fingers could gain a firm grip and pull his head down so she could kiss his lips.

Another decade passed before his tongue entwined with hers, mimicking the carnal dance of his lower thrusts. Charging. Retreating. Making her crazy. Driving her wild. She moaned and he responded by deepening his kiss, his conquest of her body. She accepted his challenge, giving as well as she received, holding him to her until the last vestiges of her sanity slipped away, making her a prisoner of their passion.

Galen groaned and rolled to his back, taking Thea with him. He arched his hips, filling her deeper, finding his own release as she reached ecstasy for the second time. He held her tight, fought to regain his wits, his breath. Thea lay still upon him, the length of her hair falling to cover his neck, his shoulders, and the spread of his hands over her buttocks. He kept her from moving too soon, not wanting to give up the pleasure of holding her, of feeling himself still buried deep inside her tender sheath.

Moments later, he arched his hips to judge her reaction and received a soft moan in response. He kissed the top of her head, slid his hands up the small of her back, and buried his fingers into her hair. She turned her head into the side of his neck, and Galen felt a shiver run down the length of his body when her moist tongue touched his flesh.

He shifted his arms as he raised himself from the mossy ground, supported Thea's buttocks, cradled her close, and wrapped his arms about her waist. He stepped into the moonlit pool.

Thrice more, they reached one shattering wave of rapture after the other, until they fell exhausted to the mossy bank and slept the darkness away, entwined in each other's arms.

CHAPTER 27

"Thea."

Thea kept her eyes closed, resisting the intrusion of a new day, a day that would drastically change her life and that of those she'd come to love and admire.

"Thea?"

She sighed. This rising they were to leave the safety of Borderland and travel across the Tundra toward an uncertain future. No matter how much she might wish otherwise, her destiny called.

She opened her eyes to find herself lying on the thick furs in Galen's cave, the mystical darkness they'd shared no more than a cherished memory. Galen had obviously been awake for a while. He was fully clothed, his possessions packed and stored by the cave entrance, waiting to be carried to his equox.

Thea offered a silent prayer that their journey would be safe, their battle successful, then rose from the fur. She folded the gown she'd borrowed from Mya's, placed it upon the bedding, then donned her own woolen robe and tied it about her waist. She gathered her warm boots and the wool and fur cloak she'd worn from Glacia and stepped to Galen's side.

"Thea--"

"No, Galen. There are no words to say. What must be done, must be done." She took one more glance around the cave, remembered all she'd learned about Borderland and the people who'd become so dear, then left the cave.

Thea walked slowly among the people gathered in the center cave. She looked into their eyes, read their sorrow, and felt it mirrored in her own heart. She touched the tawny hair of a small boy, smiled down at several young girls who grasped her robe, returned Mya's hug, and kissed Deja's sleeping face.

The silence in the cave was unsettling. No one spoke. The children were unnaturally still. A tremendous blast of thunder echoed through the caves, scaring the two northern equox saddled near the cave entrance. Several warriors hurried to calm the beasts, and the chilling calm was shattered.

Galen placed his hand upon her shoulder. He pulled her against his chest.

She looked up at him. "I'm afraid," she whispered.

"We all are."

She forced a smile. "I love you, Galen."

"And, I love you, Thea of Glacia." He bent to kiss her lips as a great cheer erupted in the cave.

Thea buried her head against his chest to hide her embarrassment, then drew a deep breath and turned to face the people of Borderland. "I shall miss every one of you," she said. Then, before tears began to fall, she walked to her equox and accepted Thor's assistance into her saddle.

She closed her eyes, concentrated on the days ahead, and drew strength from all Gustoff had taught her. She didn't hear Galen's parting words to his people, didn't realize he'd mounted and joined her at the mouth of the cave until he touched her hand.

"Destiny awaits us. Come." He spurred his equox and left the cave.

She followed.

* * * *

Glacia

The impatient slap of his riding crop and the tap of his boot heels echoed off the stone walls as Berezan paced the meeting chamber. He strode through one of the archways that led to the balcony, paused at the rail to look down over all he commanded.

The slippery streets were empty. Shadows from the mountains cast the tiny houses with smoke belching from stone chimneys into darkness. League after league of snow and ice crept up steep mountains with jagged, snow-capped peaks that reached the clouds and beyond. Hundreds of docile citizens huddled inside their tiny shacks, afraid to come outside, afraid to face him.

But his victory felt hollow.

He'd searched every inch of the Keep from the steam baths to Gustoff's tower and hadn't found the Sphere of Light.

Berezan shook his fist to the sky and damned Gustoff for the hundredth time since arriving in Glacia. He cursed Elsbar for never explaining all he would encounter in Glacia.

He closed his eyes and remembered the old man who'd been more of a father to him than his own sire. Elsbar had been correct. Gustoff was a worthy adversary. Even in death, he protected the hiding place of the Sphere of Light.

Yet, it had to be in Governing House.

Or, close by....

Berezan turned abruptly and entered the meeting chamber. He stomped toward the table. He hurled his riding crop to the table's center, then leaned forward to wrap his fingers around the edge of the carved wood. He tensed the muscles in his arms and hands, raised his head, and stared into the lumastone chandelier.

Incantations--strange, foreign--once again spilled from his lips.

His heart raced. His lungs burned. He gripped the edge of the table hard to stabilize his body as he entered a seeking trance and willed his essence to the imaginary form of a hawk.

He spread his imagined wings and flew high above the Keep.

Cold air rushed past his face, stung his eyes. He looked down to the frozen ground, watched a black shadow--wings spread wide--sweep over the snow. Three strokes of his powerful wings took him higher, above the frosted peaks, beyond the wispy clouds, to an altitude where the air was thin, the sunlight blinding.

He mentally ascended higher. Higher still.

The village of Glacia, the Keep, and the mountains filled the panorama beneath him.

Honing his senses, he concentrated on any power greater than his own and began to circle, each pass taking him lower, closer to his domain. He flapped his wings to ease his descent, extended sharp talons to grasp the crumbled edge that remained of Gustoff's tower, settled his wings close to his body, then searched all directions.

Nothing.

His heart rate soared. Blood pumped frantically through his veins. A predator's vision caught the figures of a woman and child hurrying across the roadway.

Black rage consumed him. Wings extended, he caught the wind that whipped around the tower, lifted from his perch. He collapsed his wings, talons extended, and dove.

"Master?"

Berezan jerked his head toward the sound of his commander's voice. R'han ushered three old men toward the enormous table that took up almost the entire meeting room. Berezan clenched his fists harder to his sides to subdue the impulse to lash out at the three men in anger.

"This is Elder Faudrey, Master." R'han pointed to the bent old man garbed in a white robe belted with gold, supported at each elbow by two other men in gray. "These are the Messahs Thaddius and Jermaine." R'han indicated the men cloaked in gray at the Elders left and right, nodded, then stepped away to stand at attention before the chamber door.

Berezan strode across the chamber floor and paused before the men, looking down on them from his imposing height. He swallowed hard, vowing to control his fury until he had the answers he sought. He blew out a disgusted sigh. "You were summoned to arrive at Governing House three moonrises ago."

"We were delayed by the Elder's health, Master," the man introduced as Jermaine explained. "Elder Faudrey has been suffering from a weakening that has severely limited his mobility."

Berezan studied the old man under discussion. His face, pale as the robe the Elder wore and lined with wrinkles that resembled the parched deserts of Solarus after a season with no moisture, lifted slowly. Sunlight filtering in through the three draped archways defined each whisker in his sparse silver beard. Tiny bloodshot eyes of a color Berezan could not determine peeked through lids barely open and, his mouth, no more than a slash beneath an overlong mustache, was tightly closed against pain.

"Why did you bring this old man to me?"

Jermaine bowed his head, exposing his bald pate. "We held a conference in the Temple of the Peaks, Master. The Elders searched their memories for any recollection of the item for which you seek. None have any knowledge to offer you. Elder Faudrey has seen one hundred and forty-three winters. He alone remembers stories told by his ancestors of the Sphere of Light."

Berezan stepped forward and grabbed the old man by his robe. "Tell me what you know, old man. Your time is close, but I can make it that much closer if you deny me."

The old man did not blink at Berezan's threat. He raised his withered hand and grasped Berezan's, digging his long, bent nails deeply into the exposed flesh. "I see much in your eyes, Berezan," he said with a raspy voice. "I see great hatred, and an evil so dark it consumes you. Even with all the powers you claim to have, you have no weapon to use against me. You cannot take from me what I refuse to give. If you insist on killing me, you will never know what secrets I carry to the everafter.

"I have heard the stories of your childhood you have spread since your arrival in Glacia, Berezan. Anyone who might doubt you are anyone other than who you claim needs only to look into your eyes and see your father, Lars Asvaldr. I understand how you could believe you have the right to claim your place as heir."

The old man shook his head. "But, I look into your eyes, your soul, and see the evil Gustoff must have sensed when you were but a small boy."

"Old man--"

The Elder raised his hand. "I understand you have destroyed Gustoff." He pointed a twisted finger at Berezan. "By committing that crime, you have forfeited any right you might have had to govern."

Berezan raised his hands. Jermaine and Thaddius stepped forward to shield the Elder. Fire flew from Berezan's fingertips, striking the Messahs, reducing them to ashes.

The Elder looked down at the remains of his companions, then back at Berezan.

Tears streaked down the old man's face. "I pray Gustoff will be forgiven in the everafter for what he did to you as a child, but I am sorry he did not destroy you when he had the opportunity."

The Elder collapsed to the chamber floor, drawing his last breath and taking any secrets he might have disclosed with him into his next life.

CHAPTER 28

Thea huddled deeper into the mounds of fur. She drew her knees to her chest and crossed her feet. She raised her hands to press the thick hood that covered her head closer to her ears to block out the sound of the wind howling beyond her tent and blowing through the seams the women had stitched, causing the tiny fire at the tent's center to sputter.

She wished for Borderland's heat to still the trembling of her body. Sighing, she recalled she'd been warmer in Borderland than she'd ever been in her life, and free from the restrictive layers of clothing that did little to hold out the cold of the Tundra.

She silently cursed the chattering of her teeth, not welcoming as she had on her first journey through the Tundra the sound that echoed in the wind. She needed sleep. Blessed oblivion that would chase away the cold, the memories, the thoughts of what lay ahead. Sleep would restore her powers for her confrontation with Berezan.

Day blended into night. Had it only been ten sunrises ago when they left Borderland? She remembered their departure from Cree, the gallant way the warriors of Borderland marched through the jungles, the crystal-clear springs that flowed up from cracks in the earth along the thaw line. The way the air grew cooler, the vegetation more sparse the farther north they traveled.

Galen spent more and more time with his men, leaving her alone in their tent. At first, she'd welcomed the privacy, using the time to remember the lessons Gustoff taught her. All he'd told her of Berezan, and what she'd seen take place in the valley of ice.

Now, the hours of loneliness bred doubts, and doubts bred fear.

Be strong in your convictions, Thea Asvaldr, Last of the Ancient Ones. Hold true to your feelings. See your destiny through.

Gustoff's words haunted her. Thea missed the old man deeply, wished he'd confided his plans to her before he left Glacia and met Berezan alone in the valley. She squeezed her lashes against the tears that threatened to fall, fearing the moisture would freeze upon her face.

Moments passed. The wind continued to howl. The fire sputtered.

Thea tossed restlessly, attempting to find a comfortable position to sleep. After several minutes and no success, she struggled into a sitting position and shook her head.

It was no use. Until Galen decided to return to their tent, she'd never be able to relax enough to sleep. Or be warm enough.

Over the past three moonrises they'd shared each other's heat, cuddled close during the long night hours, but little more. Thea missed the touch of his hand upon her flesh, the feel of his big body pressed intimately against hers. The taste of him.

She groaned. She thought of Elijah and Nola, the plans they'd made before she and Galen left Glacia. She prayed her friends had been successful in their efforts to evacuate as many of the people as possible to Dekar before Berezan's arrival.

Thea visualized the battle she'd witnessed between Berezan and Gustoff. She wiggled her hands free from the long sleeves of her cloak, held them over the tiny fire for warmth, then raised her hands above the fire to stare at the tips of her fingers.

She whispered incantations Gustoff had made her recite repeatedly as a child. Warmth flowed from her shoulders, down her arms, her hands, to the ends of her nails. Tiny sparks of blue flame danced on the tips of her extended fingers. She wiggled her fingers. The flames swayed back and forth, disappeared when she closed her hands.

She opened her hands, recalling the spell that came quickly to her now. The flames ignited again. Stiffening her fingers, and curling them like talons, she concentrated harder. The height of the flames neither increased nor diminished by her efforts.

"It's no use," she whispered in frustration. "I can light a fire, a candle, warm hands. However, what good will this do against Berezan? If I only knew what form the power of the Sphere would take with me, maybe...."

The tent flap opened. A cold gust of wind blew across her face.

Galen huddled in the doorway, snow and ice caked in his hair, across the bridge of his nose, in the fur that hugged his neck.

Thea looked away, unable to face him, unable to explain her failure.

"Thea?"

She shook her head, listened while he crawled into the tent, secured the flap then shook away the snow when he removed his outer cloak.

"Thea," he whispered.

She bowed her head. "I can't create anything more than a flicker of light. I've tried, but I don't--"

His cold fingers touched her lips. "Don't do this to yourself. Perhaps, it was never meant to be that you meet Berezan with his own magic." He grasped her hands, kissed each trembling digit. "You told me Gustoff explained there was no way to know how the Sphere would react in each different Guardian."

He smiled. "You punish yourself needlessly."

"I know, but--"

He hushed her with a kiss. "Gustoff was adamant in his believe you would succeed. He never doubted you. You shouldn't doubt yourself." He pulled her close to his chest.

"I believe there is a power within me that will destroy Berezan's evil. Gustoff would never have left me to do this task alone if there was any chance I might fail." She raised her hands, spread her palms against his cheeks, and called forth her inner fire to warm his flesh.

"I have faith, but I'm still terrified," she whispered against his neck.

Galen kissed the top of her bent head. He pulled her with him as he lay down on the thick fur that made up the tent floor. He covered them both with another fur and slid her into the curve of his body to shield her from the cold.

He lay awake long after her trembling subsided and her breathing became slow, regular.

He didn't dare think of what the future might bring, nor plan or dream beyond their journey to Glacia. Instead, he thought over the strategies he and the other warriors discussed earlier. He reconstructed the Keep in his mind's eye, saw each corridor, doorway, and the alcove his army might use for a hiding place while they awaited the opportunity to strike Berezan's forces.

He refused to consider Thea's part in the upcoming confrontation. Hearing the frustration in her voice was enough to send his heart into palpitations. His anxiety turned quickly into anger. He cursed fate, Gustoff, and himself for placing Thea in danger, for taking such a delicate creature and demanding she destroy or be destroyed.

Galen held Thea tighter, cuddled her closer. He smelled her hair, remembered the first time he'd inhaled the mysterious fragrance that enticed him more and more as each day passed. He stroked her arm, her side, and finally cupped the fullness of her breast. Swallowing hard, he buried his lips in the wild tangles of auburn at the crown of her head. "I love you, Thea. I will do all within my power to protect you from harm," he whispered.

* * * *

Thea wrapped her cloak tightly around her and climbed to the top of the small ice-covered hill. She stood for several moments, feeling the cold breeze swirl up under her heavy woolen skirt and circle her legs. She looked down upon their camp, wondering at the peace that settled over the Tundra as the warriors took to their beds. Turning, she studied the higher peaks of Glacia in the moonlight, the snowcaps that glistened pearly white, the black night sky, and the countless stars in the heavens.

Coming home touched her deeply. Warmth grew within her, reaching outward to heat the tips of her toes, her fingers. She thought about the people of Glacia, those she'd never come to know. Were they safe? Had Berezan's arrival in Glacia changed their simple lifestyles?

Her thoughts turned to the women and children left behind in the caves of Naro. She remembered each trusting face, every smile. Her heart beat a little faster. Another glance toward the camp below caused her heart to pound against the walls of her chest.

Galen and the warriors of Borderland were trained and ready to give their lives to ensure the safety of their families.

The few gentlemen she knew in Glacia, so different from the proud men who slept below, came to mind. How many had died if they refused her command and engaged in efforts to save their own from Berezan's wrath?

"Thea?"

She hadn't heard Galen approach. His arm draped around her shoulder, drawing her nearer, offering strength and warmth. She leaned against him, accepting his offer, and listened to the thundering of his heart.

She closed her eyes and remembered his pledge given on the eve that seemed so long ago. His sword, his heart, his life.

Could she offer him any less?

"We should reach the Keep by moonrise tomorrow," he whispered.

Thea swallowed hard. They had one plan. One opportunity to reach Berezan and put an end to his tyranny.

"Come." Galen steadied her steps down the hillside, led her to their tent, then cradled her close for long hours before Thea finally closed her eyes.

* * * *

"It has to be here." Galen ran his fingers over the rough stone, feeling for the doorway he knew had to be located in this area. He stepped back, studied the wall of granite that filled the ravine on the southernmost side of the Keep.

Glacia's Governing House was built inside the mountain. The abandoned tunnel he'd found was but one of the numerous caverns and corridors that twisted away from the center of the Keep.

He looked up. The stone climbed upward for fifty spans before disappearing again into the side of the mountain. He glanced over his shoulder toward his warriors huddled in the shadows created by the full moon.

"The moon will be directly overhead soon, Galen. Our cover of shadow will be lost," Thea whispered. "Perhaps, we should use the exit Elijah led us to when we left the Keep."

Galen looked up into the sky then around at his warriors standing near. "There's no time to circle the mountain and enter through another passageway."

Thea stepped forward and touched the cold stone. A flicker of recognition flared inside her. She ran her palms over the rough surface, pausing a moment when the strange feeling grew sharper. Moving on when it faded. "Something is here, Galen," she whispered. She traced the stone she'd just passed.

"Gustoff!"

Galen touched her shoulder. "What is it?"

"Gustoff's been near, Galen. He's touched this stone. I can feel his essence, though it's very weak." She trailed her finger down to the snow-covered ground, then up again, outlining a perfect doorway in the stone. "This is an illusion, Galen. What appears to be solid rock is not." She stepped back, raised her hands into the air, and uttered several strange words.

After a moment, she shook her head. "I can't undo whatever he did."

"It's an illusion?"

Thea reached up, touched Galen's temples. "Concentrate. Look at the wall. See only what you wish to see, not what your mind tells you is there."

"The doorway."

"Reach out. Touch it. Feel the seams with your fingers."

Galen did. He turned to Jakar. "Give me a pike." He placed the hard edge into the seam he'd visualized, applied all of his strength.

Jakar stepped forward, adding his strength to Galen's. Within moments, a gaping rectangular hole stood in the surface of solid granite.

The warriors of Borderland wasted no time on awe. They gathered their packs, hurried into the dark, cold corridor, took seats along the stone wall, and awaited further instructions.

Thea walked among the warriors, uncapping the ancient lumalanterns that lined the walls. Bright light filled the corridor, illuminating each face, each pair of eyes.

She listened as Galen again explained his strategies, studied the acceptance in each man's expression. She looked to the far end of the corridor, at the old wooden door shielding them from the lower level of the Keep. She wondered what went on beyond that door.

Three deep breaths calmed her heart rate, slowed the blood flow through her veins. She exhaled slowly, counted to ten. Images of the steam bath, the bedchambers, the hydro-gardens, and Gustoff's tower flooded her mind.

Chills crawled over her flesh. Every cell tingled.

Concentrating on the interior of the Keep, she opened her senses and found her essence standing at the head of the circular stairway, the chandelier of lumalights dangling thirty spans below her. She focused on each closed door, searched beyond to find empty chambers. One after another, she searched the corridors and passageways of Glacia's Keep, finding no trace of Berezan or his army.

Thea then visualized Gustoff's tower. She almost lost control when she discovered the destruction that had taken place. The enormous bookshelves, which held Gustoff's cherished scrolls and ancient books, were destroyed. Bits and pieces of wood were scattered about the interior of the stone chamber.

She looked up. Moonlight poured in through what had once been a wooden roof. Great piles of ashes littered the stone floor. Only scraps of the primitive leather bindings remained of thousands of years of recorded history.

Thea felt herself weakening. The tower room began to fade. Cold crept along her limbs. She inhaled deeply, drawing more strength from the energy within her, wanting to hold on for a while longer.

"Thea!"

Thea jumped. Galen's hands were on her shoulders, shaking her. She blinked several times to clear the fuzziness in her head.

"Thea?"

She stared into his face, gasped a deep breath, and held it to slow the thumping of her heart. "Berezan's not in the Keep," she said.

Galen's face was pale, his movements frantic. "Thea, what's wrong? Are you ill?"

She forced a weak smile. "I'm fine. Please." Thea shrugged her shoulder beneath his hand. "You're bruising me."

Galen dropped his hand to his side. "You're so pale, so cold."

Thea closed her eyes and remembered the destruction she'd seen. The emptiness she'd felt. She prayed the Keep was vacant because Elijah and Nola had been successful. "I've searched the Keep, Galen. Berezan is nowhere to be found."

Thor took a seat at Galen's side. "If Berezan is not here, what do we do now?"

Galen placed his hand upon Thea's back, leaned his head against the stone wall, and closed his eyes. "We wait."

CHAPTER 29

Thea sat straight up out of a dead sleep. Her heart raced, her pulse pounded, and perspiration dampened her forehead. She drew several slow breaths to calm herself. She then looked down the darkened corridor, over the warriors asleep along the wall, and studied each one carefully to attempt to identify what had awakened her so abruptly.

Galen shifted at her side. She glanced at him. His big body was bent in an unnatural position, but he appeared to be in deep slumber.

She closed her eyes, searched within for an answer to her question. When it came, the answer sent chills along her spine and caused her entire body to tremble.

Berezan.

Thea could sense him, feel his evil crawl over her flesh like static.

* * * *

Thea stood in the enormous meeting room her father used to conduct Glacia's business. She looked around, noting the smoke-darkened stone surrounding the three open archways and the ashes on the floor. She gazed up at the lumalights suspended overhead, remembering Gustoff in this same room, the Messahs, the hundreds of times her father had sat at the head chair.

Something moved in the shadows at the other side of the chamber. Thea held her breath, knowing the time had come to fulfill her destiny. She braced herself, clenching her hands so tightly her nails dug into her palms.

A man stepped from the shadows and paused about thirty spans away. The lumalight reflected off a long emerald cloak that swayed around his booted feet, but stopped short of revealing the man's face. He took another step.

Light flooded his features.

Thea gasped. Her father's essence filled the chamber, reached out, drew her closer. She took a hesitant step.

The man took another.

She looked into his eyes, into pools of brown that mirrored her own. The light reflected off streaks of red in his brown hair. Thea glanced down at a tendril of her own hair resting against her breast, at the color reflected by the light, then up again to study his face, wanting to find her father's smile, the mustache of auburn she'd touched as a child.

She found nothing of her father's kindness.

The man brought his hand to his head and rubbed it through his hair, apparently analyzing her as she studied him. She noted his fingers were not wrinkled with age, but were long, strong, and straight.

Another chill raced up her spine, freezing her foot in place as she prepared to take another step closer.

"Who are you?" she whispered.

A familiar, evil laugh filled the chamber.

"Ah, a little sister."

Thea gasped. It couldn't be. It must be an illusion. This could not be the same man who'd faced Gustoff in the valley of the Tundra. "No. You can't be--"

"Your brother?" Berezan crossed his arms over his chest, spread his booted feet wide. "Why not? Do you not believe it possible to have a brother you knew nothing about? I certainly had no idea you existed."

Thea shook her head, denying what her eyes told her was true. It couldn't be. Her father would not have designated Erik as his heir.

"It's not possible. Gustoff would have told me about you."

Berezan's evil laugh again filled the chamber. He took a step closer, out of the shadows so Thea could get a good look at his face, his body. "Gustoff," he growled. "That wonderful old man who stole a child of six from his bed and sent him to the deserts of Solarus to meet his death."

Thea shook her head adamantly, not knowing how else to respond to the ridiculous accusations this man, her brother, cast at the mentor she'd known and loved her entire life.

She watched him tap his fingers against his biceps, noting his facial expressions were those she remembered from her father. The hair. Those eyes. Tiny seeds of doubt sprang to life in her mind.

Why would Gustoff lie to her about Berezan?

Why had her brother's name never been mentioned during her childhood?

"Come closer. Let me get a better look at you."

Thea took two steps back, resisting the mesmerizing quality of his voice that attacked her willpower. He was a tall man, almost Galen's height, but his shoulders weren't as wide, his legs not as muscular. He stood with his shoulders squared, his chin held high, his hands once against planted firmly upon his hips.

"Do not be afraid of me, little sister." He held out his left hand to her. "I would harm only those who stand in my way as I claim the destiny denied me so many years ago."

Thea turned away. She refused to look into his eyes. "I don't know you."

"Of course you do. Look at me."

Something touched her, sent a chill over her body and forced her to do his bidding. Thea struggled against his hold, but she had no will of her own. She met his gaze.

"I am Berezan Asvaldr, son of Lars and Dimetria." Berezan raised his hands into the air. "Behold all that is around you, sister. Know it is and shall always remain mine."

No matter how hard she tried, she could do little more than stare into his eyes. Fury flashed through her nerves like lightning. She gasped for breath, held it, counted to ten, and repeated the ritual three times. It didn't relieve her temper, nor did it calm her nerves.

"You have no right, Berezan. You're evil. You've destroyed and killed. Glacia will never belong to you."

Berezan shook his head. "Is it evil to try to redeem all taken away from me? I think not." He stroked his hand through his hair again. "Besides, my army, thousands strong, waits in the village. No other power in our world is strong enough to defeat me or say nay to my claim as leader."

Thea closed her eyes, blocking out Berezan's image. She thought about Gustoff, Galen, and the people of Glacia, of Borderland. Anything to distort the visions her brother's words planted in her mind. It took every ounce of willpower she possessed to overcome the mysterious hold Berezan had over her, but she persevered.

Galen's face appeared, along with those of the warriors of Borderland huddled in the hidden corridor.

Galen! Please hear my words. Berezan's army is in the village. Go there, my love. See your mission through!

* * * *

Galen came awake with a start. He pushed past the wild palpitations of his heart and concentrated on the words that replayed in his mind. Thea's voice. He heard her words as clearly as if she'd been standing next to him.

"Jakar!"

His warriors were immediately on their feet, weapons at ready. They stood at attention, awaiting orders.

"It's time, old friend." Galen drew his sword then grasped Jakar's arm. "Come."

Galen led his warriors to the exit Elijah had shown him when he and Thea left Glacia many days ago to follow Gustoff. They flooded out into the streets of Glacia, taking Berezan's warriors by surprise. At the sight of the warriors of Borderland, fully armed and ready for battle, many of Berezan's men turned and fled down the slippery roadway.

"Jakar."

Jakar turned to engage the warrior charging toward him.

Galen stepped to his flank and raised his sword to do battle with another of Berezan's minions.

* * * *

Thea opened her eyes to stare into eyes like her own.

"Your beloved Gustoff stole me from my bed, told our father I died in my sleep, and paid a servant woman to take me into the deserts of Solarus and dispose of me." Berezan paced back and forth under the lumalight.

"Fortunately, the servant was greedy and sold me to an old hermit for six crystals." He stopped pacing, placed his fisted hands upon his hips, and stared into her eyes. "You have been the fortunate one, little sister. Since you grew up in luxury, there is no way you could know how it feels to be abandoned by a father you loved, cast out into the desert where your thirst was never quenched, your flesh never clean."

Berezan turned to pace again. His emerald cape billowed out behind him as he walked. "My one stroke of good luck was that the man who purchased me, Elsbar, treated me kindly, and taught me all he knew of the arts of the Ancient Ones."

Berezan now stood with his head held back, his hands at his sides. "Glacia is mine. I am the rightful heir to all around us."

He turned, folded his arms over his chest. "Gustoff used the magic of the Ancient Ones to kill Elsbar, little sister. He murdered a defenseless old man."

Thea thought about what Berezan had told her of Elsbar, of the dark magic he obviously possessed, and knew Gustoff had not murdered a defenseless being. He'd destroyed a part of Berezan's evil.

"The Ancient Ones never used their powers for evil, Berezan. This old man Elsbar spoke false."

"Did he?" He raised a dark brow. "Perhaps, your limited knowledge has been tainted by Gustoff's words, little one. Elsbar once believed he and Gustoff were the last in the world to carry the Ancient Ones' powers, but he was wrong. When Elsbar saw in me what had caused Gustoff to cast me out, he knew I was destined for higher things."

You're wrong, Berezan. There is yet another chosen one left!

Thea had to bite her lip to keep from hurling her thoughts at Berezan. Instead, she searched deep inside her heart, waiting for some spark, some hint of the affection she felt should be present for one of her kin. She saw only the city of Cree, the sad faces of the people of Borderland, the destruction this man left in his wake as he journeyed to reclaim his heritage.

She shuddered, thinking the same thing could happen to Glacia, remembered a sample of his malevolence in Gustoff's chamber, the battle that had taken place between him and Gustoff in the valley of ice.

In the place of kinship, she found evil, an evil she knew must be destroyed.

But how? Gustoff had tried and failed.

The passing of the Sphere of Light gives you the knowledge of the Ancient Ones to be hidden in the depths of your mind until the demand for such knowledge surrounds you. When needed, a voice will come, whispered through thousands of years by generations.

Cherish the truths and confidences you have been taught, for if you allow doubts and uncertainties to fester and grow, the power of the Sphere will be weakened.

Bless you, Thea, daughter of the Ancient Ones.

Gustoff's voice filled her mind, speaking words she remembered hearing before. The warmth of his love flowed through her. "You are the one who's wrong, Berezan. Glacia will never be yours," Thea said as she listened to the foreign words that whispered through her mind. She repeated the sounds, forming her tongue to create the garbled tones.

She raised her hands into the air, felt the energy within her flare, heating her flesh, her hands, surging through every blood vessel, every nerve. Her fingers filled with brilliant white light, pulsing, growing, and encompassing her hands, her arms.

Berezan cursed himself for a fool thrice over. He listened as his sister spoke words in the tongue of the Ancient Ones, watched as her eyes grew almost twice their normal size. His hands shook, his body trembled, every inch of his flesh tightened and contracted.

He dug his fingers into his hair, closing his eyes against the light that grew stronger and brighter with each word passed from her lips. He reached deep within, summoning the dark power that would destroy this weak girl and allow him to possess what was rightfully his.

* * * *

Arcs of red fire sprang from Berezan's fingertips and streaked across the chamber toward Thea. She braced for impact, held her hands higher to shield her face, not knowing or fully understanding the power she held in her palms.

The Sphere of Light absorbed Berezan's fire and grew larger.

One after another, red arcs crossed the chamber, collided with the stone wall behind her, burned craters in the granite, upon the floor at her feet.

The walls shook. The floor vibrated, making it extremely difficult to maintain her balance.

Her hands trembled. She didn't know how much longer she could hold on, how many more of Berezan's evil strikes she could stand. She offered a silent prayer, seeking

Gustoff's guidance, listened for his words of instruction, but found only silence.

"Give that to me. It's mine! You have no idea how to control the Sphere. It will destroy both of us." Berezan's voice echoed around the chamber.

Thea could do no more than shake her head at his demand.

"The Sphere is mine. Give it to me. Now." Berezan began a chant of his own, speaking words Thea didn't understand. The red arcs of fire spewing from his fingertips grew stronger, merging to form a huge burning globe that encompassed half of the chamber.

The chamber became unbearably hot. Perspiration dripped into her eyes, blurring her vision. Heat siphoned more of her energy, weakened the muscles in her arms, and burned through to the very marrow of her bones.

She swallowed hard and shook her head. She needed to lower her hand, wipe the moisture from her eyes. She held fast.

"No. Gustoff passed the Sphere to me for safekeeping, Berezan. I will not allow you to possess it. I'll see it destroyed before it falls into your hands."

The Sphere absorbed several more arcs of red fire.

Berezan cursed, shaking his fist in the air. "Give it to me, sister, or I will destroy every living soul who lives within these mountains."

Tears wet her lashes, but she couldn't release the Sphere to wipe them away. She could only stare into the white light in her hands, feel her body quake, and hold her arms out.

Another barrage of red fire filled the chamber, this time aimed not at her but at the chamber walls. Horrendous blasts of thunder echoed over her head, shaking the walls, dislodging mortar, sliding the stones from alignment. The floor trembled violently beneath her feet as large blocks of granite fell one atop another, crumbling the walls, breaking away huge chunks of the ceiling.

The floor split beneath the weight of the fallen stones, leaving a gaping chasm that grew wider and wider. She heard Berezan's evil laughter over the noise of his destruction.

The floor shifted again. Thea fell to her knees, tearing her flesh on a chunk of stone. She shifted her legs to support her weight, disregarded the debris that fell around her, the smaller pieces of rock and mortar that struck her arms and jostled her hold on the Sphere.

As she watched all she'd grown up with and loved disintegrate before her eyes, anger grew within her. She allowed the energy flowing through her to feed on that anger. The Sphere pulsed within her grasp, growing larger, brighter, until its luminescence filled the chamber. Suddenly she became multidimensional, her essence no longer contained within the shell of her flesh.

Thea stared through the white light, the red blaze that shielded Berezan, into the evil that poured so freely from Berezan's eyes, and saw the elation he felt at the destruction he created.

Thea met Berezan's gaze and held it. "No! You will not do this. You will not destroy Glacia."

The sound of his laughter again crawled over her flesh. "I will destroy all I cannot have."

"You will not!"

"Stop me."

Thea raised her arms above her head. Warmth from the Sphere radiated outward from the center of her chest to flow through her shoulders and arms until it tingled against her fingertips. A strange blue light, more powerful that any she had accomplished over time, wove itself through her fingers, over her palms, down her arms.

Voices from the Ancient Ones long passed suddenly whispered through her mind, telling her the Sphere had vanquished evil over thousands of years. And, to use it she must call the light within her, to bask in the magical Sphere she held in her hands.

She listened to the voices, each telling her that the Sphere of Light had the power to vanquish the evil she faced. Forged with the Ancient Ones magic, the Sphere was capable of destroying whatever force worked against lasting peace.

Another, familiar voice echoed in her mind. Believe in the Sphere of Light, Thea.

Ancient, garbled words filled her mind. Words she could not understand. She repeated the words over and over, each time louder and with more conviction.

"With the power entrusted to me by the Ancient Ones to wield the Sphere of Light, I destroy you, Berezan Asvaldr, Son of Evil."

The light emanating from the Sphere of Light turned a deep yellow, almost blinding Thea with his glow, hiding the sight of Berezan's flesh being torn from his bones, his body sagging to the floor in a blaze of yellow fire, then disappearing.

* * * *

Galen clutched his side, staring down at the warm stickiness that flowed over his fingers. He pressed hard against his torn flesh to stem the blood flow, then wiped the Blood of the Solarian who'd given him the wound off his sword on the dead warrior's clothing.

He turned, stumbled as the frozen ground shook beneath his feet, and looked up to the Keep a hundred spans above his head.

Galen tried to keep a tight rein on his nerves, forcing himself to look back at the battle going on around him instead of overhead. He ignored the constant spasms in his stomach, the cold sweat running in torrents beneath his woolen tunic, the ache in his shoulders, and the pain in his heart.

Jakar stepped to his side, drawing his attention.

"Hundreds of Berezan's warriors have fled down the mountainside, Galen."

Galen looked at the carnage strewn over the icy main street of Glacia. Fifty or so men were still locked in mortal combat. Hundreds of bodies littered the snow. Blood froze in pools that shimmered in the sunlight. Discarded weapons lay where they were dropped or had been kicked aside in the heat of battle.

Thankfully, though his warriors suffered many wounds, none seemed serious.

"Galen."

Galen turned and engaged swords with another member of Berezan's army. He lunged, locking hilts with the warrior's bloody sword, pinning it back against the stone of the mountain, while he grasped the knife protruding from the interloper's belt with his free hand and slashed upward across the man's exposed throat.

"What's happening?" Jakar shouted, his voice barely audible over the howling of the wind.

Thunder rumbled overhead. Shadows crossed the ice, blocking out the sun. Galen looked up. Thick black clouds, reminiscent of the ones he'd seen over the ice valley where Gustoff and Berezan had met, filled the sky. A strange red glow flashed like lightening through the arched windows, reflected from the dark clouds.

The thunder grew stronger. The ground quaked beneath his boots. Wind whipped over his body, picked up energy, wound through the streets, between the stone houses and whistled through his hair.

Galen brushed the hair from his eyes. His heart did a somersault in his chest. His blood ran like iced water through his veins. "Thea!"

Jakar grabbed his arm. "Go to her."

CHAPTER 30

"Gustoff?"

Gustoff stood before Thea enshrouded in mist. The brilliant purple robe she remembered seemed lavender, translucent. The wind blew in gentle ripples around his frail body, but Thea could feel no wind. She looked into his eyes, studied the opalescence of his flesh, and understood Gustoff was not with her in body, but in spirit.

"Come with me, child." Gustoff held out his hand.

Thea grasped his hand but felt no substance, only the warmth of his love. "Where are we going, Gustoff?"

"To a place where you will learn everything I have not had time to teach you."

"But, Berezan--"

"Is destroyed. Come. There is much to tell you and little time."

Thea concentrated on placing one foot before the other as Gustoff led her toward a light. She followed eagerly.

"Why did you not tell me Berezan was my brother, Gustoff?"

Gustoff looked over his shoulder at her. The light breeze rippled through his beard, fluffed his white hair. "It would have served no good. You could not have faced your destiny knowing you must destroy your own brother."

"But, Gus--"

"Berezan was my mistake, Thea. His malevolence grew out of his hatred for me and the things I took away from him. I should have destroyed him. Instead, I exiled him. I will pay in the afterlife for my weakness, but I could not pass my misdeeds to you." He turned away, refusing to offer more.

The light suddenly grew nearer. Brighter. A hundred faces filled her path. Thea reached out, tried to touch one, but her hand passed through the image.

"Explain this place to me, Gustoff."

"Listen to the voices, child. Concentrate and hear what is your true destiny."

Gustoff's image faded away. "Remember, I will always love you, Thea of Glacia. Go in peace."

"Gustoff! No. Come back. Don't leave me," she cried, but Gustoff was no more.

The hundred voices spoke as one within her mind.

"Child of Destiny. Hear our words. Know these as truths that shall be honored for all times."

Thea turned about, watching the ghostly images float all around her. A mysterious calm filled her. Soothed her.

"The Sphere of Light you have been given to hold has but a simple purpose. When the Sphere is possessed by good, all things evil will be destroyed. Should it ever fall into the hands of evil, all that is known as good in our world will forever perish.

"Your life must be spent protecting the Sphere until the time comes when you shall pass it on to its next bearer, the male child who grows within your womb."

Thea dropped her hand to her stomach, but was distracted by the next words that filled her mind.

"The Sphere has completed its task. Speak the words. Call it back into yourself. Hold it dear."

Strange words fell from Thea's lips, words that were familiar yet she couldn't remember ever hearing them before. She looked down, saw the Sphere draw its brilliant yellow light back into itself, watched it shrink until it became no more than a pulse of light in her hands.

"Place your hands upon your breasts, child. Feel the warmth that flows through your body."

Thea followed the directive of the strange voices. She watched in awe as the Sphere disappeared, leaving no more than a warmth in the region of her heart.

She closed her eyes and succumbed to the darkness.

* * * *

"Thea?"

She opened her eyes and looked up.

Galen knelt within a hand's span of her, his blue eyes paler than she'd ever seen them, and so filled with his emotions her heart beat wildly within her chest. His distraught face streaked with blood. His woolen tunic clung to his flesh like a second skin. Blood seeped through the cloth at his waist, darkening the beige fabric to almost black. His hair, that glorious flow of blond and platinum hugged his muscular shoulders, was matted and wet.

He'd never looked more handsome.

Thea swayed forward. Galen's arms were suddenly around her, clinging to her tightly. She melted against the muscles of his chest and sighed in relief as he smothered her mouth with his.

Reluctantly, she pulled away. "It's done."

"Bless you, my lady."

* * * *

Galen glanced over his shoulder to find one of Berezan's warriors standing at his back. He watched in awe as the man dropped to his knees before Thea, reached out to touch the hemline of her gown.

"Bless you," he repeated.

Galen withdrew one hand from Thea's back, placed it upon the man's shoulder, and pushed him away. "What are you doing here?"

R'han met his gaze. "Surrendering, my lord."

Galen looked at Thea, then back at the man still kneeling.

"I was Berezan's commander, my lord. Many sunrises ago, the people of Solarus lived in peace. Then Berezan killed the rulers of Solarus and the lives of every person of the desert changed. We, the members of Berezan's army, followed him not because we believed in his cause, my lord. We had no choice. Families and homes were threatened, livestock destroyed. Our livelihoods were taken away."

R'han bowed his head. "I beg you for the lives of my men. I pledge myself to see that the army of Berezan is disbanded if you will allow us to go home to our lands, our families, and live once again in peace."

"Galen."

Galen turned to Thea.

She reached forward, touched the bronze medallion that hung against his chest. "It's your decision whether these men live or die. By right, you not only rule Borderland, but the whole of our world."

Galen grasped her hand, pulled it from the medallion, then raised her fingers to his lips. "No, Thea. The right to rule Glacia is yours."

Thea shook her head. "I cannot. The Articles--"

"Will be changed," Galen finished.

"But, the Elders...."

"Were not here to protect Glacia from Berezan, nor were they in Borderland, or Solarus. Those who would call themselves leaders, yet stand by and relinquish their beliefs to the evil of Berezan, have no say in anything that will happen from this day forward."

R'han cleared his throat.

Galen turned to the warrior of the desert. "Do you have a family who awaits your return?"

"A sister and her children."

"Would you return with the army to Solarus, then gather a delegation of trusted men? And women?" he added with a smile. "Have them travel to Glacia with you for a celebration that will take place at the next full moon."

R'han bowed. "I would be honored, my lord." He looked at Thea. "My lady."

The shuffle of boots drew Thea's attention from Galen and R'han's conversation. She gazed over Galen's shoulder to find Jakar and Thor standing in the center of the chamber. She raised her hand and beckoned them forward.

"Galen," she said, softly. "Jakar and Thor are here." She smiled up at the two warriors. "I would ask you to join us, but my legs have lost all feeling."

Galen immediately understood. He stood, bent, and picked her up in his arms. "See that this man gets adequate provisions and clothing for the men of Solarus to make a safe journey home."

Thea chuckled and ducked her head to the side of Galen's neck when she witnessed the startled expression on the two large warriors' faces.

"I have given Berezan's army my leave to travel home in peace."

Jakar nodded.

Galen clasped R'han's hand. "Go in peace."

Thor stepped forward. "Any orders for me, Regis?"

"See that the people of Glacia know it's safe to come out of their homes then return to the Keep with Jakar. Find chambers for my warriors to rest, healers to take care of their wounds, then seek me out at sunrise and I'll fill you in on everything that's about to take place.

"But, for now, Thea is exhausted, and I intend to do everything in my power to see that she receives proper rest."

Without a backward glance, Galen left the meeting chamber, cradling Thea in his arms.

He took the granite stairs two at the time, pausing before the huge carved door of the chamber he'd used many sunrises ago. He positioned Thea so he could open the door, then walked inside to place her in the middle of the high poster bed.

"You should now use my father's chamber, Regis," she whispered.

Galen shook his head. "I happen to like this chamber just fine," he answered as he walked across the floor to loosen the cord that held the tapestries open. The fabric swished together, shutting out the light, leaving only the faint glow of one lumastone to guide him back to the bed. He shrugged out of his tunic, slipped the medallion from his neck, dropped both to the floor, then discarded the rest of his clothing.

"Galen." Thea held out her hand to him, touching his side, healing his wound. "I've had a strange vision."

Galen looked down at his side then back to Thea. "Tell me about it later. I've waited too long for this moment."

Thea shook her head. "But, I remember something I think you should know."

"Later." He fell upon the bed, upon her, twisting her over until she lay on top of him. He made quick work of her gown then, changing positions, smothered her with his body, placing warm kisses on every inch of her accessible flesh.

"It's cold in here," she murmured against his ear.

"Not for long."

* * * *

Hours later, Galen stirred, pulling the thickness of the fur about his shoulders. "What was it you wished to tell me earlier?"

Thea twisted in his arms until she faced him. "What type of celebration to you plan for the next full moon?"

"Hmmm?" Galen had already been distracted. Positioned as she was, with all of her glorious charms readily within reach, he'd forgotten he even asked a question. He stroked her arm, her side. She arched to meet his touch. He raised his hand, caressed her breast, then eased his way down to the heat that burned between her thighs.

"Galen." She squirmed beneath his touch.

"Hmmm?"

"What type of celebration do you have planned for the next full moon?!"

He groaned. "As you heard, I've invited a delegation from Solarus to hear our plans for lasting peace."

"Will Borderland also send a delegation?"

Galen nuzzled the tender flesh of her neck. "Of course."

"Women and children, too?"

"Thea!"

"Answer me, Galen. It's important."

"Every last person of the jungle is welcome to our celebration." He gave up, realizing Thea wasn't about to allow him another bout of lovemaking until he answered all of her questions. He flipped over to his back and stared at the ceiling.

Thea watched him in the faint lumalight. He'd closed his eyes. His mouth pressed into a taut line. All that glorious hair tangled about his head, teasing her fingers. She leaned across his body, kissed the harden plane of his chest, licked his breastbone, his nipple.

"Good. Now, tell me what type of celebration you have in mind," she said between kisses that worked their way slowly down the length of his body, nearer and nearer to the part of him that gave such pleasure.

Galen groaned. He grasped her shoulders and pulled her back until they were eye to eye. "A proper joining, Thea. I plan a great feast to celebrate our joining."

"Perfect." She tangled her fingers in his hair and pulled him closer. "I wouldn't want our son to be born without one."

Galen bolted upright, dislodging Thea, who sprawled beside him on the soft mattress. He reached to place one hand on each side of her body and stared into her laughing eyes.

"A son?"

Thea nodded then raised her hand, placed her fingers upon his shoulder, and pushed the mammoth warrior over as if he weighed no more than a feather. She scrambled up, spread her legs over his chest, then lowered and opened wider to welcome the thickness of his erection.

She sat straighter, undulating her hips in an erotic dance that caused the ends of her hair to sweep his abdomen. Reaching down, she traced each band of muscle, the arrow of dark blond hair that grew downward to where their bodies joined, then lifted his hand to her belly.

"Our son," she whispered.

He entwined his fingers into her hair and drew her down. He used his lips, his tongue, his body to express the words of love his mind failed to supply, all the promises he would make to her and his unborn son to keep their world safe, to reunite the three regions into one, and to join her in protecting the Sphere of Light.

He skimmed his hands over the warmth of her breasts, the contours of her back and buttocks. He held her, embraced her as the ripples of ecstasy washed over them, fusing them together as one.

EPILOGUE

Thea stood on the balcony and watched the sun slip slowly behind the peaks and streaks of gray and purple gathered in the sky. She wrapped her arms around her waist to ward off the chill that increased with the coming darkness. She looked down upon the multitudes of people gathered in celebration on the icy streets, their faces lit by thousands of lumastones decorating the houses and shops of Glacia. The people were all garbed in warm clothing befitting Glacia's climate. Thea couldn't tell Creean from Solarian or Glacian.

Joining day. A day that would be remembered in history, for not only had she taken her warrior as mate, but the boundaries of their world had been dissolved. The people were now free to travel as they would, experience all the wonders each region offered.

"Thea?"

Warm hands wrapped around her waist and pulled her back to rest against a solid chest. Large, callused fingers slipped to cradle her belly. "Your subjects await you, love."

Thea smiled. "Our subjects, Regis."

Galen bent his head closer. "Is that your Nola by Thor's side?"

Thea eased forward and glanced toward the couple before the smith. "Yes, I suppose it is," she whispered, then snuggled into her warrior's arms. She'd never confess she'd sent Nola to Thor's side for answers to her numerous questions about Borderland.

"Do you suppose we could skip the celebration for a few hours?" Galen asked.

"Do you have something more important in mind, warrior?"

He stepped back and held out his hand. "Walk with me, Thea." He led her into the chamber and closed the tapestries tight against the night air.

The End

CHECK OUT THESE OTHER FUTURISTIC ROMANCES NOW IN PRINT FROM NCP:

Armageddon by Kaitlyn O'Connor ISBN 1-58608-775-4

Barbarian by Amanda Steiger ISBN 1-58608-718-5

Butterfly Scales by Evangeline Anderson ISBN 1-58608-746-0

Endless Night by Andrea Dionne ISBN 1-58608-659-6

Illicit Pursuits by Marie Harte ISBN 1-58608-786-x

Intergalactic Bad Boys by Jaide Fox ISBN 1-58608-686-3

Love's Captive by Myra Nour ISBN 1-58608-689-8

Naughty Men by Jan Springer and Lauren Agony ISBN 1-58608-740-1

No Holes Barred by Kimberly Zant, Shizuko Lee, Angelia Whiting, Shelley Munro ISBN 1-58608-789-4

Promises to Keep by Janet Miller ISBN 1-58608-706-1

Sky Pirates by Jaide Fox, Shizuko Lee, Ashley Ladd ISBN 1-58608-747-9

Teasing Danger by Autumn Dawn ISBN 1-58608-081-4

Tripping Through the Universe by Ellen Fisher, Jaide Fox, Ashley Ladd, Shelley Munro ISBN 1-58608-729-0

The Warrior Prince by Michelle M. Pillow ISBN 1-58608-732-0

Printed in the United States
52383LVS00001B/79-87